THE MAID'S DAUGHTER

BROOKLYN KNIGHT

1

WILLIAM

BEAUFORT, S.C., 1952

*T*he sliver of light coming from underneath Naomi's door told me she was awake. Not that I'd had any doubt. It was time for final exams and the girl was no slacker. She was the type to study even when there wasn't a test. The kind of girl who could recite passages from *Across the River and Into the Trees* like nobody's business. There was no doubt in my mind she was sitting at her scrap-paper-covered desk, scribbling notes and memorizing facts and figures.

I inched closer to the door, glancing over my shoulder. Narrowing the gap until I was standing in front of it, I lifted my hand to knock. Normally I wasn't apprehensive, but tonight was different. For one, it was eleven o'clock at night, and secondly...

I cleared my throat and tapped my knuckles against the door before rubbing my palms together and looking behind me again.

The hallway would have been completely dark had it not been for the soft glow of light seeping from the sconces on the wall. My parents' bedroom was on the third floor, so I wasn't concerned about them coming around the corner. Naomi's room was on the second floor, but Miss Carole's bedroom was right around the bend. The last thing I needed was for her to come out for a glass of water and see me standing in front of her daughter's quarters.

Naomi didn't answer.

Imaginary sounds filled my mind, like the shuffle of patrolling footsteps and the clinking of crystal glasses transported through the mansion. My breathing quickened. I reached up to knock again but before I made contact, Naomi pulled the door open and stared at me. The light from her room now flooded into the hallway, threatening to blow my cover.

"Well, it's about time," I grunted.

"And hello to you," she said, peering around the door and into the hall. "Will, why are you standing outside of my room like this?"

"I knocked, didn't I?"

She made a face. "That's not the problem." She looked at her watch and back up at me, crossing her arms over her chest. The top of her pink and white striped pajamas was buttoned all the way up, and the ankle-length bottoms flowed around her tawny legs. Noticing my inspection, she pulled her robe closer together.

"So, what are you doing?" I asked with a shrug.

"You know what I'm doing. I'm trying to study."

"Me too."

Her eyes narrowed.

I cleared my throat. "I need your help with something. That's why I'm here."

"You need my help? That's a first," she said as one of her eyebrows raised. "Where are your books?"

I rubbed the back of my neck. "They're in my room."

"Really? And how am I supposed to help you if you don't have books or notes or anything?"

I looked back into the hallway again. "I left them because—"

She started talking before I could conjure a response. "Will, this is no time for games."

"What makes you think I'm playing games?"

We stared at each other.

"Alright, fine," I said. "You got me, okay? I don't need help with anything."

"Then what do you want? It's late."

"Yeah, I know...which is why I'm wondering why you still have me standing in this hallway like a stranger." I tilted my head to the side and lowered my voice. "Can I come in or what?"

Naomi stepped to the side and spread her arms with a sigh. I entered her bedroom and closed the door behind me. Shoving my hands into the pockets of my housecoat, I looked around the room as if it were my first time inside. The room had a pink color scheme. Powder-pink walls sprinkled with pinky-white flower blossoms matched a pale pink rug laid in front of the bed. Although the cover on her bed was white, it too had a pink floral border around its edge. Under a sloping ceiling, a narrow closet held some of Naomi's pink Sunday dresses and church shoes. In front of a quaint window was her desk, which, as I'd predicted, was covered with an assortment of books and notepaper. Further study materials lay strewn haphazardly across the bed and floor.

She sat on the edge of the poster bed my mother insisted she have and rested her hands in her lap. I sat at the desk. A light evening breeze made the curtains flutter against the open window. Feeling like I needed to do something to distract from the silence, I pushed the curtain to the side and pulled the window halfway down.

"Will, you're stalling. What's really going on? Is everything okay?" Naomi's voice ripped me from my pointless exercise.

I pushed the window completely closed and turned to face her. Her eyes were the color of rich terracotta, yet they were bright and vibrant, dancing against the décor of the room. She was five years old when she moved in with her mother, but now, at sixteen years old, puberty had turned her into a woman. Where her chest had once been flat, I couldn't help but notice soft mounds pushing themselves against the stripes of her pajama top. Her hips were swelling, curving. Her legs were longer and shapelier. The rich complexion of her skin had always been fascinating to me, especially the way it glowed in the early morning and evening light.

"Everything is okay," I said. "Something's on my mind, that's all."

"Well, what is it? Is it something you want to talk about?" She looked at her watch again.

I felt the sweat under my arms, despite the shower I'd just had. I paused, trying to redirect nervous energy as I drew air into my lungs and rubbed my palms together. This is the reason I came here tonight. Unable to deny it any longer, I needed to put it out there. It was plaguing me day in, day out. Now was the time. I couldn't turn back.

"I was just wondering," I said and paused. "Do you ever think about...you know...boyfriends?" My feet shuffled against the carpet.

Naomi's neck snapped back. "Boyfriends? You mean like boys that are friends or—"

"No, like go-steady boyfriends."

She laughed at some joke I'd missed. "Are you serious?" she asked.

I stared at her, my lip pinched between my teeth.

"Is *that* what you wanted to talk about? Really? Right now?"

"Just answer the question, Nay."

"I know what you're doing, William."

She'd used the full name...

"You're trying to distract me," she said. "Every time I'm studying, this is what you do. It's like you can't bear the thought of me being productive."

"I promise, I'm not doing that this time," I replied.

"Is this about Danny Hightower, the boy at my school?"

I pinched my lips together. "As much as I want to know about Danny Hightower, it's not about him either," I responded.

"Good, because I already told you, it's nothing serious. Yeah, he wants to get jacketed, but I'm not ready for that."

"So, to be clear, you *don't* want Danny to be your boyfriend?"

She groaned. "So it *is* about Danny?"

"No, it's about boyfriends in general. I told you that. So do you think about them or not?"

The whispering match was getting out of control.

She sliced through the air with her hand and turned toward the books on her bed. "This can wait, Will," she said. "I have a math test on Monday, and you have that economics paper due. Have you even started working on it?" She waited for a second for my response then sucked her teeth. "Listen, I need to get back to work. I'm already behind and it's late."

I groaned. "You're not listening to me."

She didn't answer.

I strode over to the bed and took the book out of her hand, throwing it on the pillow.

She gasped. "William Cooper! Have you flipped your lid? What's the matter with you?" Her eyebrows drew in.

I stood in front of her, raking my fingers through my hair. "I'm sorry," I said, "It's just that I have to tell you something and it's really important. It's been on my mind all day, all week actually. The way you're acting, it seems like you don't care one bit about what I've been going through." I sat on the edge of the bed and dropped my head in my hands.

"Will, you know that's not true. I'm always there when you need to talk." She sighed and scooted closer to me so our thighs touched.

Beneath the shield of my hands, I looked at the point of connection. Fire burned my skin where my leg brushed against hers. I wanted to touch her with my hands, but I had never done that before. At least not the way I really wanted to. Deep down inside there had always been this fear of being rejected by Naomi. We had known each other for so long, lived under the same roof for so long, yet there was no way I could predict how she would respond to what I was about to say. Did she see me as a friend? A brother? And to make matters more complicated, her mother was the maid. Surely the way I felt about Naomi was unpractical, but my feelings were too strong and there was no way I could hide them any longer.

I looked up to find her big, beautiful eyes gazing back at me. My eyes roamed over her face, taking in the details of her perfection; the way her lips pouted and the small, round shape of her nose.

My heart felt heavy, like whatever was in it was about to spill out.

As if on cue, we looked away from each other at the same time.

"You're such a Cooper," she said.

"What's that supposed to mean?"

"It means that you're spoiled," she replied. "You get what you want all the time. You want my attention and you're supposed to get it. Isn't that how it's supposed to go?"

I groaned and stood.

"Fine," she said, "since you're so serious about all of this boyfriend business..." She ran her toes through the rug. "No, I don't think about boyfriends because I don't have time for any of that."

"Why not?" I asked.

"Well, I just started piano lessons. Miss Anna insisted."

"You don't have to do what my mother says all the time you know, Naomi."

Her neck whipped back. "Of course I do," she said. "She takes good care of my mama and me. You know that, Will."

I shrugged. "Well, what else you got going on?"

"Then there's the reading your father assigns and there's homework. You know he always wants me to read. He says it'll make me head of the class." She paused. "And sometimes I have to help mama with her chores—"

"About that," I interjected, "I can help with the chores, you know, if y'all ever need help or anything."

Naomi smiled.

I continued. "I'm just saying because I know sometimes it can be a lot, especially when Mom has her parties and meetings and socials and—"

"I think Mama and the rest of them got it," she assured me. "I just like to help out sometimes. Give Mama a little break."

I nodded, my head feeling like a bowling ball on my neck. An awkward silence followed.

"Oh," Naomi added, "and not to mention that both our mamas would kill me if I ever thought about bringing a boy home. I can hear Miss Anna now asking me where I think I'm going with some raggedy old boy. She'd say I was going to ruin my future if I had a baby." She sighed and frowned a little. "Anyway, I'm getting good grades, Will. I'm trying to stay focused so I can get into nursing school after I graduate, but that's not gonna happen if I have a boyfriend or if you keep barging in my room in the middle of the night asking me about them."

"I knocked," I reminded her.

We smiled.

"Naomi, you have nothing to worry about. You've always gotten good grades," I said.

"That may be true, but some of us have more to prove than others, especially if they want to go to college."

I grimaced.

Naomi leaned closer to me. "Your father says if I can keep up the good work, he'll loan me the money for nursing school."

"That's...great," I said.

Naomi's perfect smile faded. "You don't sound like you're really happy for me. I would've thought you'd be more excited."

I sat back down on the bed. "I am excited," I said, "It's just..."

She turned to face me. "Will, you know that I know when something's not right with you. So you can either be straight with me and tell me what it is or—"

"Naomi, listen," I said, raising my hand slightly. "I'm asking about boyfriends because I'm on the hook with someone."

She stared at me. Her eyelashes fluttered. "With...whom?" She squared her shoulders. "Wait, I know who it is. Sandra Glasgow."

"No, it's not Sandy. It's—"

"Jessica McCarthy? The new girl down the street?"

"No, Nay, not her either. The girl I'm on the hook for is—"

"You know what? You don't even have to tell me." She twisted a loose thread on her pajamas. "I'm sorry for being so nosey. It's none of my business."

"Naomi, it's not Sandra and it's not Jessica, and you're not nosey. The girl I'm on the hook with is you," I blurted out.

Naomi's fidgeting stopped.

I tried to swallow the lump in my throat, but it wouldn't go down.

Naomi opened her mouth but closed it. Then she opened it again. "W-what?" She shook her head like she was clearing it. "Will, what are you on about now?"

"You heard me," I said, moving closer to her. "Don't act like you didn't."

Silence.

"And don't act like I'm the only one who feels this way either, because I know I'm not."

"Ex-cuse me?"

"I see how you look at me when I'm getting ready to go on a date, Nay."

"I have no idea what you're talking a—"

"And anytime I come to ask you for advice about girls, you rush the conversation or act like you don't hear me. Like you're doing now."

"Okay, now I know you're imagining things," she scoffed. "I do not—"

"Nay..." I reached over to touch her hand, but she lifted herself off the bed and turned away.

I followed her. "Please don't walk away from me."

She grunted.

"It's bad, Nay. In fact, I'm real gone. I think I'm in love with you."

She spun around. "Cut the gas, Will," she snapped, crossing her arms and hugging herself. "You can't say that."

I continued to approach her, ignoring her protests. "I dream about kissing you almost every night," I whispered. "Sometimes I dream about more. When I'm around you, I get this heavy feeling right here." I pointed to the left side of my chest.

Her eyes tracked my finger.

I was standing right in front of her as my chest heaved in and out and my heart pounded against my ribs. I paused, gathering courage.

"I know you said you don't have time for boyfriends and all, but I want you to be my girl."

She stumbled over to the desk. Her hands lifted and stuck to her cheeks, pulling at them, making her eyes sag. "Oh my God.

William Cooper, you've done it now. You've lost your ever-loving mind."

She turned around and stared into my eyes.

"Why are you saying these things?" she asked, looking around the room the way I'd been looking around the hallway, running her hands over her hair. "You need to stop with this mess. What you trying to do? Do you want to get me in trouble or something?"

"What are you talking about?"

"What am *I* talking about?" She strode closer to me and her voice lowered to a whisper. "You know better than me that it's not possible. A Negro girl and a white boy? A Cooper, no less?" Her hand clutched her neck as if she would strangle herself. "That's not acceptable 'round here, and you of all people know that. I'm scared to even think about it." She shivered.

"Well, how 'bout we make it acceptable then?" I said. "I don't care what people say or think. I never have, and I reckon I never will."

She shook her head, denying everything I was saying as her freshly pressed hair bounced around her shoulders. Staring into the distance, tears collected in the corners of her eyes.

"You can't make it acceptable," she whispered. "There's no way you could, even if you wanted to. And it doesn't matter if you don't care what people say and think. They're going to say and think it anyway." She looked up at me. "You need to go. Go back to your room before Miss Anna comes 'round here."

"I don't care about my mother," I said, closing in on her and tilting her chin up with my forefinger. "Answer my question. Do you?"

"Do I what?"

"Feel the same way?"

Naomi sighed. "I don't know what you're talking about."

"The hell you don't, Naomi," I said.

Her mouth trembled as she twiddled her fingers, and her eyes shifted around the room until they landed on me. "A lot of girls say you're a playboy, William. How many girls did you go steady with last year? It was more than four."

"How many girls I went steady with last year doesn't matter.

There's only one that I want to go steady with right now, and right now I want to know how she feels about me. That's all I'm asking."

She didn't answer.

I touched her face. It was my first time touching her like this, though I had imagined this day for a long time. My pale fingers ran wispy circles on her cheek and lingered down her jawline.

Naomi closed her eyes and covered her hand with mine. The heavy rise and fall of her chest was obvious against the pink and white pajamas.

"Do you know the courage I had to build to come in here and say this to you?" I whispered, watching as tears escaped onto her cheeks through closed eyelids.

Unable to take any more, I bent my neck forward and gently placed my lips on hers. I rested there, waiting, fearful that if I moved too quickly something might go wrong.

For a second, nothing happened. Then her mouth responded and her hand, almost reluctantly, rose to the nape of my neck. My breath caught against the back of my throat. I guided her face closer to mine, deepening the kiss.

She pulled away.

"What are we doing?" She gasped and took a step back, but I pulled her towards me and her chest smashed against mine. "We can't do this," she said.

"We can do whatever we want," I responded. "It's just you and me."

2

NAOMI

BEAUFORT, S.C., 1953

"*W*ill, I'm not saying I don't love you, because I do. It's just that sometimes I wonder if getting jacketed was the right thing to do..." I exhaled and stared at myself in the mirror.

I started again.

"Will, something's been on my mind. I just don't know what the point of this relationship is. Maybe we should call it quits before it's too late."

I groaned. That was worse than before. Besides, William would never believe me.

I didn't even believe me.

My eyes were too soft and my tone was too weak. I needed to toughen up if he was going to take me seriously. William was strong-willed. If I expected him to believe what I was saying, I would need to be stern and show him I meant business this time.

I squared my shoulders and hardened my eyes in the mirror. "William Cooper," I started again. Yes, that sounded better already. "We need to talk. I've been thinking, and this relationship just doesn't make any sense. It's a dead-end street, and I think we should cut the gas on it."

I nodded at myself in the mirror.

"Now, I know what you're thinking," I continued, pacing back and forth. "You think I'm being silly and paranoid. You think I don't know what I'm talking about, but I do. I'm not saying I don't love you, because we both know that's not true. It's just—"

Three knocks on the door cut into my diatribe, causing my breath to catch in the back of my lungs. In an instant, a throng of butterflies erupted in my belly. I scurried towards the mirror to arrange my hair and run my hands over my belt and skirt, smoothing out imaginary wrinkles.

The knocks sounded again.

"I'm coming," I called out. Composing myself, I walked to the door and inhaled before pulling it open.

William stood on the other side, leaning on the doorpost wearing dungarees and a matching jacket. His soft brown hair was stylishly slicked back, a loose strand falling carelessly in his face. My eyes fell to his peach-fuzz framed mouth. I felt my mouth dry up as he caught his lower lip between his teeth.

"Hey, bean," he whispered, walking into the bedroom. He eased the door closed, turned the lock, and pulled me into his arms. Before I could foster a desire to protest, he lowered his head and kissed me. The electricity from his touch zipped through my body and I closed my eyes, debilitated by his presence. His mouth was sweet, like peppermint candy, and he smelled like Barbasol. I moaned, lost in the moment created by the kiss.

As always...

All the resolve I had attempted to conjure up fizzled into thin air and I melted into him, slinking my arms around his neck to bring him closer. His hard hands sent a tremble down my spine as he caressed the length of my back. Soon, our displays of affection slowed and we rested our foreheads together, staring into each other's eyes.

"You're early," I whispered. "We aren't supposed to meet until eight o'clock. It's only seven-thirty."

"I saw my parents leave a few minutes ago," he said. "They won't be back for hours. That means we have extra time to be together."

I smiled at the prospect, but then reality started to bleed back in.

Dread and disappointment settled in the pit of my stomach and my heart started to race.

William's eyebrows drew in. "You're doing that face," he observed. "What's the matter? You don't want to see me tonight?"

I pulled away from him and walked over to the bed. Weight crushed my shoulders as I dropped onto the covers and sighed. "Of course I want to see you tonight. I want to see you every night," I said, shaking my head.

"Then what's the problem?"

Now was the time to tell him, I realized. I'd been practicing since the week before and had several script options. Suddenly though, my mind was blank. I tried to recall the words I had rehearsed a few moments ago. "William, you know I love you," I began.

Wait—that's not how I'm supposed to begin.

"I love you too," he said, approaching me. "Don't I tell you every day? There's no other girl I want more than you." He sat next to me on the bed and held my hands. My throat tightened when I looked down at the contrasting skin tones of our intertwined fingers. I pulled my hands out of his and got up from the bed.

Lines creased his forehead as he jumped up to follow me.

"Listen, Will, we really need to talk," I started over. "This relationship...I mean...getting jacketed...maybe it wasn't the right thing to do."

"What are you talking about? Of course it was the right thing to do. How long were we supposed to go on hiding our feelings?"

"Okay, maybe it was the right thing to do," I reconsidered, "but it's a dead-end street, us acting like we're boyfriend and girlfriend and—"

He cut me off. "Not this again," he muttered, scrubbing the back of his neck. "Baby, you talk about this all the time. At least once a week."

"That's because I'm real worried about it, Will," I said. "Sure, we love each other and we spend a lot of time together, but does it really make sense?" She lowered her voice. "Did you hear about Molly Anderson and Tommy King?"

He groaned and slumped back onto the bed, running his hands over his face.

"When Molly's father found out she was seeing a black boy, he got kicked out of school and his daddy got fired from his job." I stared at him, waiting for a reaction. "Isn't that scary, Will?"

After a moment of silence, he stood. "Yes, Nay. It's pretty scary."

"I know!" I huffed. "I really think we ought to talk about this. About us."

"Okay, we can talk about it," he said, placing his palms on my shoulders. "But how about we do it later?"

"Later? Will—"

He hushed me with a soft kiss then gazed at me. "I promise," he said. "You trust me, don't you?"

"Of course I trust you, Will."

"Then quit worrying, okay?"

I watched him walk over to the window and throw it open. Smiling as he inhaled the fresh breeze, he turned to face me and extended his hand. "Let's go."

"Where are we going?"

"To the dock," he said. "Let's sit on the chairs and count shooting stars. We can make wishes."

I rolled my eyes at him, yet a smile turned the edges of my mouth. The thought of being with him under the glow of the moon made my skin tingle. "The last time we went to the dock, we didn't see any shooting stars," I said.

"I bet tonight will be different," he said. "Come on. I'll go out the window first then I'll help you down."

I stared at him, chewing on the inside of my lip, pondering his suggestion. The air was crisp outside, but it was a perfect fall evening. The keepers were off the premises and my mother had been given leave for the week, so there was no way anyone would catch us. I'd be a fool not to take advantage of having unrestricted time with him.

William pushed my desk to the side with ease and climbed out of the window. He scaled the ample ledge and hopped to the ground as I nervously stared down at him from the safety of my bedroom window.

"Go on," he said, looking up at me. "Climb out and then I'll catch you. Just be careful."

"Are you sure?" I asked. "You'd better not miss, William Cooper! If I break a leg, I'll never forgive you."

"I was the MVP for my baseball team this year. I won't miss."

Laughing at his unwavering confidence, I gathered the edges of my skirt in one hand and lifted my leg over the sill. With both feet carefully placed on the outside ledge, I soon found myself standing in the same spot he'd been in moments earlier. I glanced back into the bedroom and then down at his extended arms, ready to receive me. Before I could second guess my actions, I tiptoed to the end of the ledge and quickly shimmied off. Instantly, the wind whipped through my hair and billowed up my skirt as I free-fell the short distance down. William's grasp was firm around my waist as he eased me to the ground.

"I told ya' I wouldn't miss," he whispered with a smile. "Come on! Let's not waste any time."

We hurried through the grounds until we reached the edge of the property, where the dock stood surrounded by soft ripples fanning across the surface of the water. Two lawn chairs waited patiently for occupants on the edge of the dock. William and Mr. Cooper sat in this spot whenever they went fishing after dinner in the lazy, humid summer evenings, while I stared out of the window on the top floor and watched them. Off to the side was the Cooper's private beach, with its soft, white sand sparkling under the moonlight.

William and I walked side by side, our hands coiled together between us, before we came to a rest and sat down.

"It's such a beautiful night," he said softly after a while, staring up at the sky. "These are the moments I look forward to. The ones where I'm with you and there's nobody else around."

"Me too," I replied. "We get to imagine that everything is perfect. I wish it could be like this all the time."

Displaying a mischievous grin, Will leaped to his feet and started taking off his jean jacket, then I watched him unzip his jeans.

"What in the world are you doing?" I asked with a smile.

"Let's go skinny dipping," he said. Even in the darkness, I could see the sparkle in his eyes.

"Have you flipped your lid? I can't get my hair wet. I just pressed it yesterday. Besides, how will we get back into the house dripping wet?"

"The same way we left," he said, stepping out of his pants and taking a step toward me. My eyes dropped to his hands as he played with my belt.

"It's cold out here," I said, staring into his eyes.

"That's never stopped us from taking our clothes off before," he reminded me. I laughed, shaking my head.

"You're a bad influence. What would people think if they knew I was out here naked with a boy?"

He shrugged. "Who cares what they'd think."

In no time at all, standing at the edge of the dock, we both peered down at our naked reflections in the water.

"So, who's gonna go first?" he asked, shivering.

"I think you should. After all, this was your idea."

Without warning, I shoved him off the edge and he sailed through the air with flailing arms, landing in the water with an almighty splash. He came to the surface laughing. "You're gonna be sorry you did that," he warned.

I jumped in next to him. "You'll have to catch me first."

Racing over to the seashore with William in hot pursuit, I turned around every so often and splashed water at him. He grabbed me at the first opportunity and we wrestled in the water, laughing, splashing, and squealing before I swam away again.

Now in the shallows, I climbed onto his back but he threw me off in an instant. The water splashed around me as I became momentarily submerged before bobbing back to the top. William swam over to me and wrapped me in a hug. Sending another wave of water over him, he laughed, fighting against me until I was under arrest.

Water dripped from his eyelashes and his eyes softened as his gaze melted into mine. Under the water, I could feel his manly anatomy hard against my body. William exhaled and ran his fingers through my hair, which had transformed from stark and straight to soft and curly.

"You fascinate me," he whispered, twirling a lock around his finger.

My cheeks flooded with emotion and warmed as I placed a tender kiss on his lips.

William's hands glided up the sides of my face as our kiss intensified and we began a slow and passionate dance in the waves. My chest threatened to explode and tears leaked from my eyes, mixing with the salty water as he filled me with his passion. My nails raked his bare back as I buried my face in his neck to muffle my cries of pleasure. It didn't take long for us to reach the pinnacle of emotion, and we held onto each other, shuddering in the cold water.

William lowered his lips to my face and tenderly kissed me as we waded in each other's arms.

"We are not a dead-end street," he whispered. "I promise you that. I want you to believe me."

"How can you make that promise?" I asked.

"I don't know." He wiped water from my brow and his eyes shifted away from me. "But I'll find a way."

As if on cue, a shooting star whizzed across the sky.

"Look," I said, pointing up.

William looked up just in time to see two more stars zip through the dark sky. "Quick, close your eyes and make a wish," he urged.

I squeezed my eyes together and made my wish. When I opened them, I looked at Will. His eyes were still closed.

AN HOUR AND A HALF LATER, we were ready to head in. After we'd finished swimming, William used his shirt to dry my body off before I stepped into my skirt and buttoned up my top. He stepped into his jeans and threw his jacket across his naked back. We walked through the grounds and back to the ground floor, just outside my open window. William climbed up onto the landing and pulled me up after him. We both climbed through the window and stood in the warmth of my bedroom. William dropped his damp shirt on the bed and pulled me closer for a final hug.

"It's late," I said. "You'd better go."

"I know, but I hate leaving. Just a few more minutes." He nuzzled my nose and started in for another kiss, but the sound of his mother's voice made us stand to attention.

"Naomi?"

Miss Anna called from the hallway and started knocking on the door. I turned to look at William, my eyes as wide as saucers.

"Oh my god, Will. It's your mother," I whispered. "She can't find you in here. What are we going to do? You've got to leave. Now!"

"Don't panic," he said, grabbing my shoulders.

Miss Anna knocked and called again.

"The door is locked, so she won't just walk in." He looked around the room and pointed to the closet. "I'll hide in there," he said, scrambling off in the direction of cover. "Open the door and act normal."

I nodded and hurried to the door, trying to ignore my hammering heart. I gave a final glance towards the closet to ensure William was out of sight, then unlocked the door and pulled it open.

"Naomi," Miss Anna said. Her eyebrows were drawn together.

"Miss Anna. I'm sorry to have kept you waiting. I was just about to change for bed."

"It's after nine o'clock, dear. Why on earth are you still dressed?"

I looked down at my clothes and tried to think of a sensible response.

Miss Anna started talking before I could say anything. "You shouldn't lock your door, darling. Suppose there's an emergency and someone needs to get to you quickly?"

"You're right, Miss Anna. I won't lock it again. I'm sorry."

She sighed and walked further into the bedroom.

"It's been such a long night and I'm pooped," she said, "but I wanted to come and remind you to have your chores finished before the weekend arrives."

"Yes, ma'am," I said, nodding my head slightly. "I have a lot of homework to do, but I certainly won't wait until the last minute."

"Yes. And Mr. Cooper has decided he wants to take you to the ice cream shop on Saturday, but that will only happen if you've done everything you need to do." She smiled at me, but then her head tilted to the side. "Naomi, what happened to your hair?"

My hand lifted to the top of my head. Anxiety seized me.

My hair...

How could I explain why my hair was suddenly in an afro when it'd been in shoulder-length ringlets a few hours ago? A million thoughts rushed through my mind. I sorted through them, trying to find a believable one.

"I showered earlier and forgot my cap," I sputtered. "And after all the work I did to straighten and curl it. I guess I'll have to press it again for the weekend."

"Well, I should say so," she said. "You know I prefer the straight look to *that* one." She smiled, but it faded again as her eyes shifted around the room. She looked at the repositioned desk and then the bed.

I pressed my shaking arms against my sides, fighting the urge to twiddle my thumbs.

Don't panic. Act normal.

She walked over to the bed and picked up William's shirt. "Naomi, what is this doing in here?" she asked.

I opened my mouth, willing believable words to come out.

She walked towards me, and I saw her hands tighten around the clothing. "And it's wet."

"Miss Anna, I..."

Her chin dropped and her eyes hardened before I could say any more. "Naomi," she started, her tone lowering to a whisper, "I hope you're being honest with me." The icy glare served as a warning. "Now, you've always been a good girl from the moment you got here. I would hate to think I was wrong about you."

My head slowly dropped until I was staring at my bare feet. "No, Miss Anna," I said, forcing my gaze to return to hers. My eyes quivered. "William stopped by earlier to help me with math homework. Maybe he forgot it when he left."

Miss Anna's eyes narrowed as she cleared her throat and straightened her shoulders. "Well, in that case, I'll have to have a chat with William. I don't quite like the idea of him being in your room so often. I know the two of you study together sometimes, but I'm not comfortable with it. You're growing into a woman, Naomi, and it's not proper for a boy to be coming into your room like that. Things happen to girls like you, and I'm sure you know what I'm talking about. Not that anything would ever happen between you and William, but it's the principle I'm talking about."

My mouth tightened, but I nodded.

Miss Anna smiled and reached her hand out to stroke my head, but then she pulled it back and her fingers rolled into a fist.

"Make sure you straighten that tomorrow," she said, heading for the door. As she was about to exit, she turned back and looked around the room again. I stood, stuck to the floor. My pulse pounded against my ears like a set of drums in my head.

"Good night." She smiled at me one last time and slipped through the door, closing it softly behind her.

When the coast was clear, I finally released the breath I'd been holding and hurried to the closet just as Will stepped out. His face was red, and his eyes were hard and wet.

"Are you okay?" he asked, grabbing me by the shoulders.

"I'm fine," I said, but my voice was shaking. "Just hurry outta here before she comes back or something."

He nodded and started for the door, but I grabbed his arm.

"Uh-uh. Use the window," I instructed. "She could still be in the hallway, and then I'd really be in trouble."

William stared at me but quickly turned and headed for the window.

I watched him slink through onto the outside ledge, and then he reached back in and pulled me close. Placing a firm kiss on my mouth, he then pulled away with sincerity in his eyes.

"I'll find a way, okay?"

My lips trembled and I nodded. After giving him a final quick kiss and hurrying him off the ledge, I changed my clothes and buried myself under the covers.

3

WILLIAM
BEAUFORT, S.C., 1954

*I*t was late at night, and I was in Naomi's room with my arms wrapped around her. We were exhausted after several rounds of slow and deliberate lovemaking. The time for my departure to Harvard was drawing near, so we had been sneaking in as many encounters as possible. At 11:30 p.m. the house was quiet and dark. It had been the perfect opportunity for us to spend uninterrupted time together.

I dotted a trail of gentle kisses over her face under the glow of the nightstand lamp as she wriggled and giggled under my caresses.

"We need to stop this," she whispered through a labored sigh.

"How can you say something like that with such a serious face?"

"Will, this is very serious. You're really askin' for trouble coming in here every night. Remember what happened last time?"

I rolled my eyes. "Last time, as in, last year?"

"It doesn't matter that it was a year ago," she said. "It was a close call. We almost got caught."

"But we didn't," I argued. "So much time has passed, my mother doesn't even think about that anymore."

"How can you be so sure?"

"Remember how she used to sneak around like Sherlock Holmes, gathering clues and evidence? After we decided to lay low, we threw her off our scent."

"Laying low was all my idea," she reminded me. "If it were up to you, she'd have uncovered a ton of *evidence*." She sighed. "You're leaving in three weeks, Will. I need to get used to the idea of you not being around here anymore. No more midnight walks in the garden. No more holding hands and touching. No more of this..." She paused. "The more time we spend together, the more I realize how much I'm going to miss you when you get on that big old airplane and fly away from me. Far away too. It just doesn't seem fair."

My jaw tightened as the reality of the situation was again forced upon me. I placed a tender kiss on the side of her face and turned so I was lying on my back, looking at the roof of her poster bed.

"You know what else isn't fair?" I said. "I'm going to Boston, and you have to go to Seattle. And *that's* far away." We fell silent for a moment before I sighed. "Sometimes I dream about us leaving and getting a place together. Can you see it, Nay? We'd meet after class, walk down the street holding hands and nobody cares. We'd be together and you wouldn't have to be afraid of what anyone thought or said."

Her mouth drew into a straight line.

I swallowed before continuing. "You know I found a nursing school in Cambridge. Why won't you consider that? We'd be able to see each other every day. Nothing would have to change. No one would even know. The keepers wouldn't have a clue."

She chuckled and shook her head but still didn't say anything.

I grimaced. "What does that mean?"

"This isn't the first time you've mentioned that school. Will, we've talked about it over and over." She sighed. "I cannot go to the school in Cambridge because your father and mother have chosen the school I'm going to. It's a great nursing school, and I'm really excited about it."

"The school in Cambridge is also a great nursing school. In fact, it's an excellent one. Massachusetts is the academic capital of the United States, you know?"

"That may be true, but how exactly would we explain to everybody—"

"Everybody as in, my father and mother?"

"No...I mean, how would we explain why we're all of a sudden wanting to go to the same state?"

"I don't know, but we could easily make something up."

Naomi shook her head. "Me going anywhere else is out of the question. You know that. How would it look if I suggested another school?"

I grunted. "Why do you always do everything they say anyway?"

She looked at me as if the question was a stupid one. "Do you know how much your parents have done for me and my mama, Will? Mama is always quick to remind me. I was five years old when my daddy left us with nothing but a crocheted blanket and the clothes on our backs. There was no milk, no food, and there was no house to live in. We bounced around, from house to house, staying with friends and sometimes strangers. I remember having to wake up early with Mama so we could go walking around rich, white neighborhoods, knocking on doors, begging white folk to let her cook and clean for them. Before we left, she would scrub my cheeks and tell me I had to be a good girl so someone would take us in. I always tried my best to be good. I didn't ask Mama any questions and I didn't cry or pout, even though I was so hungry I didn't think I could walk another mile next to her. It took more than two months, Will. Mama would knock and knock. Black people would answer the doors and close them in her face in one swift motion." Naomi paused. "Then, one day, your father opened the door. And you were standing next to him. Do you remember?"

My throat felt dry. "Yeah. I remember."

"Mama says there was a connection. Your father let us inside, and we've been here ever since. So you should already know why I do everything your parents say. They care about me and want the best for me. If it weren't for them, nursing school would be out of the question, no matter how smart I am."

I inhaled, taking in the severity of the situation.

"If I suggested Cambridge, everyone would be suspicious. We would blow our cover."

I threw my head back against the pillow. "You're right, I know. It doesn't make sense and it's not possible. I guess I just feel desperate because we're going to be apart soon, and there's nothing we can do about it."

We lay in silence for a second, each of us looking up at the canopy above her bed. The air in the room was thick and heavy, a stark contrast to the lighthearted atmosphere we'd enjoyed earlier.

I turned my head to look at her silhouette. "Do you wanna know what I think about *our cover,* though?" I grabbed the bedspread and ripped it off her, revealing her gloriously naked body.

Naomi squealed with laughter as I pounced on her, and we fooled around in the sheets. After a few minutes, she pushed me off the bed and handed me my pants while laughing hysterically.

"You need to get out of here," she said. "It's Wednesday night."

"So what does that mean?"

"Wednesday night is the night your mother has her committee social. She could be home any minute."

"And…" I pressed her.

"Will, if she were to catch you coming out of here…" Her bottom lip caught between her teeth as a wave of anxiety registered across her face.

"Do you really think I care if my mother knows about us?" I asked, trying to soothe the lines of concern etched deep into her forehead.

"You might not care, but I wouldn't want anything bad to happen to my mama or me. This is all we have, Will."

I sighed and kissed the worry away as she pulled a robe across her body.

"I'm sorry," I said. "I just hate that we have to hide 'us' all the time." I took my pants from her hand and stepped into them. She watched me from the bed with a twinkle in her eyes.

I chuckled. "You're saying you want me to leave, but the look on your face is suggesting something entirely different."

Her smile dropped a little. I fastened the button on my pants and approached the edge of the bed. "What's the matter?"

Naomi swallowed and tried to smile. "I'm going to miss you. I'm going to miss this...us."

Emotion caught in my throat as I pulled her off the bed and walked her to the door.

"You remember what I promised, don't you? I'll find a way. Don't give up on me." Her eyes looked hopeful, but her withering shoulders revealed the true thoughts going through her mind. I drew her close to me and squeezed her body, delighted at the way her petite frame melted into mine. She was always so warm and soft, with a scent reminiscent of new spring flowers.

We stood in silence as I basked in her potent presence.

Suddenly, the door flew open, knocking us back and revealing my mother standing before us. Her eyes widened, and her skin turned red beneath the layers of expensive makeup.

Before either of us could react, my mother marched into the room and ripped us apart. She gripped Naomi's shoulders and shoved her away. Naomi's back hit the wall with a thud and she shrieked, wincing in pain.

My brain took forever to register what was happening. "Mom, what are you doing?" I sputtered.

She spun on her heels. "What am I doing? I should be asking that of you!" Her eyes bulged. "Were you touching her, William?"

I looked at Naomi, who was cowering against the wall.

"I was...I was hugging her. I—"

"What have you two been doing? I can't believe you are in her room after I told you not to go in there anymore! Don't tell me you were in her bed, William. Were you in her bed?" My mother's words were like rapid fire. Her eyes were bloodshot. Her breathing was ragged.

Words disappeared deep in my throat.

My father hurried around the corner with his eyebrows knitted together at the apparent commotion.

"Anna, what in God's name..."

"I don't know, Bill." She stopped to catch her breath, pressing one hand against her chest and the other against her forehead. "That's what I'm trying to figure out, but your son refuses to answer. Maybe *you* can get something out him."

My father observed her for a second and then turned to me, but I couldn't look at him. As my eyes fell to the floor, my shoulders stiffened. The heat rising in my chest made me feel like I was going to burn from the inside out, and all of a sudden, a feeling washed over me as if my body was about to collapse in on itself. I was concerned for Naomi, but I couldn't look at her either. I had to do something, but I didn't know what.

"Son, what is going on?" he whispered.

"Nothing...I mean..." I finally made eye contact with Naomi. She was still slumped against the wall, her paled skin and her wide-eyed stare crying out for help.

My father's voice cut off the nonverbal exchange. "If you won't answer, then I guess I'll have to ask Naomi."

"Really, Bill? Is that how you propose to handle this situation?" my mother demanded. "Do you really think she'll tell us the truth? I asked her before and she outright lied to me. I pray to the good Lord above that the two of you were not doing the unthinkable. You would be a disgrace to this family, William. An absolute disgrace!" She scoffed and turned to glare at Naomi. "And as for you, missy, if you think that living here has given you a license to get close to my son, then we can certainly remedy that!"

Naomi tried to respond. "Miss Anna, I—"

"Don't you dare talk back to me, little girl," my mother barked.

Naomi's head fell.

"And you make sure to look at me when I'm addressing you."

Naomi attempted to lift her head, but it looked heavy.

My mother marched over to Naomi and yanked her up from off the wall. My heart caught in my throat.

"Mom, stop it!" I cried.

"Anna!" snapped my father.

With my mother's attention momentarily distracted, Naomi

pulled away from her and sprinted down the hall, disappearing from sight.

My muscles vibrated throughout my tense body, and my jaw tightened as I briefly glared at my mother before turning to follow Naomi.

"I think you should go to your room, son. I'll get Naomi. You and I, we will talk in the morning," my father said.

I ignored him and kept walking, my legs quivering like strands of overcooked spaghetti.

"You'd better listen to your father, if you know what's good for you," my mother shouted.

I stopped, but didn't turn to look at either of them. "I know what's good for me," I whispered through tight lips. "And I'll have it in as little as three weeks." I stomped away, the sound of my mother's screaming voice in the distance still ringing in my ears.

HAVING SEARCHED EVERYWHERE for Naomi for at least fifteen minutes, including the library, the backroom, and the kitchen, I'd finally found her out on the dock. I could see the top of her head rising just above the back of one of the lawn chairs on the edge of the wharf. This had become our favorite place to sneak off to late at night when everyone was asleep, though we had christened several other spots around the house too. Smiling, I imagined the soft beams of moonlight sprinkling through the boughs of the azaleas and falling on her body, creating a heavenly glow.

A deep, purple-blue curtain of darkness had long settled over the clearing far beyond the lake, and the full moon shone a luminous path across its surface. The tall lamps leading down to the dock twinkled against the darkness, and somewhere in the distance a heron flapped its wings, taking off into the night.

I paused and drew in a snatch of the humid July air before making my way towards her. My sneakers thudded against the grass and scraped along the splintered wooden planks of the dock.

"I've been looking everywhere for you," I said.

She didn't reply. She didn't even look up. A choir of crickets sang an almost-harmonic melody in the background.

"Why are you avoiding me?" I huffed. "What good will that do?" Still, no reply. I groaned. "Nay, can we please talk?"

"About what?"

I dragged the vacant chair closer to her and eased myself into it. I stared at her profile and moistened my lips. "About what happened just now." I swallowed. "About my mother."

She turned to look at me. Her eyes were hard and puffy, but she laughed. It sounded like something scraping against her throat. Turning away again, she threw her head back and smeared the tears across her cheek.

"It's not funny," I mumbled, trying to ignore the thickness in my throat.

"No, you're wrong," she snapped. "The fact you want to talk about what happened tonight, like you even *understand* what happened, is a big tickle."

"Of course I understand it," I said. "My parents...The things they said were wrong. It was hurtful, it was disrespectful, it—"

"Was all of that, yes, I know," she interrupted, "and you..." She swallowed, fighting the well of tears behind her swollen eyelids. "You didn't even say anything in my defense."

"What was I supposed to say?" I asked, leaning closer.

She shook her head. "If I have to tell you—"

"Okay, no, you don't have to tell me, it's just..." My head dropped. "It was a nightmare. It was my family, it was you..."

"And your family won. You said you didn't care about what anyone thought about us, but that was just apple butter. You weren't being straight! Miss Anna only saw you hugging me, and it totally rattled her cage!" She exhaled a ragged sigh as her shoulders drooped in front of her body. "You promised me you would find a way, but that wasn't true either."

Her eyes shimmered and fresh tears splashed down her cheeks.

Naomi wrapped her arms around her body and stared at the water as the heron glided back across.

"I can stand up to her," I whispered.

"You shouldn't have to," she said and sighed. "I've been thinking, William."

I groaned and rolled my eyes. That phrase was the universal prelude to bad news. "Naomi—"

"It's not gonna work. I think we both know that. We knew it two years ago. We knew it last week."

"What are you talking about?"

"Our relationship, if that's what it even is   "

"Of course that's what it is. That's what it's been since I first came into your room and told you how I felt about you."

"It's been two years of nothing but secrets and lies," she said. "I've had to be in the shadows because it was too dangerous for me to be in the light. We can't go anywhere unless it's with your parents, and now that they know something is going on between us, I'll never be able to go anywhere with you again."

"You can go wherever you want," I said. "*We* can go anywhere we want. You're nothing to hide."

"It sure didn't seem that way when Miss Anna was ripping us apart like I had some disease."

I shuddered. "I didn't know what to say, but I do know I'm not ready to give up on us and lose the one thing that means more to me than anything else in the world."

I took her hands in mine and placed my lips on them. Rubbing my face against her palm, I desperately wanted to make her see that everything was going to be okay.

"I have never seen Miss Anna look like that," she whispered, almost to herself. "She has never, ever looked at me like that. It was like..." Her breath caught. "Like I didn't know her, and she didn't know me."

I buried my head in her lap, trying to force her affection. Her fingers tousled my hair and I squeezed my eyes closed, secretly trying to erase the tears.

"You say you're not ready to give up on us," she repeated, "but maybe I am." She pulled her hand away from me and scooted the lawn chair backwards a touch.

Taken aback, I straightened my posture. "What are you saying?"

She chewed the inside of her lip. "Maybe I should stick to dating people who look like me," she whispered with a nod.

The muscle in my jaw cinched. "You mean like Danny Hightower?"

"Don't make this about him. These are your people, Will. This is *your* life. I'm only a part of it because I live in your house, because my black mama works for your white father and mother. You will never understand my life, no matter how much you think you do."

"Baby..." I reached out to her, but she instantly backed away.

"Cut the gas," she said. "You're leaving for Harvard in a few weeks anyway."

"What's that got to do with anything?"

"There'll be other girls where you're going. White girls. Girls you can relate to. Girls your parents will approve of."

"I don't want any other girl," I barked, pounding my fist on the arm of the lawn chair. "I've told you. I am coming back and I'm coming back to you, Naomi."

"I'm going to be in Seattle...that's if your parents even want to do anything for me anymore. Either way, it's not going to be the same."

"Nothing has to change."

"You're wrong," she said, shaking her head. "*Everything* has to change. In fact, it already has."

I glared at her until I could look no more. My heart clamored inside of my chest.

"It's over, William. Let's just...try and act like this never happened. I'm going to apologize to Miss Anna. I'm going to assure her I will never make a mistake like that again." She grunted and raised from the chair before slowly walking up the dock and towards the dark shadows of the house.

Standing alone, I stared at the lake, trying to make the complex puzzle pieces fit together. I understood what she was saying. I knew what her fears were because they were mine also. But maybe she was right. Maybe I didn't really understand. Maybe I never would. It didn't matter to me. All I wanted to do was try my best to understand. I had let Naomi down. How could I blame her for wanting to end it? I should have said or done something more.

My father's boat bobbed back and forth on the rippling water of the lake.

"I can fix it," I blurted out at nothing but the water. Turning to look after her, I shouted, "I can fix it! Marry me!"

The shuffling of her feet came to a halt, though I could barely see her through the curtain of my tears. "When I graduate from school, let's get circled. Right away."

"You've flipped your lid," she said.

"You might be right," I said, "but I would definitely flip my lid if I let you go back to that house without telling you I can do without this life. I can do without my parents' approval. I don't need their house, I don't need their money, I don't need any of it if it means I won't have you."

She was frozen.

"You *can* depend on me," I said. "I was wrong for not defending you tonight, but I promise you, I'm going to fix it." I pointed toward the house. "I'm going to tell my mother how I really feel about the terrible things she said and the way she acted." My voice was shaking. "I'm going to tell her I love you and that there is nothing she can do about it. I *will* defend you, Naomi," I said. "I will defend *us*."

Naomi stared at me. The look in her eyes led me to believe she wanted to trust me. The way her body trembled told me she wanted to run into my arms and never leave them, but instead of trusting me, instead of running towards me, she burst into tears and bolted in the other direction.

My heart twisted in my chest. "Naomi!" I called after her.

She was gone.

4

WILLIAM

BEAUFORT, S.C., 1954

hree Weeks Later

The dreaded day had arrived. It was the day of my departure to Massachusetts and the official severing of my relationship with Naomi. It was a busy and steamy Saturday morning in early August, with crowds of people and their luggage filling every corner of the airport. The queue for the American Airlines flight was snaking beyond the ropes and spilling into the main walkway. It was a depressing scene. It matched my mood perfectly. Only my mother and father walked beside me; although I had searched high and low for her, I had been unable to find Naomi. In fact, we hadn't really spoken since the debacle three weeks ago. I had tried to talk to her. I had tried to reach out her, but she was distant. I'd walked the gardens alone at night hoping I'd bump into her. I'd knocked on her door at midnight. I'd even tried to walk in without knocking, but she soon started using the lock to keep me out. She had made herself inaccessible, both physically and emotionally.

I dragged my Louis Vuitton luggage across the floor, listening to the wheels clacking against the tiles of the Hilton Head Airport. My mother was too close for comfort, enthusiastically snapping pictures with the new Polaroid camera my father had bought for her. It was like she was trying to make up for what she had done, but it was too late. She would never be able to make up for the way she treated Naomi, or for ruining my relationship.

The irritating whizz and whir of pictures shooting from the mouth of the device was grating my ears, second only to the flash that was constantly blinding me. I swiped my hand across my face. "Mom, are you serious with that thing? I'm begging you to stop."

Snap.

Taking the flap that protruded from the bottom, she fanned it around in the air. "William, just because you're eighteen and you have hair on your chin and lip now, dooon't mean I can't treat you like my baby." Her thick, southern accent seeped with overbearing affection as she grabbed my cheeks and pinched them between her slender fingers.

My father stepped forward and clapped a manly hand on my shoulder. "Your mother and I are very proud of you, William. I'm looking forward to hearing great things from Harvard. You've worked very hard to get to this place. I know you'll take full advantage of the opportunity you've been given." He lowered his head and peered at me with raised eyebrows.

"Your father won't say it, but I will," my mother added, her posture turning ramrod straight. "We were very worried. For a minute, we thought you'd squandered this opportunity. You've made some silly mistakes along the way...some careless decisions, but thank God everything has worked out just fine."

"What are you saying?" I asked, tugging at the open neck of my shirt.

"We needn't beat around the bush," she said. "There'll be a lot of girls over in Boston." She looked around and lowered her voice. "Now, I know you're upset at the way I handled Naomi a few weeks ago, but your friendship with her will survive that. You'll make new friends. And of course there's always that nice girl, Evelyn."

"I don't need relationship advice from you, Mom," I said. "And speaking of Naomi..." I looked around the airport. "Where is she? Where is Miss Carole?"

"Miss Carole had some things to do around the house," she answered, fixing the elaborate double string of pearls around her neck.

My father shook his head and took a step closer. "Yes, she has work to do, Anna, but I gave her permission to come and see Will off," he said. "I know how much she means to you. Both of them. Naomi has been like a sister to you. I'm sorry about what happened a few weeks ago as well, just as your mother is."

My jaw tightened, but my racing heart began to settle. If I couldn't see Naomi before I left, I would have considered changing my ticket.

Scanning the airport showed no sign of either of them, and the line to the ticketing agent was moving more rapidly than I would have liked. With each step closer to the counter, my heart sank deeper.

She wouldn't do this to me, I told myself. In two weeks, she'd be off to nursing school and the chances of me contacting her would be even more slim. At least there was the hope of seeing her during the holidays. That offered me some comfort.

I was two passengers away from the ticketing agent and my neck was on a swivel. My mama kept clearing her throat and trying to initiate conversation, but even that couldn't distract me.

Where the hell is she?

As if on cue, Miss Carole's voice broke through the din. I spun around in the direction of her familiar tone. She was wearing the yellow sheath dress, which I knew she only wore on special occasions, a fashionable tam on her head, and a simple purse hanging on her wrist.

"Oh my! William." She hurried up to me and gathered me in a warm, maternal embrace, squeezing and shaking my shoulders so hard I could feel my cheeks starting to wobble. Her kindheartedness permeated every inch of my clothing. "Oh my god, you look so handsome, William," she said, holding my face between her palms. For no reason, she began to adjust my collar and pick bits of imaginary lint off the edges of it. "You're making your father proud, you know?

You're making us all so very proud. You go on over there and study good, you hear?"

I smiled at her. "Thank you, Miss Carole. And yes, I will."

She lowered her voice and looked at me through lowered eyes. "And you keep those vulture women away. Once they get a look at you—a good looking and broad-shouldered—they'll be all over you, but you stay focused, you hear?"

"Yes, ma'am," I said.

Her eyes twinkled as she smiled.

"Carole." My mother's voice sliced through the moment.

Miss Carole took a step back as she turned to look at my mother. Her posture stiffened. "I know what you're gonna say, Miss Anna. Everything at the house is taken care of. I made sure to wake up extra early so I could see this fine young man off." She turned to me, smiling again, and picked more lint off my shirt.

My father cleared his throat. "You don't need to explain, Carole. We wanted you to be here for this." My father looked at me.

I looked away.

"Right, well," my mother said through tight lips, "we don't need to waste anymore time now, do we? We need to get moving." She smiled and took another picture.

I was still holding onto Miss Carole. "Miss Carole, where's Naomi?" I whispered.

She stared at me. When she spoke, it matched my volume. "She outside. Said she needed to catch some air, but I don't think she coming in. She told me to tell you goodbye."

My eyes shifted to the exit.

Miss Carole gently touched my cheek. "She says she okay, but I don't think she ready to see you go, Will. You two been together since you was children. She's going to miss you bad, Will."

With eyes like wide spheres of anticipation, I turned to look at my mother. "Hold my spot, Mom. Naomi is outside and I need to say goodbye to her."

My mother shoved the Polaroid against my father's chest and marched over to me like a soldier approaching an enemy. "I don't think that's a good idea," she said. "It's almost your turn to check in and you cannot miss this flight. Now, I said it's time to go and I will not have you disobeying me, William Cooper." She looked at Miss Carole. "Carole, go and fetch Naomi. Let her know William would like to bid her farewell."

Miss Carole nodded. "Yes, ma'am."

As she turned to head for the exit, I put my hand on her arm and stopped her. "I'll go," I said, glaring at my mother. My father cleared his throat, an unspoken command, and my mother stepped back with her tongue in her cheek. Before anyone could say anything else, I rushed out of the airport and onto the sidewalk.

The hot August air smacked me in the face, causing beads of sweat to break on my brow in an instant. Travelers bustled everywhere; rich white families with children and their colored nannies, and students going to school for the start of a new semester. I scanned the crowd, looking for Naomi. There weren't many black people amongst the masses, especially not our age, so I figured it should be easy to spot her.

Finally, I saw her, sitting on a bench at the entrance of the terminal. She was wearing a sleeveless, pink cotton halter dress that fanned out from her trim waist like a flower. Her smooth, tawny shoulders, the ones I'd run my hands over so many times, glowed against the sun's rays. A fashionable pink scarf tied around her neck and matching pink pumps brought the outfit together. With her chin pressed against her chest and her hands folded around a handkerchief in her lap, the altogether sorrowful demeanor was completed by several ringlets of hair falling down over her face.

I looked around and steadied myself before making my way over to the empty space on the bench next to her.

She didn't move.

I leaned over and whispered in her ear. "The first time I saw you in this dress was the day we went to the ice cream shop. Do you remember? I convinced you to order the mint chip ice cream. You always get strawberry, but that day you tried something new."

She pressed the hanky to her nose but didn't say anything.

I caught my bottom lip between my teeth and continued, leaning closer. "Then...we got back to the house and I took you out of the dress." I chuckled just thinking about it. "I love this dress. You wore it for me, didn't you?"

She shifted on the bench but still didn't look at me.

I sighed and tried to swallow my Adam's apple. "Please tell me you weren't gonna let me leave without saying goodbye, Nay."

She shrugged her small shoulders. "I was going to write you a letter," she said, pursing her glossy lips. "I was going to write it tonight and give it to the mailman tomorrow. You would've gotten it soon enough."

"It takes a long time for a letter to get from South Carolina to Massachusetts, Nay," I said.

Silence.

"Why are you shutting me out?" I shuffled closer to her. "I'm going to do right by you, I promise. You just have to trust me and be patient."

For the first time since I sat down, she looked at me. Her eyes were red and watery. "How can you say something like that? Patient? Trust you? I've been telling you for months we need to call it quits. I'm only here because..."

I waited for her to continue.

Her tone softened. "Because it would be wrong for me to not say goodbye."

I reached out and gently brushed my knuckles against her silky smooth cheek.

A group of white college boys passed us. One of them gave us a condescending look.

"You only feel that way because you don't believe we can really do this," I said. "If we love each other, if we want to be together, there's no one that can stop us."

"Except the world."

"What are you talking about?"

"Will, look around," she demanded. "There are people over there staring at us right now, and we're not doing anything 'cept having a conversation. Is your head that deep in the sand?"

I glared at her, angry with her and whomever she was referring to. I refused to acknowledge what she was saying. Heat rose in my chest.

"Admit it, Will, it was fun while it lasted, but it's over now." She swallowed. "I'm sure you'll find the woman of your dreams very soon. Miss Anna and your father probably have it all arranged by now." She huffed and folded her arms across her chest. "So I guess it's goodbye, Will," she said, standing and putting an end to the conversation and our relationship all in one fluid motion. She turned and started to walk away.

"Naomi, please don't leave me like this," I begged, fighting the rising current of raw emotion. "The dock was one thing. Not speaking to me for three weeks after was another. But if you walk away now, I swear..." My heart plunged as she continued her departure. My feet were stuck to the pavement. I wanted to chase her, but it wouldn't make sense. I thought about going back into the airport, but now, I wondered if that made sense either.

Miss Carole's hand on my shoulder jerked me back into reality. "William. It's time to go," she said softly.

I closed my eyes as tears crowded in the back of my throat, threatening to flood at any moment, and my shaking hands clenched into fists so tight I could feel my nails leaving indentations in my palms.

We stood in silence for a second, and then she said, "I know you love her, Will. I know your secret. It's safe with me."

My eyes shot open and I looked at the woman, searching her face for confirmation. I instantly found it in her sad smile and pulled her into another firm embrace, her narrow shoulders almost crumbling under the pressure. I released her and walked into the airport with my head held high, vowing that I would see Naomi again one day. And when I did, I wouldn't let her get away.

5

WILLIAM

BEAUFORT, S.C., 1957

"Where's your father to cut the turkey?" my mother said as she rounded the corner holding a casserole dish full of steaming, bright green beans and pork bits. Not too long after, Miss Carole entered the room with a dish of golden cornbread. She set it down on the table and wiped her hands on her apron.

"Carole, don't forget the chitterlings, now," my father reminded her with a playful wink.

She offered him a small smile and nodded once. "No, sir. I'd never forget your chitlins. I know how much you like 'em." She pointed to a dish next to him. "There they are right there, Mr. Cooper. Right next to you where you can get 'em easy."

My mother groaned, swiping the back of her hand over her forehead. "Jesus Christ, I hope you cleaned them right this year, Carole. Last year was an absolute disaster." She took her usual place next to my father, who was sitting at the head of the table and wriggled his shoulders, settling in for the monster feast.

Miss Carole acknowledged my mother's concerns with another polite smile, but this one shivered on her face. "No, ma'am. This year they done right."

My father leaned closer to my mother. "Carole didn't prepare the chitterlings last year, darling," my father said gently, placing his hand over my mother's. "It was the new girl we took on, Adrianne. Remember, she'd never done it before?"

My mother grunted, reluctant to shift the blame, especially if it meant an apology would become necessary. "In that case, Carole should have supervised better," she mumbled under her breath.

"Well, I made sure they up to snuff this year, Miss Anna. Wouldn't want you disappointed again now, would we?"

My mother grunted and Miss Carole quietly left the room.

I shuffled in my chair, hating the fact that it was yet another Thanksgiving. I'd never really bought into the holiday. The unspoken tension that lingered between my parents made it a little hard to find something to be thankful for. They were cordial in public, but before I'd moved to college, I used to hear them arguing up on the third floor. I'd never been made privy to the nature of the argument but my mother was always crying and shouting at my father, who always seemed so cool and nonchalant in his responses.

The unnecessarily long dining table was decked out with the finest of china and gold-plated cutlery. Down the center, a smorgasbord of culinary delights released aromas that made my mouth water.

I pushed my linen napkin down the front of my shirt and leaned back in the chair, throwing my arms over the sides.

My Uncle Steve, my mother's brother, and his wife, Elise, had flown in a few days before. They'd brought my three cousins with them, Bruce, Amy, and Alice. Evelyn Dandridge had also been invited to the feast at my mother's insistence, and she had already tried to catch my eye from across the table. She was wearing a navy blue polka-dot petticoat and skirt, and if I'd have bothered to look at her for long enough, I would have noticed the way her breasts perched against her chest. Her choice of fancy perfume was just shy of competing with the aromas of the Thanksgiving meal.

The table was full. But not full enough.

There was no Naomi. Again.

In fact, this would make the third Thanksgiving she had missed.

I didn't understand it. Why wouldn't she want to come back home and see everyone? Her mother? Me? Every year felt worse than the one before. Around October, I'd get my hopes up real high. I'd call the house and pray Miss Carole would answer, and when she did, I'd ask her if Naomi would be home for the upcoming holiday. Miss Carole could never answer my question. How could I expect her to? She had no say in whether Naomi came home for the holiday. It was all up to my parents. Every year, the disappointing reality would set in once at the Thanksgiving dinner table. Just like it was setting in now.

Late at night, when everyone was asleep, I'd walk past Naomi's room, push the door open and peek in. Everything inside was the same. Nothing had changed. I swore I could even smell the burning from her hot comb in there. My mother hadn't touched the room. Despite her disdain for our relationship, I knew she loved Naomi. She was like the daughter she'd never had. But the more I thought about it, I wondered if she had really cared about Naomi the way she wanted everyone to believe she did. All she'd ever really done was dress her up like a doll; an object. Maybe she never had cared about Naomi's feelings at all. All she had ever really cared about were her own.

My father, sharpening the carving knife with the big, glazed bird sat in front of him, snapped me out of my thoughts. The feast was about to begin.

"That meat is lookin' mighty good over there," Steve said, licking his lips and rubbing his hands together. His belly sat on top of the table as well as beneath it. For him, it looked like he celebrated Thanksgiving every day. His beady eyes seemed too small for his face, and his false teeth were so loose I wondered how he kept from losing them in his food.

His son, Bruce, was an exact replica of his father at twenty-two years old. And the girls, Amy and Alice, looked like not much food was ever left by the time it got to them, perhaps explaining their smaller frames. It was in their best interest because, even as it was, they'd never place in a beauty pageant. They had inherited their father's beady eyes, but their long, golden hair had come from their mother, who was slightly more normal looking. It was obvious she had married Uncle Steve for his money.

"It took the staff an hour to catch this bird," my father said through a cheesy grin. "He knew all along what his fate would be, having been born and raised for this momentous occasion."

Everyone around the table laughed.

Bruce elbowed me while eagerly readying his napkin. "Thinking about hitting the hop tomorrow night," he said, referring to the big party that happened every year around this time. "You coming or what?"

"Not sure if I'm up to it this year," I said.

He frowned. "What do you mean not sure?" he asked. "Man, you gotta come! Hey, we can double date." He leaned closer and whispered. "I met a mighty fine thing downtown last night. She asked me to meet her at the hop. I was hoping you'd come along. You always know what to say to the ladies." He looked towards Evelyn. "What you say, Evvie? You, Will, me, and that girl I met yesterday."

Evelyn clasped her hands in front of her. "I think a double-date would be groovy," she said. "Of course, Will would have to ask me. A real lady never asks a guy to go out on a date with her, you know. That's what my mama says anyway."

I rubbed my brow. "I'm sorry, guys, but I'm not interested in going to the hop...or going on a date, for that matter," I said. "I got a lot to do and—"

"Evelyn is a lovely girl," my mother said. "I don't care what you have to do, William. I think the three of you going to the hop is a fine idea. It'd be nice for you to get out and socialize for once. All you ever do when you come home is sit in your room and..." Her words and smile faded in unison. "Evelyn, I'll call your mother after dinner."

"It would be good for you to get out, son," my father said. "But, Anna, maybe it'd be best to let Will decide what he wants to do tomorrow night. If he doesn't want to go to the hop then—"

"Bill, if we left it to William he'd never go anywhere. He'd never have a girlfriend and then we'd never have any grandbabies."

I groaned and slid further down in the seat of my chair.

Aunt Elise laughed. "And we must have our grandbabies, isn't that right, Anna? I'm so looking forward to the day when Bruce Junior and the girls give me some little ones to spoil." The two women giggled.

I looked at Evelyn, who was smiling at me with a flushed face and fluttering eyelashes.

Miss Carole returned to the room, bringing the final trimmings to the table and nodded respectfully before turning to head back to the kitchen. That was where *the help* waited to be summoned.

"Carole?" My father held his hand up, stopping her in her tracks.

"Yes, sir?"

"Why don't you join us this year?" He gestured to an empty seat at the corner of the table. "We would like that. Steve, move over. Let Carole squeeze in there."

Steve looked at my mother with questioning eyes, but scooted his chair to the side nonetheless.

Miss Carole didn't budge. "Now, Mr. Cooper, you know that's not necessary. I can find my place with the others in the kitchen. You may need something, and I'm in charge back there."

"She's right, Bill," my mother said. "Carole, you go on back there. We'll save a special plate just for you. After all the hard work you've done, you deserve it."

My father shook his head. "Carole..." Their eyes locked for a second before Miss Carole's gaze dropped to the floor.

"Well, that's mighty kind of you, Mr. Cooper," she said as she eased herself in the seat next to my uncle and offered my father a small smile.

My mother pursed her lips.

"Don't speak of it," my father said. "This is the time of year when family should be together. You've not seen Naomi on Thanksgiving for a few years now. I know it's tough. And we *are* your family."

My chest tightened. I jumped up, grabbed another set of bone china and gold cutlery from the cabinet, and laid them out on the table in front of her.

With the roles reversed, Miss Carole smiled but it was obvious she was uncomfortable with her new-found place at the table.

The dinner progressed, and everyone laughed, talked, and reminisced about days gone by. Everyone except Miss Carole and me. I wanted to speak to her but she was sitting across the table, next to Evelyn, and the conversation I wanted to have with her was no one else's business. I'd tried to catch her attention, but it was glued solely to her plate. Every now and then, I'd feel my mother's eyes fixed on me.

"Have you spoken to Naomi, Carole?" my mother asked, smothering cranberry sauce over her meat.

"Not as yet, Miss Anna, but I expect to hear from her before the day is out. She always wait until it's late before she call. She got a whole lot to do up there in Seattle."

"Instead of calling, it might be nice for her to actually come home for once," I grumbled. "You must miss her terribly."

Evelyn's eyes turned in my direction.

Miss Carole shrugged, cutting into her food. "She up there studying hard, Will. That's very important to me."

"To all of us," my mother added, taking a dainty sip of her beverage.

Some excuse.

"And she can't expect to be traveling back and forth like money grows on trees now," Miss Carole continued with conviction. "Your mother and father were gracious enough to pay her way through nursing school. She can't get too carried away. It wouldn't be proper and I always taught her that, for a young woman, it important to be proper."

"I wondered how she'd been able to afford college," Evelyn said.

"Me too," Amy added.

"She's a lucky darkie, that's how," I heard Alice whisper back. The girls snickered.

As my teeth clamped down on my turkey, I opened my mouth to address them.

My father cleared his throat and interrupted me. "Well now,

Carole, if Naomi wants to come home, I'm sure I can make arrangements for that to happen. You miss her, and so do I."

My mother's head swung around to face my father, while everyone else turned to stare at me as the sudden screeching sound of my knife scraped across my plate.

"Sorry," I mumbled, shoving a forkful of ham into my mouth.

Miss Carole's eyes fluttered. "I appreciate your kindness, Mr. Cooper, I really do. But I don't think Naomi wants to come home," Miss Carole said, shaking her head. "She never mentions it anyhow. No, I think she happily settled over there. Let's not worry ourselves about it."

"Well I, for one, think she should come home," I spat. "She doesn't know anybody over there. It shouldn't matter what she wants to do. We are her family, right, Dad? She should be sitting at this table with the rest of us."

Miss Carole looked back at her plate.

Evelyn's brow creased over her scornful stare.

"You sure seem very passionate about this topic, Will." My mother's voice pierced the silence. She was looking at me through narrow eyes. I met her gaze, but was the first to look away.

"I miss her," I mumbled.

"What do you mean, you *miss her*, Will?" Evelyn asked, frowning. "I'm sure the two of you were good acquaintances but—"

"We were more than acquaintances." I paused, carefully considering my next words. "We were friends."

"Well, we all miss her, Will, but that's no reason for her to travel home for every holiday, is it?" my mother suggested.

"Every holiday? She's not come home for even one, Mom," I said. My tone was sharper than it should have been. I tried to dial it back. "I wish she would come home some time, that's all."

My father rested his fork down. "Maybe we can talk to her and see what she wants to do," he suggested with his usual calm tone.

My mother shook her head. "Carole is right, Bill. Money doesn't grow on trees, and Naomi's got a lot going on up there in Seattle. We all know that. Don't we, Carole?" My mother glared at Miss Carole and then at me. Miss Carole's cutlery rattled in her hands as a chilly silence enveloped the room.

My father cleared his throat again.

"We'll see her when she's graduated, dear. I think that'd be best," my mother finalized.

Steve peered around the table through downcast eyes. "Well, now. It seems as if William here has a little crush on the maid's daughter, the little darkie. Maybe that's why he doesn't want to go out tonight with Bruce," he said.

"How absurd," Evelyn said.

Almost everyone at the table laughed.

My mother's napkin shot to her mouth, like she was trying to contain a guffaw.

My father's mouth and eyes dropped simultaneously.

As my hands rolled into tight fists, I could feel the blood draining from my knuckles. I chewed hard on my bottom lip until the metallic taste of blood filled my mouth.

"We don't engage in that kinda talk 'round here, Steve," my father said through his teeth.

"He was only joking, Bill," my mother said, cutting into her turkey. "Lighten up."

"Yeah, Bill. It was just a joke," Uncle Steve added without looking up from his food.

My father put his cutlery down and tugged uncomfortably at his collar.

Steve slowly looked around the table until his eyes landed on Miss Carole. "It was just a joke, miss," he snapped. "I'm sorry, I didn't quite catch what they call you, but I didn't mean no harm by it. It's Southern humor. Just trying to evoke a few chuckles."

"Just a joke?" I muttered, putting my own cutlery down. "Wow, Steve, I had no idea you'd gone into comedy. But with shitty material like that, I sure hope you haven't quit your day job."

Aunt Elsie gasped.

Evelyn's eyes fluttered, but she still managed to paste a weak smile onto her face.

My mother slammed her hands flat on the table and leaned toward me. "William Cooper, that is absolutely no way to talk to your uncle, and we certainly don't use that type of hooligan language in this house. You apologize at once!"

I leaned forward in her direction. "I can't say *shitty,* but he can call members of this family *darkies?* Gimme a break, Mom."

"William!"

"I'm twenty-one years old, Mom. Do you really think you can talk to me like I'm a kid?" The legs of my chair scraped across the floor as I pushed it away from the table.

"William, you are out of line and if you don't apologize—"

"Apologize?" I shook my head. "You'll keep waiting for that." I threw my linen napkin on the table. "In fact, you'll be lucky to ever get an apology out of me." I stormed around the table towards the door.

"William, you're overreacting," Evelyn said. I ignored her.

Miss Carole tried to grab my hand as I passed her. "Will—"

"No, Miss Carole. You may not have it in you to stand up for what's right, but I do, and I'll be damned if I'm gonna sit at this table and let them talk about you like you have no feelings."

"William!" My mother shouted after me, but I'd already stomped out of the dining room. Barely able to see anything for the rage that was blinding me, I marched up to my room and fell on the edge of my bed. I dropped my head in my hands, willing it not to explode.

It wasn't long before a knock on the door disturbed me from my internal rage. It couldn't have been my mother; she would've barged right in. It didn't matter, though. Whoever it was, I didn't feel like talking.

"Go away," I demanded.

The door slid open and my father peeped in. His face was sagging. Deep lines creased his forehead and the sides of his mouth, but I suspected I hadn't been the one to put them there.

He closed the door and cautiously took a step into the room. "What's this all about, son?" he asked, folding his arms across his chest.

I ignored him.

He proceeded further into the room. "You were disrespectful to your mother and your uncle. I didn't like the things they said either, but there was no reason to lose control."

I rolled my eyes and started examining my fingernails.

My father nodded and walked over to my dresser, passing his hand over the tops of my baseball and tennis trophies. He looked up at my graduation photos and certificates.

I saw his head bend to the side before he reached up to pull a picture from behind one of the frames on my desk. In an instant, I sprung off the bed and ripped it from his hands. My fingers curled around it until the flimsy Polaroid plastic dented between them.

"Why are you here, Dad? What do you want?"

He sighed and sat on the edge of my bed. "I had a feeling this would happen," he muttered. "In fact, I should have known." He scratched his cheek. "William, Naomi is a very nice girl, but there is no way you should be thinking about her as anything more than a friend...a sister."

My eyes tightened as I stared at him. "What are you talking about?"

My father stood and walked toward me with uneven steps. "I know you like her, but—"

"Like her?" I echoed. "You're wrong. I more than *like* her, Dad," I said. "I love Naomi. In fact, I have for years, and both you and Mom know it. That's why you're not bringing her back for holidays and vacations. You're trying to keep us apart, aren't you?"

My father's pale face developed a red hue as his lips bunched up. "I am not trying to do anything other than give you a good life," he said, almost whispering.

"What does that mean?"

"It means that I know what's best for you."

"It means that you're no better than Uncle Steve and Mom," I shot at him. "Admit it. You feel the same way about Naomi and Miss Carole as they do."

"I am not like them," he said, raising his voice back to a normal level and stabbing his finger in the air. He started pacing the room. "And for the record, I had no clue about how deep your feelings were for Naomi. How was I supposed to know? You don't talk to me about anything. You keep everything bottled up. You don't ask me for advice. You never let me be there for you. Your mother, on the other hand..." He grunted. "She's been saying it for a long time, but I never listened to her. Just figured she was overreacting the way she always does." He stared at me, opening his mouth a few times like there was something he wanted to say but wasn't sure how to begin. "So is the rest true then?"

I groaned and walked away from him. "Now is not the time for rhetoric, Dad."

He spun around. "I asked you if it was true," he said, his unusually loud voice shaking my bedpost.

"Yeah, it's true," I shouted back, "and if you think coming in here and giving me some stupid lecture is gonna change anything, then—"

My father raised a thick hand high into the air, aiming for the side of my face. I stood in front of him, refusing to cower beneath him. He could hit me. In fact, I wanted him to hit me. I didn't care.

But he didn't.

Instead, he threw his head back and rested his arms over his face. He sighed. "You're making a mistake, Will. A huge mistake."

"Then how about you let me make it?" I demanded. "You can't control my life. Mom can't control who I love."

"You watch your tone with me, young man," he whispered. "I am not your mother or your Uncle Steve, you hear?"

I lowered my head, trying in vain to keep my lip from trembling.

"There are some things we have to protect you from, William. Things *I* have to protect you from." He shook his head as if he was trying to clear it. "Naomi isn't coming back here. You need to forget about her and move on with your life."

"You can't be serious," I spat.

He started to head out of the room

"You just told Miss Carole you'd think about bringing her home. What's different now?"

"What's different now is that I know what your mother was saying is true. I'm trying to protect you. I know what's best for you, but you don't see that."

I didn't see it. I wouldn't.

My father sucked his teeth and left the room, slamming the door behind him.

I stared at the closed door. A fire singed the inside of my chest as I threw myself onto the bed, slamming my fist on the mattress and rolling up into an emotional pile on top of the comforter.

Through a curtain of tears, I looked down at the wrinkled picture in my hand. Naomi and I stood side by side during a family trip she'd come on, my arm draped around her shoulder. I'd held the camera up in front of our faces and snapped. She was looking into the camera, her smile competing with the Hawaiian sun, and I was looking down at her, my eyes brighter than the flash.

I un-creased the picture as best I could and placed it back on my bureau, in plain sight.

Then something hit me.

Maybe my father was right. Maybe it didn't make sense to be in love with Naomi. I had no idea when or if I'd ever see her again. Obviously, she didn't want to see me, or she would have come home by now.

I was beginning to question whether I really was a fool for holding onto shadows and placing my confidence in ancient memories.

I thought about Bruce and his invitation to go to the hop tomorrow night. Then I thought about Evelyn.

I lifted the picture from the dresser and shoved it in the back of the drawer—way, way back—figuring maybe I'd forget about it if I pushed it far enough out of sight. Then I dove back on the bed and tried to fight through the pain crushing my chest.

6

WILLIAM

"So she's going to die, then?"

Gerald, my driver of over thirty years, had such a way with words.

He raised his eyes to the rearview mirror and caught my attention. I stared back at him, noticing his forehead was creased and his eyebrows were drawn into a straight line. Every now and then, he'd rub his hand over his wiry mustache as if his nose itched.

"So are you, Gerald," I said. "In fact, we all are." In the back seat of the limo, I absently flipped through the pages of the newspaper.

"Yeah, but she's gon' go before us. That's what the doctor is sayin', ain't it?"

I didn't answer.

Gerald shook his head. "I dunno, Mr. C. I'm sixty-three years old and both of you are younger than I am. That just don't seem right."

I refolded the paper and shoved it back into my briefcase before tilting in the backseat and digging into the inside pocket of my blazer, pulling out a Cuban cigar. "It's just breast cancer," I said.

"Just *stage four* breast cancer…"

"They'll cut her titty off, she'll get chemo, and she'll be fine."

"Eloquently put, if I do say so myself," Gerald said, peering at me through the rearview mirror again.

I groaned and rubbed my brow. "I'm sorry, Ger, I know you're concerned. It's bothering me too, it really is. I just don't know what to say right now. I don't know what to think or feel. We all have to make that appointment sometime. I guess I just never considered I'd be dealing with something like this at my age." I thought about the irony of the circumstance for a second then cursed and ran my thumb against the lighter. Lighting the end of the fat cigar, I drew in a few deep puffs, settled back into the seat, and closed my eyes.

"Maybe you should put that thing out, sir. Both you and I gon' be next at the rate you goin'. All that second-hand smoke you releasin'. You been smokin' for years and this is your second cigar since I picked you up."

"Well, maybe I *should* be next." As I stared out of the window, my eyes started to sting with unshed tears. "I ain't been the best husband, Gerald. You know that better than anyone else. If anybody deserves to go, it's me."

"We ain't got to go there, sir," Gerald muttered.

I continued anyway. "Not coming home nights, working late, leaving her all by herself, the other woman..."

"In all fairness, sir, she ain't been the best wife either."

"She's dying, Gerald. It's not right for you to be talking about her transgressions at a time like this."

"That may be true, but it ain't right for you to go on this big old guilt-trip either. What about all the nagging? What about the inter-fering in your business matters," he said, as if trying to provide more evidence for why she should die. "She almost screwed up that Tokyo deal." He snorted.

My jaw tightened but I forced it to relax. "It wasn't the Tokyo deal, Gerald," I corrected him. "You need to make sure you get your facts straight before you start spouting off at the mouth. And what wife doesn't nag, Gerald? That's nothing out of the ordinary."

"Mm-hmm," he said. "Well, you ain't the only one that's been unfaithful. Let's not forget, she's had other men too, you know?"

I lurched forward. "It was one time, and it was one guy."

Gerald grunted. "And you ain't never had no other woman. Not a real one anyway. Only been one thing you been pining for, and you ain't seen her since you were eighteen years old. That's the story you've been telling me, anyhow. How many years is that?"

He had a point. Sort of.

"On top of all those things," Gerald continued without prompting, "Miss Evelyn is meaner than a pit bull tied to a tree on a short leash."

"Okay, that's enough," I said. "Evelyn is dying, and it ain't right for me to be engaging you in this kind of conversation. If that's how you feel about her, that's your business, Gerald, but this is my wife and you need to show some goddamn respect when you talk about her, you hear?"

Gerald pressed his lips together and flicked on the indicator.

I lit the cigar again and lifted it to my lips between trembling fingers. "If I didn't know any better, I'd think you wanted her gone. You're making a pretty good case for it. I know she hasn't been the nicest person, but she's been good enough to you, hasn't she?" Whatever that meant.

"Now, now Mr. C., I'm a God-fearing Christian man," he said. "I'm not keen to wish death on anyone, no matter how evil they are."

I grimaced. "Well, good. Evelyn is at stage four, but it's not the end," I said. "Doctors can turn it around. I've seen it happen a thousand times."

We fell silent.

"The Good Book says the arm of flesh will fail us," Gerald muttered.

"What the hell is that supposed to mean?" I asked.

"It means you can't depend on them doctors, that's what it means," he said. "But who knows? The good Lord might have pity on Miss Evelyn. He might heal her up real good. He did it for my mama."

"I'm glad he did it for your mama," I agreed, waving my cigar through the air. "All I know is, I need to do all I can for Evelyn. I need to be there like I've never been there before. We need to find her a good nurse who can take care of her and help her transition through the emotional and physical stages of this goddamn disease. I can work less," I suggested. "Maybe start coming home early."

"Well," Gerald said. He sounded like he was about to preach a sermon. "Only the good Lord knows what fixin' to come down the line. But this one thing I do know. I done worked for you for almost thirty-six years. I been driving you around in this here car day in and out and you're like family to me, Mr. C. You been mighty good to me and my kinfolk. That means I got your back. I always have and I always will. So, whatever you need, you just need to let me know and I'll do my best to make it happen."

I cleared my throat. "Well, I appreciate that, Gerald. Hearing you say that means a lot to me. And you certainly know how I feel about you, Louise, and the kids."

Gerald caught my eye again and nodded. "So what will Ethan say?"

"He'll be devastated," I said.

It was a lie.

"She doesn't want anyone to know though, and that includes him," I added.

Gerald frowned. "He's y'all's son *and* he's a doctor."

"I know that."

"He might be able to do something."

"I know that too."

Gerald *tsked.* "Blasted women," he said. "It don't make one iota of sense. Well, I'll respect y'all's wishes. I ain't gonna tell a soul about this little dilemma. My lips are as good as sealed."

"Thank you, Gerald."

"Yes, siree. Maybe it's best Ethan doesn't know about it yet. I'm sure right now the only thing on his mind are his upcoming nuptials."

"You might be right," I said, feeling the buzz of my Nokia cell phone. "I was shocked as hell to find out he was dating someone, let alone getting married. He's been consumed with work and studying, and I didn't think he had time to think about anything else." I reached inside my blazer and pulled it out. I frowned. It was Ethan.

"Shit..."

"What is it?"

I held up the phone, showing Gerald Ethan's number, which had popped up on the phone's screen. Gerald frowned and turned into the airport terminal.

"Mrs. C. arrived this morning...there's only one reason for that phone call."

Before I could scold him, he jumped out and opened my door. As he was pulling my luggage from the trunk, I accepted Ethan's call.

"Dad!" His voice was loud and spoken through heavy breathing.

I switched the phone to the other ear. "Ethan, are you okay? What's going on?"

"What's going on?" he echoed. "Who's bright idea was it for Mama to come up before you? Really, Dad?"

So, Gerald was right.

Evelyn's voice in the background competed for attention; the thick, southern drawl, lecturing and scolding. I held the phone away from my ear and groaned as Gerald walked up next to me.

"I don't want to say I told you so..." he whispered, dropping luggage onto the sidewalk.

I ignored him. "Ethan, relax," I said.

"Relax? How is it even possible to relax with her here? You know how she is, Dad. You know how *we* are."

"I'm at the airport now. I'll be there by five o'clock," I said, trying to reassure him.

"And not a moment too soon," he replied.

"Just try to play it cool for a few more hours. I'll handle her when I get there."

"What were you thinking letting her get here before you anyway? If anything, it should've been the other way around. We could've set a game plan." He groaned.

"Don't talk about your mother that way," I said, attempting to concoct some conviction to go along with it.

"I can't believe you, of all people, are saying that. You know better than me how she is. I can't take her, Dad. I don't know how you have for so long!"

I rubbed the back of my neck. "What is she upset about? She's only been there a few hours."

"She always finds something to be upset about," he said. "This time it's Dakota."

Dakota?

"Who's Dakota?"

"My fiancée, Dad. My wife-to-be." He let it sink in. "Apparently, Dakota isn't the kind of girl Mom expects me to be with. Do you think I care what she thinks or has to say?"

"Now, Ethan—"

"She judges everyone. I'm in love, Dad. What else matters?"

My eyes narrowed.

"I'm coming, Ethan. You hold tight. Everything is going to be fine, you hear me? Just..." I paused to select my words carefully. "Just don't do or say anything that will upset your mother. She's going through something right now, and the added stress won't help her none."

"Her and me both," he said and hung up.

AT 4:45 P.M., I was in another limousine, being whisked away from Logan International. Thirty minutes later, the limo was weaving through the narrow streets of cobblestone and came to rest in front of the colonial-style, red-brick two-story home in Beacon Hill. Flowerboxes adorned the four windows with purple hydrangeas spilling from them, and a welcome mat with potted plants at its side laid in front of the door. The chauffeur pulled my door open and I stepped out, heading toward the porch.

Before I could knock, Ethan flung the door open, displaying wide eyes and a disheveled mop of golden-brown hair. I imagined he'd been raking his hands through it since his mother arrived.

"Thank God you're here." He gripped me, pulling me into a tight embrace. He was taller than me, so my beard was securely planted against his neck. "You should've used the private jet. You'd have gotten here sooner." Ethan pulled away from me. "You have to do something, or I swear to God—"

"I'll talk to your mother," I said, slapping his back. "I don't know what this is all about, but I'm sure it's nothing that can't be settled over a bottle of wine and some caviar."

The chauffeur had lugged my bags up the steps and was ready to put them in the house.

Ethan nodded, granting him entry. We watched him disappear inside and Ethan pulled the door closed.

I looked at my son and smiled. He resembled me when I was his age with his strong, set jawline and thick build. Pride consumed me. Despite Evelyn's protests, I had chosen not to follow the tradition of naming him after me. William Cooper was a strong name, but it came with legacy, one which I didn't subscribe to. I had been glad to give him his own identity.

What had I been doing at his age?

I had been making money and missing Naomi, but of course, I'd been doing that for years. It was nothing new.

I grimaced and myself. "Well, big things are happening this weekend, hey?"

The concerned look was plastered across Ethan's face like a bad paint job. "How the hell am I supposed to think about this weekend with *her* in there going crazy?"

The door flew open and my wife stood in the entrance with her hands on her hips. Her chest was heaving in and out, her feet spread apart like she was ready to charge. I rubbed my brow in anticipation of the inevitable.

"Will, I don't know what you're going to do with your son. He has no respect for us. No respect for the way he was raised. Absolutely none. And with everything I'm going through..." Her hand darted to her forehead.

Ethan gripped the bridge of his nose. "Mama, I'm trying really hard not to be disrespectful, but you're making it very difficult."

Evelyn was shaking so much her black bob wig rattled around her ears. She pointed a finger at him, the red polish from her fresh manicure glinting in the sun. "How dare you talk to me, your mother, like that, young man! You may think you're getting married, to some hussy no less, but you're still my child and you will respect me until my dying day!"

Ethan threw his hands up in the air and pushed past her into the house.

I looked after him and then back at my wife, who had turned to hurl her insults after him through the open door. "You get back here this instant!"

I inhaled and touched her shoulder. "Evelyn, what's the problem?"

"What's the problem?" She glared at me and pointed over her shoulder in Ethan's direction. "I don't know what he thinks he's doing, talking about getting married to some girl neither you nor I have met or approved of. Who is this girl, Will? Has he said anything to you about her?"

I tugged at my earlobe. "No, he hasn't," I said.

"Precisely." She lowered her tone. "Her name is *Dakota*..."

I cleared my throat. "Yes, I heard."

Her neck snapped back. "So he *did* tell you about her, then?"

"That's all I know, Evelyn. Listen, you need to relax," I whispered. "You're not well, you know this. We came up here to have a good time and meet the boy's fiancée. All of this drama is unnecessary. It's not doing anyone any good."

"Unnecessary?" She huffed. "Let me be the judge of that, why don't you? Once we meet this *Dakota* woman, you'll see just how necessary it really is.

The chauffeur returned, interrupting the exchange. "Will that be all, sir?"

I groaned and dug into my pocket, pulling out a fifty-dollar bill. "I think that's all. I appreciate you," I said.

Evelyn ran trembling hands over her hair and face while I completed the transaction.

The chauffeur thanked me before shuffling down the steps and driving away.

"Look at him." Evelyn's voice was condescending. "That's probably her father or brother or something."

"Whose?"

"*Dakota's.* She can't possibly come from anything better. A chauffeur's daughter, that's what we're accepting into our family?"

I turned to look at the limousine as it turned the tight corner.

"Thank God I'll be dead and gone so I won't have to live under the disgrace!" Evelyn fixed her hands on her round hips. She'd started off like a Barbie doll, but years of access to the finer things hadn't been good to her waistline.

My head snapped around and my eyes narrowed as the descriptions Gerald had listed off earlier launched themselves into my brain. "Tell me you're not serious."

"Come on, William. With a name like *Dakota*, what kind of girl do you think Ethan is messing with? She's black, William!"

"You're assuming she's black because she's named Dakota?"

"It's an urban name, William. It has to be. Nobody we know would ever name their child after a state. She might as well have been called Oregon."

Listening to the things Evelyn was saying caused bad feelings to rise within me. Her voice, sounding like a swarm of bees, faded into the background as visions of that traumatic Thanksgiving dinner and Naomi assaulted me.

She continued. "She stalked him, I'm sure of it, and our son, my poor baby, he's so sweet and tenderhearted...he probably didn't have the heart to shoo her away, the way he should have." She huffed. "I know what this is really about, William."

"What are you on about now?" I sighed.

She pointed at me. "Don't think I forget about *your* interracial escapades. Now you're trying to live vicariously through your own son!"

"We're not talking about me right now," I said through my teeth. "And besides, that was a long time ago."

"Yet you still think about her," she accused me. "She put her African voodoo on you and it's like you can't get over her. If you had your way, you'd have married that woman. Thank God your mother had some sense."

My chest tightened as memories I'd buried away slapped me like an open palm.

I couldn't stand to listen to her anymore. "Evelyn, you are out of order and you ought to be ashamed of yourself," I snapped, walking into the house and through the foyer. She was hot on my heels. "First of all, you have no proof that this girl is black. And even if she is—"

"So you'd be okay with that?" She snorted. "You know just as well as I that it's not okay. Not for us. Some people can do it and it works out just fine, but for a Cooper..." The words died away. She shook her head. "Not for a Cooper. And I'm very sure your parents would agree, God rest their blessed souls. But like I said, you were in love with the maid's daughter at one point. What was her name? Nantucket? Nevada? But they put a stop to that, didn't they? They saved your life. It's no wonder you approve of this *Dakota* woman."

I spun around and glared at her, the edges of my eyes quivering. "I'm done talking to you," I whispered. I walked away from my wife, unwilling to process her words any longer. All of a sudden, like Ethan, I wanted to slap the woman. Her small-mindedness was grating on me. I'd never heard her speak this way before, but when I considered it, she'd never had a reason to. Where we lived, blacks and whites didn't mix much. Even while growing up, the only black people I knew were the ones who worked for my parents.

And Naomi.

But that didn't justify the sentiment. I didn't feel the way she did, and I had just as much excuse to plead ignorance as the next privileged, rich white person.

I looked around the house, searching for Ethan. I needed to find him. Hearing his voice from around a corner, I stood against the wall and listened for a second.

"Baby, I'm sorry," he was saying, "but what more do you expect me to—"

Silence, except for the muffled squeak of another voice coming from the other end of the telephone conversation. The voice sounded emotional. Irate. I winced and rounded the corner.

Ethan was in the living room, sitting on a cream leather chaise, hunched over and looking defeated. His cell phone was pressed hard against his ear while his free hand gestured in various directions. He was whispering, but the tone was fierce. When he noticed my presence, he stood and ran his hand over his hair.

"Kota, I have to go."

The voice on the other end of the phone sounded off again.

"Of course I want you to come home, but if you don't want to, I can't make you, can I?"

So they're living together?

"Fine," he said. Anger dribbled from his mouth. "Whatever." He hung up.

I approached him slowly, my eyes darting everywhere around the room but at him. This was worse than when I'd had the birds and bees talk with him. That seemed like a walk in the park compared to this. I didn't know where to begin or what I should say. One thing I did know; I needed to be supportive.

Ethan was pacing in front of a vast sliding glass door. Pristine blue water from an infinity pool outside the door glistened under the last rays of a setting sun.

I cleared my throat and shrugged out of my jacket before making my way over to the bar to pour us both a much-needed drink. "What are you having?"

Ethan responded with a groan.

I chuckled and pulled out an expensive bottle of gin and two crystal tumblers. In a fridge below the bar, I found cut limes and ice. "So is she beautiful or what?"

Ethan rubbed his eyes and finally turned to face me. "She's gorgeous," he said in a whisper. He stared up at the ceiling, and I saw a small smile turn the corner of his lips. "And she's black, Daddy."

I stirred the drinks, listening to the ice cubes clinking against the glass. "Is that why your mother is upset?"

"What does it matter if she's black though?" He strode up to me, his arms extended. "I know the kind of girl Mama wants me to be with. She wants me to be with someone like Laila or Jessica; someone who can keep the blue blood running thick through our children's veins."

I pushed a drink towards him. "What's wrong with blue blood?" I asked lightly. "It's been good to you, hasn't it? Got you through med school. Got you this townhouse too."

He sensed the lighthearted nature of my comment and laughed, dropping onto a barstool. His disheveled hair fell into his eyes as his head hung forward over the glass of gin.

I moved around the counter and sat next to him. "I'll tell you what, son. It *doesn't* matter. Not one bit." I sighed, staring straight ahead. "I don't know what your mother's on about, but I'm very disappointed in her behavior. Don't you worry. I'm going to set her straight just as soon as we settle down tonight. I'll fix it. I promise."

Ethan looked up me. "Really?"

I nodded. "Really."

Ethan smiled. "Thank you, Dad. I don't know what to say. I'm glad you're here."

I lifted the glass to my lips.

Ethan chuckled. "I met her at the pharmacy."

"Sounds romantic," I said.

"She was working the counter and I put the Cooper charm on her."

We laughed.

"She's amazing, Dad. The minute I laid eyes on her, I wanted her, you know? I've never felt this way about anyone in my entire life. She's classy, she's opinionated." He paused. "She's educated." He didn't need to say that, but I knew why he had. "And I love her."

"There's nothing wrong with interracial relationships, Ethan. Inside, we're all the same. Outward appearances never matter."

He nodded and took a swig of his beverage.

"Your mother may be upset, but I want you to know I do not agree with her. The only way I'll be angry is if you don't follow your heart and let this girl get away." I pressed my lips together. "So when will I meet her?"

"She was supposed to come home for dinner tonight, but after she heard the things Mama was saying..." He rolled his eyes, and I saw moisture in their corners.

I slapped his back.

"She's strong, Dad. She doesn't roll over and play dead."

"Many black women are like that. Their stories are different from the stories of the women we're used to. They've had to be strong. That's how they've made it. That's how they continue to make it." I thought about Naomi for the hundredth time that day. The times we used to lie together in her bed, or mine, and she'd share stories her mother had told her when she was little. But Naomi had her own stories of strength. Thoughts of the way she'd had to defend herself against my mother assaulted my conscious mind.

I gulped back the rest of my drink and stood. "Cheer up. Everything is going to be fine. You're getting *married*."

Ethan's shoulders pushed back.

I smiled at him. "I'm very proud of you." I put my glass on the counter and left him in the room looking at his cell phone.

The only way I'll be angry is if you don't follow your heart and let this girl get away. The words rung in my ears. *The way I did...*

LATE THAT NIGHT, I was sitting in Ethan's office flipping through his desk calendar. I turned the pages until there were no more to turn. How many months would I have left with Evelyn? We hadn't done much of anything together since Ethan had moved out. Summer was looming. It would be hot. Maybe we should travel a bit more this year. We'd been everywhere but nowhere. It had always been a business trip. I'd taken her along because the other fellas had taken their wives. We rarely talked. We never bonded. I owed her so much...

I sighed and adjusted the calendar back to the current day. My head dropped into my hands as the impossible weight of emotion pressed against my chest. I rose from the chair and went downstairs to be with her. She needed me just as much as Ethan did right now. I had to be a good husband, no matter how hard I thought it might be.

7

WILLIAM

BOSTON, M.A., 1996

*T*he next morning, I woke up to the sun's rays slicing through the guest room curtains. Somewhere outside of my window, a family of birds was discussing breakfast options with voices a little too loud for my liking. Then, the sound of shouting from the first floor of the house obliterated the birds' discussions.

I popped up in the bed like a jack-in-the-box and grabbed the clock off the night table. *Seven thirty in the goddamn morning?*

Evelyn's voice continued to shatter the serenity. "I forbid you, Ethan Cooper," she was screaming. "You will not marry that girl. Not only that, you'll end the relationship immediately!"

Jumping out of bed, I pulled my silk robe off the back of an armchair and raced down the flight of stairs, stumbling down the last few steps in the process. By the time I reached the kitchen, Ethan and his mother were standing toe-to-toe, ready to face off. It was reminiscent of a brewing bar fight in an old western. Suddenly, Evelyn's hand flew back and connected hard with Ethan's face. His head lurched to the side accompanied by a loud groan, closely followed by uncombed strands of hair landing like a mop across his tightly closed eyes.

My vision clouded and my throat dried out as I raced toward

Evelyn and grabbed her by the wrists. Shoving her to the side, she stumbled across the room like a discarded ragdoll.

"What the hell is wrong with you?" I shouted, shoving my finger in her face. "What are you trying to do? Make the boy hate you?"

"It's too late for that, Dad," Ethan muttered. He lifted his head and looked at his hand as if expecting to see blood from his recent injury. His shaking hands rolled up into fists.

I turned toward him. "Ethan, get on up the stairs. Your mother and I need to talk privately."

He shot a heated glare at his mother before grabbing his cell phone off the counter and walking away.

Evelyn's lips and hands were trembling. "Ethan, wait," she called out.

Tears flooded his eyes as he spun around to face his mother. "Wait for what, Mama?" He shrugged stiff shoulders. "A change of heart? A sorry? Because we all know that neither is coming."

"Now just one minute," she said.

"You won't get any more of my time," he snapped. "If you can't accept the woman I love, then there's no room for you in my life." He gave her a scathing look before disappearing up the stairs.

I turned to face Evelyn. My muscles quivered under my robe as I tried to look at her. I couldn't bear to face her, but I shouldn't have been surprised. Marrying Evelyn had been my mother's idea, and both women had been cut from the same cloth.

A sick feeling slithered under my clothes and crawled against my skin. I wanted to vomit. Covering my mouth, I pressed my eyes together in an effort to hold back the nausea.

"You need to go home," I said as controlled as possible, "back to Beaufort. I'm calling Gerald and telling him to book the next flight out of Logan."

Her hands shot up in protest. But her wide eyes and shaking head indicated she couldn't believe what she had done. "I went too far," she muttered, lowering her hands to her sides.

"Understatement."

"William." Her voice quivered. "I was only trying to help. He needs to understand. No one accepts that kinda thing where we're from. The girl wouldn't fit in. It'll be more trouble than it's worth. You of all people know that."

"Things are different now," I shouted, even though I knew it was far from the truth. "And besides, it's not up to you to choose who the boy marries."

"Your mother did," she shot back.

I gritted my teeth. "You're driving the boy away, Evelyn!"

"And I'd be happy to drive him away if it means he'll open his eyes and see he's making the biggest mistake of his life," she said. Her stone cold exterior had resurfaced. "And what about their children, Will? Where the hell are they going with some mixed kids? Where will they fit in? Who will accept them?"

I glared at her, my eyes flickering in anger. "You're a disgrace," I said, grabbing the kitchen phone from its cradle. "The doctor tells you that you have six months left to live, and you're no better than goddamn Beelzebub himself. It's like you're determined to reserve your spot in hell."

Evelyn gasped. "I'm the one who's sick, Will," she was saying. "My body is in so much pain and he doesn't care."

I dialed. "He doesn't know," I said. "And, I'm sorry, but right now isn't about you."

She continued as if she hadn't heard the last part. "And do you think that now is a good time? Look at how he talks to me? Putting some woman above me."

I put the phone to my ear.

"You said it yourself. I have six months left. It's just enough time to make a difference. If I don't tell him the truth, who will?"

"Save it," I snapped, waiting for Gerald to answer. "You've said and done things to that boy that you'll never be able to take back, and with the predicament you're in, that's not a good thing. The best thing is for you to give him space. A lot of it."

Gerald finally answered the phone. "Gerald," I said, glaring at my wife, "I need you to book a ticket back home for Miss Evelyn. She'll be returning early. She's not feeling well."

Evelyn gritted her teeth. The remorse had vanished and defiance was quickly taking its place. "I'm not going anywhere, William. You can't make me go. I still haven't seen this woman."

I briefly nestled the phone against my shoulder. "The hell I can't make you go," I said. "You've ruined everything. This was supposed to be a celebratory occasion. We were supposed to meet the love of Ethan's life, and you've come acting like some goddamn bigot. You've caused more damage in a few hours than you've done in the boy's entire lifetime. You're not staying here, Evelyn. I'm booking a flight and you're getting out of here. Go upstairs and pack. And while you're at it, think about how you'll make this up to him. You'll have the whole week to do that."

Throwing a final ice-cold glare in my direction, she stormed up the stairs like a child.

When Evelyn had disappeared from sight, I fell onto a nearby barstool and dragged my shaking hand down my face.

The sudden crackle of Gerald's distant voice made me start. "Is everything all right, Mr. C.?"

I lifted the phone back to my ear. "Everything will be fine once Evelyn is in the air." I drew in a breath. "Make sure she rests when she gets there," I said. "She's emotional. She needs to take it easy."

"Yes, sir."

"Message me with the flight details."

"Yes, sir."

"Any messages?"

"Scott called."

With a hand still draped over my face, I peeked through my fingers and looked around the kitchen to make sure I was alone. "What did he want?"

"He didn't say," Gerald replied. "He never does. He's a man of few words if I ever met one. Strange fella."

I chuckled. "Well, I'm sure he'll call my cell if it's important," I replied. "Is that all?"

"That's all, Mr. C.," Gerald confirmed.

"Good, then I'll call you later." I hung up and thought about Scott for a second before marching up the steps to Ethan's room, passing Evelyn's quarters in the process. In my periphery, I saw her pitching clothes into her Louis Vuitton luggage, crying. The sound of her lamenting sickened me. I rushed past, trying to ignore it.

Ethan was in his room, buttoning his shirt in front of a mirror. The sheets on his bed were rumpled. A sleepless night, I figured. It made sense, especially if he was used to a warm body next to him. Also, given the grief his mother had dished out, it was not a surprise.

Tonight we were supposed to go to dinner with Dakota. After my chat with Ethan a few hours ago, I'd hoped things would've gotten better, but nothing had panned out the way I thought it would.

I slid into the room. It was going to be another awkward conversation; the second in twelve hours. "Your mother is going home," I said. "You shouldn't have to take abuse from her. Literally."

He looked at me through the mirror. A red welt on the side of his face made me grimace. "Put some ice on that. The swelling will go down and the red mark will disappear."

"Thanks," he mumbled.

I shrugged. It was Pre-Med 101.

"Are you leaving with her?" he asked.

I stepped further into the room, shoving my hands into my pockets. "Do you want me to?"

Ethan grunted and yanked the knot of his tie up to his neck so hard I thought I'd need to put him on suicide watch.

"I'm not going anywhere," I said. "I told you, I'm not like your mother. In fact, I can't wait to meet this gorgeous woman of yours."

"She doesn't want to come tonight, Dad. Can you blame her? She's a progressive woman. She's successful. Why should she have to put up with this kind of behavior in this day and age?" He adjusted his tie and turned to look at me. His eyes were bloodshot and wet with dark circles underneath. His shoulders slumped.

"Maybe..." His head followed his shoulders.

"Maybe what?"

He sighed. "Maybe Mama is right."

"What are you talking about?"

"It's not worth it. I didn't expect it to be a walk in the park, but this is more turmoil than I ever would have imagined." He shrugged. "I can't subject the woman I love to this. I love her that much, I'm willing to let her go if it means she'll be at peace."

"You're talking crazy, son," I said, walking up to him. "If you let her go, neither of you will ever be at peace. You'll be tormented for the rest of your life. You'll think about her every waking moment until the day you're laid to rest. You'll marry another woman and not be able to love her the way she deserves to be loved because your heart and mind will be wrapped up in someone else."

Ethan stared at me.

I cleared my throat. "We're going to have a blast tonight," I promised. "You call Miss Dakota and tell her your father cannot wait to meet her, and he's expecting a warm hug from his future daughter-in-law when he does."

Ethan's mouth twitched before he grabbed his bag off the bed and walked past me. I looked after him, wishing I could tell him more.

8

NAOMI

BOSTON, M.A., 1996

"*S*calpel."

Heat from the surgical lights beat down on my head as I reached over to the sterilized silver tray and picked up the requested instrument. I carefully handed it to the doctor, squinting my eyes as he carefully drew a thin line over the patient's skin. In a second, blood was seeping from it.

Over thirty years later, and I still flinched at this part.

"Retrac—"

My hand was already outstretched. The doctor looked up at me and smiled through the facemask, the bright light attached to his head threatening to blind me.

I shrugged and picked up the drill. He would need it next.

"I don't know why I even asked," he muttered. "I haven't worked with you much, but I've heard about your skills. They say you're the best surgical nurse in the hospital."

"And they say you're the best up-and-coming doctor in Brigham and Women's," I said, bending my neck to watch as he pulled the flesh apart. "I'm so proud of you. I knew you were special the moment I met you."

He smiled again. "What will the hospital do without you?"

I inhaled. "I'm sure there are plenty of surgical nurses to fill my shoes after I'm gone."

"Yeah, but, there's nothing like that good old-school training," he said. "The new nurses are good, but they can't hold a candle to you. That's what all the doctors say anyway, and that's been my experience the few times we've worked together. I'm sure you're looking forward to retirement, though."

"I can't lie and say I'm not ready for it," I admitted. "It came so fast. It seems like it was just the other day I was starting out. That was thirty-five years ago."

Dr. Cooper laughed. "And it was less than a year ago when we had that chance meeting. We were on our way to the cafeteria and I asked you for relationship advice, remember?"

"I'll never forget it."

"Dri—"

I passed him the drill before he could finish saying the word.

We worked in silence for a few minutes.

"Now your time is all your own," Dr. Cooper continued, peering down at the exposed patient. "What are you planning to do? I'm sure it's something amazing."

"Well, I was thinking that maybe I could do some traveling," I said. "Europe, Asia..."

"Of course," he replied. "Hey! You might even think about going back home to visit friends and family. Didn't you say something about a son who lives in Atlanta?"

My mouth wrinkled behind my facemask; I was glad Dr. Cooper hadn't been able to see it. Go back to South Carolina? That was definitely out of the question. What was there? Miss Anna and Mr. Cooper had long since gone, and I hadn't been to either one of their funerals. Mama had been dead for years as well. All that remained in Beaufort were skeletons that were best left buried deep in their respective graves and closets. I might think about visiting Scott in Atlanta, but I'd have to be prepared. He always asked too many questions; questions for which I refused to provide answers.

Silence.

"What about that guy you're dating? Are you thinking about settling down?"

My eyes widened. "What guy?"

He prodded the patient's organs.

"How do you know about that?"

His eyes twinkled behind the surgical loupe. "Come on, Nurse Naomi. It's been the talk of the ward. Everyone is talking about the guy who brought flowers to the unit for you last week."

I smiled, shaking my head. "You doctors have nothing better to do, huh?" I joked.

"There's a lot for us to do, but we definitely welcome the distraction. We haven't had the opportunity to talk as much as I would've liked, but I feel very protective of you. I'm gonna need to be kept abreast of these kinds of things," he said. "If a man is coming to see you, I need to have him screened and vetted. He has to past the Ethan-Test."

I laughed and so did he. I was trying to keep my relationship with Lionel low key, but with such nosey coworkers, it seemed impossible. We had only been seeing each other for a few months, but I couldn't deny that the relationship was progressing and the feelings were strong.

For the next forty-five minutes, we worked in relative silence as Dr. Cooper and the surgical team began the process of removing a tumor from the patient's lungs. In a few hours, the doctor was finally removing the offensive lump and examining it in the bright light. "Got it," he mumbled.

I took the tools from him and rested them to the side. Then he began the work of closing the patient back up and finishing the surgery. When the patient had been sutured, all of the nurses and residents started clapping. I turned around in confusion.

I removed the doctor's gloves, and he joined in the celebration.

"Did I miss something?" My cheeks were hot. I turned to look at the doctor as he

began to speak.

"You're not missing anything, but we're certainly going to be missing you," he said. "It's hard to believe, Nurse Naomi, but it's true. Your time with us here at Brigham and Women's Hospital has come to an end. You're about to start a new chapter, a new journey. There are adventures you have yet to experience, accomplishments you have yet to make. You're more than a colleague to us, Miss Naomi. On a personal note, you've been there for me, both in and out of the surgery room." He inhaled and smiled.

I bit back tears as he grabbed my outstretched hand and squeezed it.

"I think I can speak for everyone when I say we wish you well on this next leg of the journey. Don't be a stranger. Stop by and let us know what you're up to."

I smiled as a tear escaped my eye.

"I will do that," I promised.

He smiled and pulled me into a hug as the team began to clear the room. He whispered in my ear. "I need to talk to you later. It's about Dakota."

I pulled away and gave him a quizzical look.

LATER THAT AFTERNOON, after a surprise retirement gathering in the cafeteria and the even bigger surprise of an expensive Rolex watch, I packed my bag for the final time. This would be my last trek through the white, sanitized hallways of Brigham and Women's Hospital.

I hadn't heard Dr. Cooper enter the locker room. "So this is really it?" he asked.

I turned to see him standing in the doorway and resumed packing to hide my stinging eyes. Over the years, I'd practiced subduing emotion. Today, it was difficult.

"It really is." I zipped the bag shut and stood tall. "After the wedding, we'll have to stay in touch," I said, changing the subject. "You need to keep me posted about your relationship with that beautiful young lady of yours. I'm so glad everything is settling down. I remember it was rough a few months ago."

Ethan rubbed the back of his neck and sat down at a nearby desk. "Yeah, well..."

"Things are better, aren't they?"

He grunted. "No? Yes?" He shook his head. "As of this morning, we were still getting married."

"Well, that's a good sign. She hasn't dumped you."

"Not yet." He laughed and paused. "Do you remember that conversation we had a few months back? It was when I first met Dakota."

I smiled thinking about it. "Of course I do. Boy, you had stars in your eyes."

The stars were there again.

"I was mesmerized, wasn't I?" He was smiling. "I was trying to pick your brain. I wanted to know all there was to know about y'all. Black women, I mean."

I laughed. "I'll never forget it," I said. Suddenly, unwanted memories stirred in my belly. I tried to swallow them away. "Tell me how the two of you met again. You know how much I love that story."

He sat down and leaned forward. "She was working the pharmacy counter and I was in the junk food aisle. I was buying snacks after being on the late shift, but I saw her standing there and couldn't stop staring. She thought I was crazy."

Smiling, I watched on as he continued his story.

"So I walked up to her and asked her what time it was. She pointed to my watch and said, 'Unless that's a knock-off Patek Philippe, it should give you a good idea.'"

"She's a riot," I said, slapping my thigh.

"Of course, I went back every night for a whole week buying random items until I could convince her to go out with me. The rest is history, as they say."

"And history is still being written, Dr. Cooper." I winked.

"We're off the clock, Miss Naomi. You don't have to call me 'doctor' anymore. Besides, you're officially retired and I'm young enough to be your son." He looked at his watch and his face dropped.

"What's wrong?" I asked.

"My parents are here," he said. "They flew in yesterday."

"And that makes you frown? Not a good sign."

"My dad is cool, but my mother..." He groaned and rolled his eyes.

I shifted in my seat. "Have they met Dakota yet?"

"Not yet," he said, sighing. "We were supposed to be going to dinner tonight, but my mom..." He trailed off again. "It got so bad this morning Dad sent her packing back home." His face hardened as his fingers curled into a fist.

The taste of lemons filled my mouth.

"You would think in this day and time..." Ethan's words faded.

I moistened my lips and grabbed my bag. "Well, for some people, the day and time changes everything, but for others, it only reinforces what they think they already know. And if your mother was raised that way, it might be hard for her to change the way she views things. It's ingrained."

"No excuse," he said. "How do you treat a person differently because of the color of their skin? It makes no sense to me."

I swallowed. "Well, I'm sorry your mother isn't open to your love, Ethan," I said, "but if one parent is supportive, things will be a lot easier."

We smiled at each other.

"Okay, now it's your turn to tell a story," he said, leaning forward with a huge grin.

I stiffened in the seat. "What story?"

"Come on, Miss Naomi. Tell me about the guy you knew when you were a kid again."

I inhaled sharply as my eyes darted around the room. I'd shared this story with him the day he'd told me about his problems with Dakota. It had been relevant then. He seemed to think it was relevant now, but I wasn't convinced. He had no idea how much it hurt to relive those details.

"Maybe another time, Ethan. I really should get going." I stood to my feet and swept my long, salt and pepper hair behind my ear.

"Fine, I'll let you off the hook this time."

I walked toward the door.

"So, do you have plans tonight?" he asked before I passed through.

I paused. "Plans to get in bed early." I laughed. "I'm sixty years old, Ethan. What's an old person to do late at night?"

"You have a boyfriend, don't you?"

"I do not have a—" I cut myself off. "It's not official."

"And who says you're old? Haven't you heard? Sixty is the new forty. You're a spring chicken."

"Why do you want to know if I'm busy tonight?" I asked.

He stood. "Remember I said I needed to talk to you? I wanted to ask you a favor."

"I'm not staying late."

"I would never ask you to, and I already told you, I'm going out to dinner."

"Then what is it?"

"As I said, my mother has gone back home," he said.

"Go on…"

"I was wondering if you'd like to fill in tonight at dinner."

Silence.

"As your mother?"

"Not as my mother, per se, but you are like a mother." He paused. "You're old enough to *be* my mother."

"You're not making your case any better," I said, fiddling with the strap on my bag. "I don't know. I mean, I get that your mother's not going to be there, and I get that we have this special bond thing going on, but it seems like such an intimate occasion. I'd be the third wheel."

"But it couldn't be more perfect," he said, walking up to me. He took my hands in his. "Dakota is dying to meet you. If it weren't for you, who can say whether we'd be together right now? If my mother won't be there, there's no other person I'd rather have present."

I shifted my weight from one foot to the other. "What will your father say? Your mother if she ever found out? I'm sure it would hurt her feelings."

He shrugged. "I don't give a damn about what my mother thinks or feels right now."

I gasped and held a scolding finger up to silence him. "Don't you ever talk about your mother that way, Ethan. Sure, she's not on the same page as you, but it's never cause to disrespect her. I'm sure she's sacrificed a lot for you, and there is no doubt in my mind that she loves you deeply."

"I apologize," he said as he glanced at his feet, "but you know what I'm trying to say. And my father, he's the complete opposite of my mother. Last night he pulled me to the side and told me to follow my *heart*. You have no idea how much that meant to me."

My hand tightened around the strap of my bag. It seemed like practical advice.

"He's a down-to-earth kind of guy," Ethan continued. "You're both around the same age, and I'm sure you two will click immediately. You can't say no."

I stretched my neck and considered what he was saying. Ethan wouldn't have asked me to do this if he didn't really need me there. I would be his moral support, his cheerleader. And I could imagine Dakota would need that too.

I sighed.

I thought I'd had it bad when I was growing up. If I closed my eyes, I'd be transported back to South Carolina; the jeers, the stares, the white girls calling Will a nigger-lover when all we were doing was going to the store on an errand. Ethan needed me just like I'd needed somebody back then. I had to be there for him and Dakota.

"Okay, I'll be there," I said through a playful groan. "But only because you did that thing with those brown eyes of yours."

He threw his head back and laughed before scooping his arms around me and lifting me off the floor with excitement. An involuntary high-pitched squeal burst from my mouth with the shock.

"What time and where?" I asked as Ethan lowered me back down to my feet.

"Seven o'clock at Sorellina. We'll pick you up."

I raised my hands in protest. "I don't need all that fancy treatment,

Ethan. I know how you rich boys do it with your cars and chauffeurs and such. If I have to be there, I'll find my own way, thank you."

"Fine," he said, "suit yourself. So I'll see you tonight?"

"I suppose," I said.

He frowned.

"Yes, Ethan. You'll see me tonight."

9

WILLIAM

BOSTON, M.A., 1996

I was trying not to stare at Dakota sitting across from me at the circular dinner table, so I picked up my menu and flipped to the wine selection on the back page. It certainly was no surprise why Ethan had fallen in love the minute he'd seen her. The gal was stunning: long black hair and big, buttery eyes, framed by lengthy, girly lashes. The rock my son had given her was perched on a long, slender finger like a monument.

"Mr. Cooper, it's such a pleasure to finally meet you," she said, displaying her straight, white teeth with a bright smile. Her voice was like Tinker Bell's.

I closed the menu. "Likewise, Miss Dakota. And please, call me Will, or Dad, or Pops, or whatever you young people call your in-laws nowadays."

She laughed. "Dad will be fine," she said. "I'd never call you Will. I was raised better than that."

"Indeed." I gestured to Ethan. "My son has told me so much about you," I said. "His descriptions didn't do you justice."

Ethan chuckled and swiped the back of his neck as his cheeks flushed. "My dad is quite the charmer."

"Well, now I see where you get it from then?" she said, laughing, squeezing his hand on top of the table.

"It certainly wasn't his mother," I quipped. We all laughed at the inside joke. I was glad to see the girl was down to earth and could laugh at the world; make lemonade, as it were. I shifted the angle of the topic. "Please allow me to apologize for my wife," I said. "Her behavior today was unacceptable."

"I appreciate your words, Mr. Cooper," she said. "I can't lie and say it wasn't hurtful to deal with, but my mother was the same way. She literally told me that if I did not stop talking to Ethan, she would cut me off. Unfortunately, I haven't spoken to her in months." She frowned at the same time as Ethan.

"I'm sorry to hear about your mother's reaction," I said, trying to ignore the post-traumatic stress syndrome symptoms creeping up on me.

Ethan shifted in his seat.

"Listen, I don't want to spend too much time on this because we're here to enjoy each other and have a wonderful time, but I want you to know that you are wholly accepted into my family," I said. "It doesn't matter what my wife thinks, or anyone else for that matter. You go ahead and protect your love, yourself, and my son."

Ethan smiled and shared an emotional gaze with me. "Thanks, Dad," he said, his mouth going tight. "I love you."

I nodded. He'd never said those words to me before, and I wondered if he'd ever say them to his mother. An unexpected rush of emotions filled me.

"I love you too, son."

I looked over at the empty seat and was reminded of my wife's absence. I'd said enough about her and was sure no one wanted the stark reminder of her intolerance. The empty seat was exactly that.

"I guess you couldn't find a smaller table?" I said.

"What do you mean?" Ethan asked.

"Your mother landed in Beaufort hours ago. You should've changed the reservation."

"Someone else is coming," he said, looking at his watch. "She's normally on time, so I can't imagine what the holdup could be."

"You didn't mention someone else," Dakota said, twisting the ring on her finger.

"It's Miss Naomi," he said. "I invited her before she left work today."

"Really?" Dakota said, her hand flying to her beaming face. "Oh my god, I have been dying to meet this woman."

"Who's Miss Naomi?" I asked, putting my napkin to my mouth.

Dakota turned to me. "Miss Naomi is a nurse who works on the ward with Ethan."

"A nurse who *worked* with me," Ethan corrected her. "Her last day was today. She's retired now. She was an incredible support to me and Dakota during the early part of our relationship, and I thought it might be nice for her to join us tonight. I know Dakota wants to meet her, and since Mom is gone..." He shrugged. "I meant to tell you earlier, but I know you're good for surprises."

Suddenly, my mouth began to dry out and every nerve in my body tingled against my hot skin.

Wait a minute...

How many nurses were named *Naomi*? Perhaps a few. But how many nurses named Naomi were retiring?

I stopped my racing thoughts.

Maybe I was getting ahead of myself.

I had no clue where Naomi had gone when she'd left Seattle. She could've been living in the house down the street in Beaufort, for all I knew. Hell, I'd not been able to find her in over forty years. It was like she had fallen off the face of the earth. Why would I allow myself to believe that I would see her tonight?

There could be no way Ethan was talking about *my* Naomi. What were the odds?

"Dad, you're sweating," Ethan said.

"Are you okay?" Dakota asked. "You look like you need some water." She called out to a passing waiter.

"No, I'm fine," I assured them. I took a handkerchief from my pocket and dabbed it against my face.

My heart was racing.

I slowly turned around and surveyed the restaurant. People entered and exited, laughing and jesting. Couples sat at tables and corner booths eating and enjoying one another's company.

My imagination was in full throttle now.

What did she look like? Back then, Naomi had been a petite girl. She was a woman now. Maybe she'd filled out. I wondered if she had aged gracefully or if the stresses of life had gotten to her.

But why was I exciting myself? There was no way it could be her.

Now I was anxious.

What was taking the woman so long? It couldn't be *my* Naomi, I thought again. She'd always been a stickler for time. She'd never been late to school. Never missed an appointment...

But tonight wasn't about me. I had come to meet my son's fiancée and that was what I needed to focus on. It just so happened that Ethan had invited a colleague; a woman that happened to be named Naomi, who'd shown him care and concern. A woman he trusted.

I turned to Dakota and opened my mouth to speak, but before I could say anything, Ethan cut me off.

"Finally, here she is," Ethan said, smiling at someone behind me. His eyes were beaming and his smile was warm, making his entire face glow.

I looked at Dakota. Her expression matched his to a tee. Whoever this Miss Naomi was, she was an exceptional woman. The kids were responding to her in a way that revealed how special she must be.

Ethan pushed his chair back and stood to greet the woman.

I stood too, but then I heard the voice. My legs became weak, almost forcing me back into the chair.

My heart stopped beating.

Time was suspended.

I could hear the flow of my own blood whooshing through my ears, and the sound of my breathing echoed in my head like a whistle in a cave.

As Ethan rushed over and embraced the mystery woman, I finally turned to settle this thing once and for all.

"Sorry I'm..." the woman started to say, but the moment our eyes locked, the words instantly disintegrated in her mouth.

10

NAOMI

BOSTON, M.A., 1996

H oly mother of God...

Ethan wrapped his arms around me, obstructing my view of the broad-shouldered, chestnut-haired apparition standing next to the table, dressed in a fine Italian suit.

There's no way on God's green earth...

I stared at him with bulging eyes, trying to make sense of it.

It can't be possible...

"Will?" I mouthed.

Our eyes locked like puzzle pieces.

I clutched Ethan's arm like it was a cane, still staring at...his *father?*

Will's lips, slightly parted and framed by a goatee, reminded of the nights back in Beaufort when he'd kiss me softly. How they'd traveled over the terrain of my flesh, leaving hot, molten trails. His brown eyes had a grey ring around them now. They were heavy, as if emotion was about to spill out of them like a cup overflowing.

I shook my head, trying to shake the intrusive memories. If the floor had opened up to swallow me whole, I'd have been grateful. I'd managed to elude this man for forty years. It had taken careful planning and the systematic ignoring of debilitating emotions to make it possible. I'd spent tons of emotional currency forgetting the man who'd made me promises he could never fulfill.

I wasn't ready for this impromptu reunion.

The question of how I missed this connection between Ethan and Will assaulted me. But then, how could I have known? There had been no clues. Yes, Ethan was a Cooper, but I'd never thought in a million years he could be one of *those* Coopers. I had never asked Ethan questions about his family or where he was from. I'd detected a southern accent, but that was nothing out of the ordinary. There were doctors from every state at Brigham and Women's. If I'd had even an inkling that William Cooper was Ethan's father, there'd have been no way I would have agreed to come tonight. I might have even quit working at the hospital long before retirement age.

Ethan released me all too soon. "You made it," he was saying. "I thought you'd stood me up."

I barely heard him. "Of course not," I said, giggling. I ran my hands over my skirt. "Why on earth would I do something like that?"

"Remember your boyfriend?" he said with a wink.

My throat constricted.

"Ethan... really..."

"You look stunning, Miss Naomi. I can't remember the last time I saw you out of scrubs. You clean up very nicely."

Will's eyes were glued to mine. His visibly labored breathing appeared to become heavier as he stepped around the chair and inched in my direction until he was standing right in front of me. He towered over me, his body thick like a tree trunk. His full hair was stylishly combed back, and his brown eyes quivered.

I began to feel lightheaded.

"You took the words right out of my mouth, son. I was going to say the same thing," he said, never once taking his eyes off me.

My fingers fiddled with the beading on my clutch purse.

"Are you going to introduce us?"

"Of course. Dad, this is Miss Naomi Jackson. She's the best surgical nurse in the world and also a very special friend."

"It is certainly a pleasure to meet you." Will's soft lips found the back of my hand, and my eyes fluttered in their sockets before I pulled it away.

"Likewise," I said, clearing a nervous rattle in my throat. I ran my hands over the emerald green chiffon skirt I was wearing, as if it was suddenly more wrinkled than it was supposed to be. My eyes flitted past Will to see a woman, whom I assumed was Dakota, was making her way towards me.

"Miss Naomi, this is such a wonderful surprise." She embraced me, giving me another welcome distraction from the impromptu reunion.

"Likewise," I stuttered. "I'm so thrilled to be finally meeting you."

Ethan gestured to the empty seat, which was next to his father. I hesitated for a second before shuffling past Will and pulling out the seat. His hand landed on top of mine as he jumped in to do the honor. The unexpected contact was like a branding iron, burning my flesh. My bottom lip caught between my teeth as I lowered myself into the offered chair.

"I hope I haven't missed much," I said, looking at Ethan and Dakota.

"Not at all," Ethan said, putting his arm around the back of Dakota. "Dad was just talking to us about relationships."

"Was he really?" I feigned interest. It was the last thing I wanted to be talking about in his presence.

"And it's funny," Dakota added. "His advice was identical to yours."

"That's very funny," I agreed. The waiter appeared and poured iced water into my cup. I thanked him and grabbed it immediately.

"It's so easy to be impacted by others," Ethan was saying. "But the both of you are right. We shouldn't let anyone else affect the way we feel about each other."

Dakota smiled. "Miss Naomi, I've never had a chance to tell you, but I really appreciate the way you supported Ethan when we were going through that terrible time with my mother. You were there for him. You coached him through it, and for that I am extremely grateful."

Feeling like I was sitting on a pincushion, I attempted a sincere response. "Of course, dear," I said, trying to be brief. She looked at me, perhaps waiting for something more profound. I straightened my shoulders and cleared my throat. "Relationships are hard, and you have to be willing to put your shoulder to the wheel if you want to make them work."

"Especially when it's the type of relationship they have," William added, leaning back in his seat.

I took another sip of water.

"The interracial aspect is tough, but it's not insurmountable," he continued. "It was tougher when I was growing up, but even then, if two people were in love, it was possible."

I forced a smile onto my face. "I can't imagine," I said, looking away from him.

The waiter trotted back to the table and asked for our orders. William took the liberty of requesting an expensive bottle of champagne to celebrate what he called 'new beginnings'.

Everyone raised their glass. I lifted mine to Will's and watched him peer at me over the edge.

"So, Miss Naomi, you promised you'd tell that story," Ethan said.

I almost choked on my drink.

Not now, Ethan...

"What story?"

"*The* story," he persisted.

I wanted to slap his face. "Ethan, you've heard it once already. I'm sure it'll be no more interesting the second time around," I said, chuckling, raking the back of my neck.

"What story are you talking about?" William asked, leaning in.

"It's an amazing story about some guy she was in love with when she was younger," Ethan said. "The relationship didn't work out, but the lessons she learned really helped Kota and I realize that what we have is special and that we shouldn't give up on it." He gazed at his fiancée before giving her an affectionate kiss.

I shoved the glass against my mouth to keep myself from cursing.

"I'd love to hear it, Miss Naomi," Dakota said. "It's true. I don't think Ethan and I would've made it this far in our relationship had it not been for you and your words of wisdom." She smiled.

I fought the urge to let my eyes roll. Now was definitely not the time for *the* story, but it seemed as though I had no choice.

I sighed, shoving my tongue into my cheek. "Well, if you insist," I said, moistening my dry lips.

William interrupted. "Now listen, if the old woman doesn't want to release the contents of her diary to you young people, how about you let her be, huh?"

Everyone laughed.

I looked at him with questioning eyes before reluctantly joining in.

"Dad, you ruined it! It's classic. It's a Hallmark movie, I swear."

"Well, it would've been had the ending been different," I muttered.

William stole a sideward glance in my direction.

"Fine," Ethan relented, still laughing, "but for the record, this woman is hardly an elder. She ran circles around the other nurses on the ward. She could easily work another ten years and no one would know the difference."

"Ethan, stop," I said, taking a sip of my champagne.

"Well, since it's story time, I have one I can tell," William offered.

I gulped my drink back and carefully set the glass down before I dropped it on the table.

After a second of thought, he started. "There was a girl I once loved. She was gorgeous, an absolute dime-piece. And she was a black girl," he added.

Ethan leaned forward. "Dad, are you serious? I never..." he swallowed. "You've never told me this."

William shrugged. "No, I haven't," he admitted. "It was never relevant until now. But I'm hoping that now you will see why I can relate to what you're experiencing and consider that perhaps your pining for women of color is genetically based."

I rolled my eyes.

"Dad..." Dakota whispered. "No offense, but I never would've guessed."

"Why? Because of my appearance? Because of where I'm from? Don't go judging a book by its cover, Miss Dakota. There's a lesson for you."

I wringed my hands in my lap.

"So what happened?" she questioned. "I mean, you loved her, but clearly it didn't work out."

William shrugged stiff shoulders again. "Well, she didn't believe me when I told her how much I loved her or how much I needed her in my life. And I couldn't blame her. The fifties down south were brutal. Interracial relationships were unheard of, or at least not discussed in the open." He paused, pressing his lips together, fighting emotion. "She thought the obstacles were too great to overcome, despite my trying to convince her that the way I felt was greater than any obstacle we would ever face. She was afraid. Perhaps she had a reason to be." He stared at the cutlery on the table, his eyes low, then he rubbed his brow and snapped out of the reverie. "Anyhow, I haven't seen her in years, but I've prayed every day that I would bump into her again."

An undefined silence enveloped the table.

"What would you say to her?" Dakota asked.

William paused. "I'd repeat everything I said to her back then. And then some." He looked at me.

I lifted my glass to my mouth. It was empty.

Ethan stared at his father. "Would you have really married her, Dad?"

William chuckled, but his features were taut. "In a heartbeat, Ethan. She meant everything to me. A day hasn't gone by that I haven't thought about her...that I haven't missed her."

"That's really sweet," I said, "but of course, in those times, marriage wouldn't have been feasible, Mr. Cooper. *Especially* where you're from. Like you said, it was taboo." My tone could've cut through the bread on the table.

"Feasibility is subjective, Miss Naomi," he responded.

"I'd say it's very objective. Culture defines what's acceptable," I said.

William shook his head. "And individuals define the culture."

Ethan and Dakota looked back and forth between Will and me as we debated the topic.

"Dad's right," Dakota said, nodding. "It's an individual thing. Individuals come together to make relationships. Individuals determine culture. Culture is a dynamic concept." She leaned over and whispered something to Ethan before offering him a confirmatory kiss.

I shifted in my seat, praying no one noticed my discomfort. Especially not Will. It was three against one.

My watch was the main focus of my attention for the rest of the night. There was no way I could stay in front of William while keeping the fact that he was the main character of my story a secret. I was a mess. The way he was looking at me and his proximity had me reeling.

I needed to figure out a way to get out of there. If I left before him, the likelihood of us doing something like *talking* would be drastically reduced. The past was exactly that. It made no sense to rehash things. I'd said enough for the night, and there was nothing more I could add to the discussion.

When the waiter came with the dessert menus, I decided it was the perfect time to head out. "Ethan, this has been lovely, but I think I should get going."

"It's early," he protested, frowning, "and I thought you didn't have plans."

"Yeah well, something came up and—"

"Oh, I get it." He grinned. "Lionel called you, didn't he?"

"Is Lionel her boyfriend?" William asked, evoking chuckles from most around the table.

"That's what he calls himself," Ethan said. "I screened him, and he's cool enough."

The skin on my face pulled tight. "Ethan thinks he's my guardian," I said with a faux smile. "He took on the responsibility himself. I can assure you, I never asked him to."

"Who else is going to take care of you?" he questioned. "Your son is miles away in Atlanta."

William turned to look at me. "A son?"

Beads of sweat formed down the middle of my back, helped little by the thickening air.

"I'm a big girl, Ethan. I'm not too old for a little hanky-panky, am I?" Now it was my turn to evoke laughter. From most.

Time to leave.

I rose. "Dakota, dear, you can call me anytime. I am here for you." I reached over and squeezed her hand. "And Ethan, I'm sure you'll stay in touch, seeing as you're my official bodyguard now."

"I'll be calling you tomorrow," he confirmed with a smile.

I stalled before turning to William. "And Mr. Cooper, it certainly was a pleasure to meet you." I smiled at him before picking up my purse and pushing my chair back.

"It was a pleasure to meet you too. I'll walk you out," he said. The sound of his chair moving away from the table made me freeze.

"You really don't have to," I assured him, smoothing the crinkles from my skirt again. "Stay and enjoy dessert with your family."

He wasn't swayed. "My son said you needed someone to take care of you."

"He didn't say that."

"Surely that means you'll need an escort to your car." He peered at me, speaking volumes without saying a word.

I turned on my heel and headed for the exit.

William put his hand on my waist, guiding me through the tables and chairs. I could feel the heat from his hand burning through my clothes and onto my flesh. He was electric. When we were out of earshot, he whispered, "You're not running away from me again, Naomi. I don't give a damn who Lionel is or isn't. You can call him and reschedule your plans because he certainly won't be seeing you. Not tonight."

11

WILLIAM

BOSTON, M.A., 1996

The stifling air outside the restaurant hit my face like an open fist. It hadn't seemed this hot earlier in the evening, so I had no choice but to assume the change was a result of Naomi's presence, rather than the elements.

She enthralled me. Her simple elegance aroused a severe curiosity in me. The simple fitted tank top she wore highlighted her perky breasts. The moon's radiance kissed her bare shoulders, making me jealous, and her shimmering skirt glittered against the moonlight. Her long hair was pulled up into a high ponytail and a simple gold necklace was laced around her graceful neck. Father Time had been good to Naomi. The woman was firm, but there was no doubt she was still soft in all the right places.

I initiated conversation. There wasn't a second to waste, especially since she was obviously trying to flee; the way she had forty-one years ago.

"Jesus Christ, Naomi."

"Stop taking the good Lord's name in vain," she reprimanded me.

I bit back a smile. "What would be a more appropriate thing to say right now?"

"Nothing." She stepped to the side and folded her arms across her chest. "Don't say another word. The kids are probably wondering what's going on. We should be acting like we don't know each other."

I laughed. "Good luck with that. I haven't laid eyes on you since I was eighteen years old, and you actually think that's possible? We were in the airport and—"

She held her hand up in the air. "Unlike the story you told at the table, I know this one."

My neck whipped back hearing the words. "You still don't believe that I would have—"

She held her hand up again. "Now is not the time for this discussion, William."

"So a better time would be when? In another forty-one years?" I almost choked just thinking about it.

Naomi's hand flew to her forehead. She was rattled, but I didn't care. There was no way I was going to let her walk out of my life again. We were children back then. She'd been afraid of what appeared to be the facts. In my adult mind, I could understand that; but now we were grown adults. There was no excuse for burying the truth.

"Who's Lionel?"

"You said you didn't care who he was."

"I lied," I said. "Is he your boyfriend?"

"I'm too old to have a *boyfriend*, Will." She rolled her eyes.

"Well, are you making love to him?"

She turned to face me, her mouth wide open. "William Cooper, I don't see how any of this is your business."

"So you don't see how much I still love you?" I stared at her, my eyes heavy, hooded, pained. "You don't see it? That if I could turn the clock back, knowing the way you shut me out, I would never have gone to Harvard?"

"You're talking crazy..." she whispered, but she knew I wasn't. "You had no choice but to go to Harvard. Your parents made that clear. Even if we could go back and do it over again, nothing would be different. Why can't you see that?" She tore her gaze away from mine and stared out across the sea of cars in the parking lot. The faint smell of her rich fragrance wafted up my nose, and I couldn't stop myself from envisioning my face buried in her neck and breasts.

"I know I made a mistake," she mumbled.

"Just one?"

She glared at me. "Well, how about you?"

"How did this become about me? You're the one who walked away and didn't look back. I was the one who was forced to marry a woman I didn't really love, trying to move on and forget about the one woman I did—oh, I'm sorry, still do—and deal with the fact that despite doing everything I knew how, she wouldn't respond to me."

She crossed her arms over her chest.

I shoved my hands into my pockets and looked into the distance. "So where is he?"

"Who?"

I stared at her. "Lionel."

"Oh, he's on his way," she said, but it was too fast. She was no good at lying. Never had been.

"If I were dating you, I would have been out here already waiting."

I saw her fingers pressing into her purse, denting it. "We already dated," she said, "and you never took me anywhere unless it was with your parents or on the down low."

Low blow. "Things are different now," I countered.

"Indeed they are. You're married."

Uppercut to the jaw. "You know, for an *old woman* your comebacks are pretty sharp."

Naomi laughed, and the sound filled me like a rushing river.

Silence.

"I'm staying at the Ritz," I said. I pointed to the parking lot. "You see that silver Lexus? It's waiting for me. I want you to get in it and go to my suite. Wait for me there."

She looked at me as if I'd lost my mind. "Wow, William," she said as sarcastically as possible. "I had no idea you were suffering from a degenerative brain disease. You seemed so lucid inside the restaurant."

"Sweetheart, my suffering from a degenerative disease is the least of your worries."

"That's debatable," she said, huffing and tucking the clutch under her armpit.

I took a step closer to her so our faces were close. Inhaling her splendor, I could now tell where the fragrance was the most potent. It was in the crook of her neck.

"I know exactly what I want," I said, pausing to let the words sink in. "You're not escaping me, Naomi. You did once, and it'll be over my dead body that it happens again. We have a lot to talk about, and we're going to talk about it. Tonight."

She didn't back away. Her eyes roamed my face. She looked at my nose, my mouth, and then into my eyes. She moistened her lips.

I knew what that meant. She used to do it when we were teenagers, right before she gave in to me.

She took a step backwards, but didn't protest.

My eyes were still glued to hers as I raised my hand. The sleek car approached the curb in one swift movement. I dug into my wallet and handed Naomi the key to my room.

"I'm not a call girl, William," she said through tight teeth.

My eyes narrowed. "Naomi, I would *never* disrespect you like that," I said. "If you don't want to talk to me tonight, that's one thing, but please don't insinuate that I would ever devalue you. I couldn't cope with that."

She looked away.

I bent down and spoke to the driver through the passenger window. "Please take this young lady to The Ritz," I requested. "I'll be ready to go when you return."

The driver jumped out and opened the back door for Naomi. Reluctantly, she gathered her skirt in one hand and ducked her head before getting into the car. The driver closed the door and I tapped on the window. Naomi wound it down.

"I still love you," I whispered, my eyes flickering. "I always have. I won't stop." I leaned in and placed a soft kiss on her trembling mouth. My eyes closed as a flash of the past whizzed through my mind. I touched her face, bringing it closer. After a second, she pulled away. Taking a couple of steps back, I watched her wind the window up as the car drove away. Then, I hurried back into the restaurant before the kids could get suspicious.

I HAD ENVISIONED myself walking into my suite at the Ritz and seeing Naomi spread across the bed, naked and ready for me to take her. Her bronze body would be swathed in the silken sheets of the bed, and the glow of recessed lighting would make her supple skin radiate. I'd climb on top of her and kiss her passionately, consuming her with decades of pent-up passion, filling her with unrestrained love, accessing the treasure I'd unlocked so many years ago.

But that might have been a little too far-fetched, I admitted to myself. It probably wouldn't happen that way...

Maybe she would be on the veranda, overlooking the commons with a glass of wine in her hand. I'd walk up behind her and slink my arms around her still-trim waist, pulling her into me with a slight jerk. She'd turn around to face me with tears in her eyes, telling me how much she missed me and that she regretted not taking my word when we were teenagers. Then I'd kiss her softly. She'd run her fingers through my hair, sending me reeling...

That scenario seemed more realistic, I thought, but of course, the actual scene that played out when I got to the room was far removed from anything I imagined. The shouting match we had was reminiscent of the ones we'd shared in the weeks before I left for Harvard. We followed each other around the room, debating, tossing blame like a hot potato and trying to get our points across. My scenarios of making love to her were way out of reach. There'd be none of that tonight. Not if she had anything to do with it.

"It's been forty-something years since you left me in that airport, Naomi. More than forty goddamn years!"

"I didn't leave you, William. You left me."

"You were the one who walked away," I retorted, taking an angry step towards her. "And when I called you, you didn't even look back."

"Look back for what?" Her chin wrinkled. She lowered her voice to an angry whisper. "Do you think you were the only one in love back then?"

I ran my hands over my face. We'd been going around in circles for twenty minutes, saying the same thing in different ways. I fell on the edge of the bed and cradled my forehead. "I don't know what to think."

"I was mad about you," she admitted. "I was head over heels. You were the first man I was ever intimate with. Why do you think it was possible for me to let you go without dying on the inside? Your parents didn't want us together. That much was obvious!"

"I didn't give a damn about my parents. They had their own issues," I said, glaring at her. We fell silent. "Thanksgiving after Thanksgiving, Christmas after Christmas," I was up and pacing the room now. "Letters, phone calls..."

Her head lowered. "I wanted to come back," she said. "I wanted to talk to you, but they forbade me. Said if I did, they'd stop paying for school and..."

I turned to look at her. My arms felt like lead pipes hanging at my sides. All of a sudden, I realized how selfish I was being. I was so busy worrying about myself, I hadn't stopped to think about what might have been going on with her.

"Why are you rehashing this?" she asked, pain seeping from her pores. "What's the point? You're happily married. You have a beautiful son." She swallowed. "I can't do this, Will."

"And I can't do another minute without you."

"Let's just forget tonight ever happened."

"And there is absolutely no way I can forget about tonight." I ran my hand down the length of her bare arms, taking care to savor the feel of her smooth skin under my fingertips.

Her chest heaved as she watched the slow movements of my hands. "Don't do that, Will."

"Don't do what?" I whispered close to her face.

She closed her eyes. "Don't touch me. Please."

"I have to touch you," I mumbled. "After all this time...Make love to me, Naomi." I lowered my head to kiss her mouth, and as my hand moved to cup her face, my fingers pressed tenderly against her cheek.

Naomi whimpered against my lips, her body melting into me. Then, as if regaining her sanity, she pulled away and shook her head. "We're not children anymore," she said, pushing me backwards. "You're a married man."

Her words disappeared in my mouth when I kissed her again. My hand found her breast. She dipped to the side, trying to wriggle away from me, but I dipped with her, deepening the kiss in the process.

She pulled out of my hold. "I can't be the other woman," she said.

"My *wife* is the other woman," I said, "not you." I smothered her with another deep and passionate kiss, groaning, famished for her love.

Naomi lifted her arms and wrapped them around my neck, kissing me hungrily in response. As she pulled me into her, we fell onto the bed in a messy tangle before I climbed on the mattress and covered her body with mine. I had waited decades for this. I had always believed it would come. Smiling internally as I bent over and kissed her face, I knew I could have devoured her whole and still been hungry for more.

Naomi's back arched as I kissed her neck and slid the straps of her top down her silky shoulders. Inhaling her delicious scent, I took my time tasting her as my mouth pressed against her delicate flesh.

She pulled away again and looked me square in the face. "I'm not doing it, Will."

"Don't do this to me, Nay," I muttered, burying my face in her neck. "Not tonight. Not after all this time."

Placing a hand on either side of my face, she forced my head up. "We can't," she insisted. "Your wife trusts you. If I were her, I wouldn't want you to give in to another woman."

If you were my wife, there would be *no other woman.*

I dropped my head and sighed. This was why I loved her. She had integrity and she was honorable. She was classy and respectable. I lifted my head. "I get it," I said, kissing her again.

As she ran her nails through the stubble on my face, I put my hand over hers, my eyes closing.

"Stay with me tonight, Nay. Lie next to me. Let me hold you at least."

12

WILLIAM

BOSTON, M.A., 1996

*I*t was three o'clock in the morning and my eyes were wide open. I looked down at Naomi, who was nestled against me. Her body fit against mine like a puzzle piece, soft where I was hard. It was just like it used to be when we were teenagers. Pressing my lips against her shoulder, I could think of nothing other than how I didn't want tonight to end. I wanted to be with this woman forever.

"You're still awake," she mumbled. Her voice was groggy.

"I don't want to fall asleep," I said, running my hand over her cheek. "I'm afraid I'll wake up and you'll be gone, then I'll realize this was all just a dream."

Naomi turned over and placed a light kiss on my cheek. "I'm here, Will. We're together and it's real."

A moment of silence filled the room.

"We need to talk," she finally said. "There's something I need to tell you."

I interrupted. "You're right. We do need to talk." I turned so we were facing each other in the bed. "But before you say what you have to say, there's something I need to tell you too, and I want to go first."

Where should I begin?

I drew in a deep breath. "My wife went to the doctor earlier this year." I paused again. "He told her that she's sick."

Naomi stiffened in the bed. "Sick? Sick, like how?"

"Like breast-cancer-sick. Stage four."

Naomi went quiet. It was dark, but I could still see the whites of her eyes staring up at the ceiling. "Oh God, Will. I'm so sorry to hear that. You must be devastated. How are you coping?"

"I don't know," I said. "Ethan doesn't know," I added. "No one does except my driver, Gerald...and now you." I pinched my bottom lip between my teeth to stop it from trembling. "I've carried the load alone for months. Sometimes I don't know how much more I can take."

Naomi exhaled and reached her hand out to touch me. At the last minute, she pulled it back and swung her legs over the bed. I watched her walk to the balcony and stare out at the twinkling city lights. After dismissing my pointless pondering, I got out of the bed and joined her. Smiling as I thought back to my earlier fanciful scenarios, I wrapped my arms around her waist and buried my face in her neck. "He said she has a few months, Nay, if that."

"If she was diagnosed earlier this year at stage four," she mumbled, "who knows how much time she has left." She trembled and her posture reduced in my arms. "Oh, God...Will..."

"I'm scared," I admitted to both her and myself in an unabashed whisper. "I don't know where to go from here. What am I supposed to do? She's my wife. It hasn't been easy but...she's my *wife*." Unwrapping my arms from around her waist, I hung my head over the cool metal rail. I could feel the tears finally rising in my chest. "I could've been a better husband, Nay. I could've loved her more. I feel like I owe her so much, but I don't know how to pay."

Since the news dropped, I'd been keeping myself busy so I wouldn't have to think about it, but now, with Naomi here, reality was hitting me hard. The woman I'd lived my entire life with was leaving me—just like Naomi had. A deep sense of dread was creeping over me. I had failed Evelyn, just like I had failed Naomi.

I was a failure.

Out of nowhere, a flood of tears rocked my body. My fingers squeezed around the rail as I swayed helplessly back and forth, half wishing I had the will to hurl myself over the edge and end the impending misery. Perhaps if I'd never seen Naomi, it wouldn't be hitting me this hard. Perhaps I would've been able to spend the remaining months of Evelyn's life taking care of her in earnest, forcing myself to give her parts of me I'd not been able to access since I was a teenager. But now, to be so close to this woman, I realized that I had never loved Evelyn the way I should have. And what was more, I didn't know if I'd be able to now. It was an excruciating reality. I didn't know if I could handle it.

Naomi's hand on my back instantly filled me with peace. "Listen to me," she said. Her tone was calm and reassuring, but it was full of emotion. "I don't know the details of your marriage and I don't want to know them, but you did the best you could with what you were given," she said. "I'm sure of that much. I *know* you." Her hand ran up and down the length of my back.

Squeezing my shoulder, she continued. "She's going through chemo and that's going to count for something. It might even save her life. In the meantime, you give her the best of what you have. You might not have been the man you wanted to be, but you can be the man she needs you to be right now, and if it doesn't go the way we want, you still have memories that can't be taken away. You'll have them long after she's gone." She paused. "I'm here for you, Will. Whatever I can do, I will. All you have to do is ask."

I stared ahead at the static lights on dark silhouettes of skyscrapers and the twinkling headlights from cars below. "You're right," I muttered, still hanging over the balcony. "I have memories, don't I?"

She nodded. "You have tons of them, I'm sure."

I turned to face her. "Remember the Spring Ball in 1951?"

She grimaced. "Will, I wasn't talking about *those* memories."

I stood. "Remember Mickey Cameron?"

She chuckled. "How could I forget Mickey Cameron? Bellbottom pants and Afro...with the pick still in it. He was the cool cat at my school, but you hated him."

She laughed, and after a second, I joined in. I did hate him.

"He was a cocky bastard, that's why," I said, "and I was jealous because I thought you were in love with him."

"What does any of this have to do with your wife?" she asked, rubbing the back of her neck.

"It's simple," I said. "Had I not loved you as much as I did, I wouldn't have had it in me to love Evelyn at all. When you left, I poured almost everything I had into her, pretending she was you."

Naomi hung her head as tears glistened in her eyes.

I lifted her chin and stared into her face. "You're right, Nay. I have a bunch of memories. Memories of unrealized dreams and love lost. I have to do right by this woman while I still can. I have to give it my best shot." I paused. "But you," my voice hushed to a whisper, "you can't go anywhere. I need you near me. I can't go through this without you. Not now that I have you here like this. I told you, I'm never letting you out of my sight again. I can't lose you like I did last time."

She didn't say anything.

Suddenly, a marvelous thought dropped into my head. I stood erect and turned to face Naomi. With my mouth suspended, I was afraid to let the words out, but there was no way I could keep them in. "I know how we can solve this."

"*We?*"

I nodded, still staring at her. "Come home with me."

"Come..." her neck jutted forward, "*home* with you?"

I nodded again.

Her mouth dropped. "What?"

"I *need* you..." I swallowed, "to come back to Beaufort and be with me while I go through all of this. I need you to take care of my wife. She's dying. She needs around-the-clock care."

Naomi took a step backwards. "Please tell me you're joking."

I stared at her expectantly.

She shook her head. "Will, I said I'd do anything for you, but—"

"And this is what I want you to do," I interrupted. "Naomi, you've retired."

"What's that got to do with anything?"

"You have the time," I answered.

"It's *my* time, Will. You can't tell me how to spend it. I'm going to Europe and China and—"

"I don't want to go through this alone." I closed the gap she'd created between us.

"You won't need me. Ethan will be there. Once you tell him, he'll drop everything and—"

"But *you* won't be there." I was in her face. "He said you were the best nurse he knew. He said it himself."

"Surgical nurse."

"You trained at the best school."

"Do not...do that!"

"I owe my wife the best. *You* said that."

"No," she said. "You're not going to use my own words on me."

My shoulders slumped. I took another step in her direction, but she sidestepped me. "Naomi..."

"I can't do that, Will. I've never met the woman, but with all due respect, she doesn't sound like the type of person I'd easily click with."

"She'd be your patient. You wouldn't need to click with her," I insisted.

"Right. I'd just need to click with you. Is that what you're saying?"

I groaned but couldn't deny that she'd read me like the business section in the newspaper.

"No," she said.

"Why not?"

"Lionel," she said. "I can't leave him."

Hearing her say the name made me want to spit. "I thought you said nothing was going on between the two of you."

She turned her back to me.

"And if there *is* something going on, he has a lot to worry about. Especially with the way you were kissing on me earlier."

"How dare you," she seethed, spinning on her heels and pointing in my face. "What *almost* happened earlier is no indication of how I feel about him."

I stared at her and her mouth started to quiver. She crossed her arms tightly across her breast and shame fell upon me. "I'm sorry, Nay," I whispered, reaching out to her. "I didn't mean—"

She jerked away from me and my heart split in half.

"Whatever, William. It doesn't matter anyway. There's no way I can go back to Beaufort after the way I left it."

"That's the past, Naomi. It's separate and aside from what I'm asking of you."

Her trembling eyes shifted. She opened and closed her mouth a few times before falling silent for a second.

"Does she know about me?" she whispered.

"What do you mean?"

She spun around to glare at me. "Does she *know* about me, William? Does she know about our past?"

"How would she know about our past, Nay?" I asked. My expression tried to deny the memories of that Thanksgiving dinner flooding my mind: the way I'd stormed away from the table; the way it had been so obvious I was in love with the maid's daughter.

Evelyn still hounded me about it. She was convinced I had never fully checked into our marriage, and she blamed Naomi for that. The maid's daughter was a measuring stick, she'd say. Even when we made love, Evelyn would accuse me of fantasizing about Naomi just so I could get my rocks off.

I exhaled and leaned against the rail, rubbing my eyes. "Yes," I said, "technically, she knows about you. She knows there was a girl I was madly in love with, but she has no idea that you're that girl."

Naomi paused. "And you think the name Naomi wouldn't ring a few bells?"

"She didn't know your name," I said. "I could barely stand to think about you let alone say your name out loud, Nay." I reached out to take her hand into mine, desperate to touch her. "I promise you, she'd be none the wiser. It'd be our secret. You'd come home, you'd take care of her, and no one would know anything more."

"Great," she said. "So it'll be 1952 all over again. I'll be *the black secret*. The girl you have to keep in the dark because no one can know about me. Is that it?"

"Sweetheart, I never said—"

"It's a horrible idea," she said. "It's not going to work. I can't believe you think I'd even consider it!" She ripped her hand out of mine. "I am *not* a house-nigger, Will. This is not the 1940s." Her lips were tight, stinging me with venomous language.

My mouth snapped shut. "A house..." I couldn't bring myself to say the word. "Wow..."

She continued. "I refuse to reduce myself to being an indentured servant at your wife's beck and call, fetching this and that, running errands, babysitting...I am *not* my mother."

"Your mother was a great woman," I mumbled. "If it wasn't for your mother—"

"Oh please," she cut me off, wringing her hands. "Think about what you're asking me to do! You want me to live in your house and exist in the same space as your wife, a woman who openly disrespects your son and his black fiancée. How do you think she'll react to me? Did you ever stop and think about that?"

"You're not making sense."

"The hell, I'm not." She stormed back into the room.

I chased after her and grabbed her arm just as she was shoving her feet into her heels. "Where are you going?"

"Home."

"You wouldn't leave me again, Naomi."

She ripped her arm from my grasp. "I would," she said. "And I am."

"So it's history repeating itself then," I muttered.

She froze for a second, but then continued to get dressed. I watched her in silence until I could take no more.

"Sweetheart, wait. Please," I begged.

She ignored me.

"Naomi, take the next few days to think about it." I forged ahead before she could interrupt my plea. "I'm here until the end of the week. We can go to dinner. We can talk about it. We can figure out a way to make it work."

She stopped getting dressed and stared at me. "Dinner? Your wife is dying, and the only thing you can think about is getting close to me? What kind of man are you?"

"I'm a man who is in love with another woman," I said, spreading my arms wide. "So if that makes me a bad person, then I've been that for most of my life. I already told you I wasn't a good husband. You're the one who encouraged me to do right by her, so that's what I'm trying to do."

"And this is your idea of doing right? By asking me to come and live with you and your family?"

My shoulders crumbled. "I'm trying. The best way I know how."

She forced her tank top over her head. "That's commendable, William, but the answer is still no. I can't do it. I can't invest that much emotional energy into something like this. I can't give you any more of me." Naomi turned on her heel and headed for the exit.

With a burst of energy, I reached the door and blocked her.

"Don't go, Nay. Please, don't leave me." I wrapped my arms around her and felt her weaken for a second, but then she slipped away and opened the door.

"I have to go," she said as she looked at me and sighed. "I'm sorry. I really am, but I..." her words died before she turned and raced down the corridor, disappearing from sight.

Staring into the corridor longer than I should have, emptiness slowly draped itself across my chest like a weighted vest. She was gone. Again. And this time, I knew she'd never allow herself to be found.

I threw my head back toward the ceiling and sucked in my emotions before heading into the abandoned quarters. The rumpled sheets on the bed served as a depressing reminder of the fact that she had been there. Her fragrance still lingered in the air; crisp and sweet.

My gaze wandered around the empty room, coming to rest on the night table where the sparkle of her clutch purse caught my eye. Her watch and cell phone lay beside it. I walked over and picked up the phone, letting my fingers run over the cold metal. She'd be back, I thought, looking at the door, even if it was just to get this.

13

WILLIAM
BEAUFORT, S.C., 1957

*B*lack Friday

Bruce knocked on my door and stood there waiting, even though it was wide open. He was leaning against the frame, wearing sky blue pants with a red vest and a checkered red blazer. It was Buttericks, for sure. My own mother had made the name famous. Of course, Miss Carole did all the sewing. My mother just about knew what a damn sewing machine looked like.

Bruce's hair was slicked back with so much LB Butch Wax, it looked like it wouldn't even move in a strong gale.

God, he's such a prick, I thought, grimacing.

After dinner last night, I'd stayed in my room, despite his knocking on the door and calling my name over and over like a broken record. After ten minutes, he got the hint; I didn't want to talk to him. I didn't want to talk to anyone. I was hoping he'd forget about going to the hop tonight, but hope had let me down.

"So are we going, or what?" he asked, pulling at his lapels. "There are some smoking skirts in the city. Way different from the chicks in the country."

I didn't respond.

He walked further into the room. "What about Evvie?"

"What about Evvie?"

"She's looking for you, man. She called the house earlier today. I heard your mother tell her you'd meet her at the hop at six-thirty." He looked at his watch. "You gotta get ready, man."

I was sitting at my desk looking through a photo album. I slammed it closed and pushed the chair back hard before stomping over to my mirror and raking a brush through my hair.

"Whoa, easy there, my man. You're gonna pull all that stuff out." He walked over to me and took the brush out of my hand. His forehead was creased, but it wasn't with concern. Bruce just wanted to know what was going on with me. He was being nosey.

I spun around. "Listen, Bruce. We can go out tonight, but don't you dare try to push Evelyn on me. I'm not into her. I don't need the headache."

"First of all, I won't have to do any pushing. I heard she's fast, man. She'll put out in a minute if you look at her for too long."

Bruce was a nosey bastard; always into gossip. He was worse than a broad sometimes. I went to the closet and pulled out my jacket. It looked at lot better than his. I was already wearing a pair of Levis dungarees with the cuff rolled up over my Converses. A leather jacket would finish the look off nicely. I could've put on a blazer and tie, but I wasn't trying to impress anyone anyhow.

"Yeah, well, don't you go encouraging her. You heard what happened last night. I don't want anything to do with her."

"So you were serious about all that? I mean, about that woman's daughter?" His voice was hushed, like he would get in trouble if anyone heard him talking about it.

"That woman is named Carole," I said.

Bruce held his hands up. "Sorry. I can tell Carole means a lot to you, then."

"She means more than a lot to me, and so does her daughter." That's all I was prepared to say. He didn't deserve details. He was none of my company.

"Hey, I'm real sorry about how that all went down last night. Some shit, huh?"

I ignored him.

"I don't think she's coming back, though. I overheard your old lady talking to that woman in the kitchen late last evening. It sounded bad."

Now he had my attention. "What are you talking about?"

Bruce sat at the desk, making himself comfortable as he threw his arm over the back of the chair. "Well, from what I could tell, because they were whispering, the girl...what's her name again?"

"Naomi," I said.

"Yeah. Naomi. Apparently, she got PG, man."

"PG?" I glared at him. "What the hell are you talking about?"

He threw his hands up again. "She got knocked up out there, man. Don't get mad at me. I'm just saying what I heard."

I stared past him, feeling the muscles in my chest tighten until I thought they would snap in half. It couldn't be true. Naomi wasn't the kind of girl who would...

"I can't be too sure about what they were saying, though," he said. "My father had gotten a few drinks in by that time and he was super loud and super blitzed, but your mother seemed pretty peeved about it. And that woman, well, she didn't have a whole lot to say." Bruce shook his head. It was such a shame, he was probably thinking.

"I can tell you like her a lot though," he continued. "She must be a real pretty nig—" he cleared his throat, "colored girl if you're that sprung. But the girl's got a baby now. That's what normally happens to them anyway, you know. You should just forget about her." He shook his head again.

My hands rolled up into fists as I tried to stop my body shaking. For a second, I thought about smacking Bruce in the nose, but what good would that do? I paced the room. Maybe I should confront my mother about this, but Bruce had been eavesdropping, and we'd all get an earful if she found out he'd told me what they were discussing.

I could ask Miss Carole about it, I thought, but did I really want to stress her out? She had enough on her plate without me bringing gossip to the table.

"You heard wrong, Bruce," I said. My voice sounded strained, like I hadn't reached puberty. "Naomi, she's not that kind of girl."

"She's a nig—" I glared at him, and he caught himself. "They're all like that."

I gritted my teeth. "*She's* not like that," I insisted. "And don't you ever use that word in my presence again. That, or *darkie*...none of 'em, you got me?" I glared at him until he looked away.

"Yeah, I got you, Will," he agreed. "You know, you're probably right, man. You know that girl way better than me. I've never even met her."

———

THAT NIGHT, Bruce and I walked into the hop. The music was bumping from a live band on stage. A sweaty drummer was slapping sticks on the skins and twirling them between two fingers, and a guitar player was strumming strings in a way I'd never seen before. The lead singer was a cool cat with more wax in his jet-black hair than Bruce had ever used, and he was wearing shades, even though we were inside and the sun had set hours ago.

A huge glittery ball suspended from the ceiling made the lights ricochet around the room, flashing off the elated faces of guys and gals ready to boogie on down and make out. People were decked out; plaid suits and crinolines everywhere.

Bruce pointed at a group of young people dancing wildly, and his belly jiggled as he made a mild attempt at the twist and then the jitterbug.

I wanted him to stop. He was embarrassing me.

"Look," he said, jiggling involuntarily now, "there's Evvie!"

I looked up just in time to see her hand rising above the dancers, waving like it would detach from her wrist at any moment. She whispered something to her friends and they all giggled, covering their mouths.

I groaned.

"Man, look at her. That girl is smokin'," he said, "and she's pinning you already. Are we gonna go over there, or what?"

He wasn't lying. Evelyn's eyes were locked on me, trying to catch my attention.

Despite my reluctance, Bruce and I passed by the wallflowers and meandered through the dancers to where the girls huddled together. We met somewhere near the center of the room where the music was louder, and crowds of excited people crashed into us from various angles.

"Hiya, Will," Evelyn said, leaning over and shouting over the music in my ear.

Even though the music was loud, I wouldn't have minded if she'd shouted from a distance. I didn't feel comfortable with her being that close to my face.

My nose pricked at the light fragrance she was wearing. Her lips were painted a cherry red and her eyelashes were real long. She had her hair fixed up in victory rolls that looked like golden scrolls.

"Hey," I said. I had to admit that she looked real pretty.

"Thanks for inviting me to dinner last night," she said.

I shrugged. "You can thank my mother for that."

She frowned a little.

"But yeah, it was nice to have you there."

Now she was smiling. "And I'm real happy you could come to the hop. You can be so shy sometimes. I always have to call your mom and ask her to get you out of the house."

"I'm busy studying, getting ready to take over my father's shipping company," I said. "I'm not really into the party scene anymore. There's too much to do."

"There's always room for a little fun, though," she said.

We were silent, standing next to one another, listening to the band jam.

Evelyn's dancing on the spot made her belt twirl around her waist and her narrow hips roll beneath her poodle skirt.

"So do you wanna dance?" she asked with glittering eyes when another song struck up. "I really dig this song."

Fortunately for me, I had prepared my no-thank-you speech last night. "No thanks. I'm no good at dancing. I'd rather watch," I said.

"Are you kidding me? Will, you're an awesome dancer. You could easily audition for American Bandstand."

I blushed. "Right."

"I've been watching you, Will...for a long time, you know?" Evelyn smiled, running her tongue along the perimeter of her cherry-red bottom lip. As my eyes tracked it, my groin started to feel warm. Evelyn's eyes twinkled just like the ball above us.

Without giving me a chance to protest, she grabbed me and pulled me deeper into the dancing crowd. The band was playing a groovy tune and before I knew it, I was moving to the beat.

I grabbed Evelyn and swung her around the floor. She laughed and put her hands on my shoulder, rocking from side to side. My sneakers squeaked across the floor as I twisted lower and lower.

Evelyn kept in step until our knees were pushed up in our chests, then we twisted back up.

The crowd screamed, egging us on.

High on adrenaline, I lifted Evelyn off the floor and swung her around my waist. Her skirt flailed in the air, exposing the crinoline underneath. With her legs straight by my side, I flung her to the other side before flipping her over my shoulder. I spun around just in time to see her land perfectly on her feet. Her saddle shoes tapped the ground, and we immediately went into the Watusi.

Evelyn dipped back and I leaned over her. Then I dipped back and she leaned over me. Her breasts brushed my chest and her eyes gleamed as she shimmied around me, twisting on her toes like a ballerina, her waist keeping in time with her toes. I stood snapping my fingers like Mr. Cool, my eyes locked on hers as she circled me.

Evelyn put her finger to her tongue and pressed it against my mouth, making a sizzling noise.

The crowd was going wild.

Soon, the music died down and the deafening chorus of clapping and cheering made my ears ring and my ego swell.

Bruce rushed over to us as a slow song kicked in. "That was awesome," he hollered.

"Yeah, well, Evelyn here is a pretty good dancer."

"No, that was you, Will. I told you. You're amazing," she said, beaming.

The vibe in the room started to change. A couple of violinists took their positions on the stage, and a beautiful black woman stepped up to the mic. The quivering sound of the strings pierced my chest as it gradually grew louder. Finally, the woman opened her mouth and the words to 'Talk To Me' by Little Willie John flowed from her vocal chords. People organized themselves around me until they had formed into distinct couples.

Evelyn was gazing at me with her hands clasped in front of her, swaying gently.

I'd already tried to use my no-thank-you excuse, and it had failed me. It didn't even make sense to try it now.

"Well? Aren't you gonna dance with me again, Will?" she asked, running her nail down the front of my shirt.

Bruce skulked away with his index finger raised to the sky.

"Of course," I stuttered as I took Evelyn's hand and pulled her close. We rocked from side to side with her head nestled against my chest. A strong scent of strawberries wafted up to my nostrils. Following the scent, I pressed my nose in her hair and inhaled.

"Will, I'm so happy," Evelyn said. "You don't know how long I've been waiting to tell you how much I dig you. I know we're in school and everything, but maybe we could..." Her words faded away.

I closed my eyes, the lyrics of the song echoing in my heart.

Talk to me, talk to me. Hold me close, whisper low. Talk to me, baby, can't you see? Darling I, I love you so.

My eyes opened and I looked at the black woman crooning on the stage. Our eyes locked and my breath caught in the back of my throat. My heart split.

Naomi?

"Are you okay?" Evelyn was looking up into my face.

My eyes shifted back to the stage. The woman stood, caressing the mic stand like it was a man, singing words that pierced me like arrows.

I stopped dancing, standing in the middle of the floor, frozen. "I'm sorry," I muttered, pulling away from her. "I can't do this."

"Do what?"

My hand swiped at my forehead. "This." I shook my head, mouth agape. "I have to go."

Evelyn grimaced and put her hands on her hips. "You can't be serious," she said, glaring at me. "Tell me this isn't about that woman's daughter, William...that black bitch!"

Heat flushed through my body and my chest tightened as I turned and walked away from her.

"William, wait," she called after me.

I didn't stop.

"I didn't mean..."

But I was gone.

I rushed out of the building like someone was chasing me. Outside the hop, I could still hear the woman crooning, torturing me with the words. Again, I could see Naomi's face in front of me like she was right there. Like I could reach out and touch her.

What was going on in Seattle, I wondered? Why *wouldn't* she talk to me? Maybe she was pregnant, I thought. That's why she didn't want to see me. Maybe she'd found another man, a black man who could love her in the open; a black man who could take her out dancing without people staring. She'd fallen in love with him, I told myself, and she'd had his baby.

I sealed my eyes as hot tears burned behind them. I leaned on the building and slammed my fist into the cold, hard bricks. The throbbing of my hand was nothing compared to the throbbing in my chest.

Bruce was right. I should just forget about Naomi. I should just move on. My mama would be happy. My daddy would be relieved. He wouldn't have to worry about me making a mistake anymore.

I looked back at the hop and thought about Evelyn. She looked pretty tonight and she smelled nice. That was all a man needed anyway. I could learn to love her...

I ran my trembling hands over my face, smearing the tears away and stood straight.

I needed to make a decision. I couldn't continue to torture myself like this.

I tugged the hem of my leather jacket down, then walked back inside to ask Evvie to dance with me. Again.

14

NAOMI

BOSTON, M.A., 1996

The smoke from my cigarette curled above my head before blowing away in the salty wind. The only time I smoked was when I was stressed. On my way home from the Ritz, I'd bought a pack of menthols and now there were only four cigarettes left. Sitting outside on my front porch, I watched the big leaves on the willow tree in the front yard sway in a breeze that was still a little too hot to enjoy. I lived near the bay in an all-white, two-story townhouse I'd called home since I moved to Boston from Seattle. Ahead of me, the waves kissed the rocky shoreline, and the smell of sea salt and a barbecue filled my nostrils. I looked up as a squawking seagull flapped its heavy wings above me, sailing through the sky. Nature normally calmed me. The sights and sounds of the environment should have relaxed my anxious soul, but it wasn't working today.

I held the cigarette to my lips with a trembling hand as thoughts about last night raced through my mind. The sun was already peeking over the horizon by the time I finally arrived home early this morning. I'd fallen onto my bed and cried myself to sleep, awakening to puffy eyes smeared with remnants of makeup. It had been a mistake seeing William. I might not have had much choice in the first instance, but I didn't have to get in that damn Lexus.

The entire drive to the hotel, I'd berated myself. I was an idiot. I was a complete fool. I had given William the upper hand, just like when we were kids. Back then he was suave and handsome. His kisses were soft; they made me melt like ice cream on a hot sidewalk. But I was a grown woman now. I thought I'd be able to handle him. That weak-in-the-knees stuff was for Ethan and Dakota, not me. I'd had a chance to get my wits about me during dinner; a chance to get over the fact he was sitting next to me, looking just as good as I remembered.

He was the man-version of what he had been when we were kids: tall, thick, and fit. It had taken all of my willpower not to swoon at the table, but I'd survived that. Yet, as I sat in the back seat of that limo, shrinking with each passing minute, it didn't take me long to realize that it didn't matter how old I was or how much time had passed, I was still a girl in Will's presence and he would have me wrapped around his finger in an instant.

I took a deep draw from the withering cigarette.

I dreamt about him last night, squirming in the bed as I recalled the feel of his mouth on my body. In the dream, we'd made love and I awoke to the sound of my primal moans and my nails raking the bed sheets. If I'd been a different kind of woman, I'd have given myself to him unashamedly. It had taken every bit of willpower I had to do the right thing, but in my dreams, I'd been free.

The house phone rang. I scrambled around on the hammock until I located it underneath me.

Lionel.

I hesitated for a split second before picking up the phone.

"Hey Li," I said, but my voice was strained. I prayed he wouldn't notice.

"Hey there," he crooned. "I was calling to confirm that we're on for tonight. I haven't seen you in almost two weeks."

"It's only been eight days, Lionel," I said. "Last Sunday we went to brunch at that new restaurant downtown, remember?"

"I remember, but it doesn't matter," he said. "You know I can't go for too long without seeing you before I go into withdrawals."

Despite all that was running through my mind, I managed to pull a laugh from somewhere. "You're so dramatic."

"And our anniversary is coming up," he said.

"Our *anniversary*?" I mocked him, amused. This was why I kept him around. His humor was refreshing.

"It'll be twelve weeks next week," he reminded me. "Twelve of anything equals an anniversary, according to my calculations."

"You're an architect, so your faulty math could be problematic. Besides, I didn't know we were exclusive," I said. "I'm old fashioned, and you never asked me to make it official."

"Well, you never know what I have planned for tonight," he said. "Do you remember, Nay?"

"What?"

"At the gala? Everyone was on the dance floor and you were sitting at that side table by yourself."

"I was letting my food settle. I'm old and I get heartburn nowadays."

He laughed. "So you say, but I think you were waiting for me to approach you. You had to have seen me staring at you all night long. You had on that navy blue gown that sparkled under the lights." He silent-whistled. "Baby, you're not old. You're seasoned, and very well at that."

I squirmed in my seat and picked up my cigarette. *If I hadn't been so strong-willed last night, I would have been good and spicy right now, never mind seasoned.*

"I tried to call you last night, but your phone kept going to voicemail."

"My phone," I said, puzzled. "I never heard it ring. In fact, I haven't seen it since..." I gasped. "Shit..."

"What's wrong? Did you lose it?" he asked.

I swiped my hand across my face. "No, I left it...um...at the dinner table," I said quickly. If only that were true. In an instant, visions of the phone sitting on the night table in Will's hotel room struck me. I wanted to groan.

"Well, if you left it at the dinner table, Dr. Cooper will make sure you get it back. At least you know where it is."

"Yeah, at least there's that," I agreed.

"Well, how was your dinner last night?"

"It was wonderful," I lied. "Ethan is so sweet and his fiancée is a doll. I was thrilled to meet her."

"I know he means a lot to you. He's like a son," Lionel said.

"He's a good boy for sure," I said.

"Speaking of sons..." Lionel paused.

"No, I haven't heard from Scott," I cut him off. I ran my hand over my face and put my cigarette to my mouth. "I thought he might've called last night, but he hasn't so..." I took a draw.

Lionel was quiet for a second. "He'll call, sweetheart. He's upset. You have to give him time to come to terms with everything."

"Come to terms?" I questioned him. "Lionel, I'm a grown woman. I'm his mother. If I'm dating someone, what business is it of his?"

"Some boys can't fathom the idea that there's another man in their mother's life."

"It's not up to him how I spend my personal time," I insisted.

"I know," he said, "but try to put yourself in his shoes. You've been single for a while and he got used to that. He's never seen you with another man. Not even his father."

My chest tightened. "Yeah, well," I was fighting the urge to stutter. "I'm still his mother and I deserve to have a life. I won't allow him to push you away, or anyone else for that matter."

"No one can push me away," he said. "It'll take an awful lot for me to change my mind about you."

I thought about Will again and blinked back sudden tears.

He inhaled. "I'll pick you up at seven. Dinner and a movie."

LATER THAT EVENING, Lionel and I were sitting in a Johnny Rockets eating hamburgers and slurping on extra thick milkshakes after our movie. A colorful jukebox was lit up playing songs from back in the day while girls in poodle skirts and two-tone saddle shoes sashayed through the restaurant. A vacuum was sucking me in, taking me back to a time when I was sixteen years old.

"Tell me more about the dinner," Lionel said before taking a huge chunk out of a hefty burger. "How was Ethan's fiancée? Was she beautiful?"

"She was more than beautiful," I said. "She's a gem. I'm happy for them. I hope they can go the distance."

"Why wouldn't they?" he asked. "They're young and in love."

"Sometimes that's not enough," I said.

He stared at me.

"It can be tough, Li."

"What can be tough?"

"Interracial relationships."

He sucked his teeth. "This isn't the 1950s, you know. Things are different. How bad could it possibly be? Interracial relationships are the in-thing now. It's all in the movies and on television." He put his elbow on the table and started counting off on his fingers. "Flipper Purify and Angie Tucci, Jeniffer Finnigan and Roger Cross..."

"Who are those people?"

Lionel shook his head and picked his burger back up. "Never mind, Nay. The point is, we live in a thriving city."

"Yes, a thriving city called Massachusetts," I said, leaning forward. "Do you realize this was the first slave-holding colony in New England? And what about the fact that Boston had the largest slave population compared to anywhere else in the United States?"

Lionel put the burger down and leaned back in his seat.

I picked up my milkshake. "And let's not talk about South Carolina, the place I was born and raised. Home, sweet home..."

"Let's not." He was staring at me. "It seems to be a sore spot for you. Every time we talk about relationships—"

"Have you ever been with a white woman?" I asked in between slurps.

"No," he said. "Not that I wouldn't, I've just never had the opportunity." We were silent. "Have you ever dated a white man?"

I played with the extra-wide straw and watched as a drop of condensation slid down the side of the glass. "A very long time ago," I whispered. "But it didn't work out, and it was *because* he was white."

"So other people drove you apart?"

"*I* drove us apart," I said. The statement slapped me. I put the straw to my mouth. "Because I'm a realist. There was no way it could've worked, so I ended it before things got messy."

Lionel tilted his head to the side, as if he was trying to see the situation from my perspective. "Sounds to me like you didn't give the guy a fair shake."

"You have no idea how difficult it was for me," I said, trying to defend myself.

"Maybe," he said with his mouth full, "but I also know how you can be. You can be stubborn."

"I'm not stubborn."

"You've got an answer for everything."

"Because there *is* an answer for everything."

"You get an idea in your head and no one can get it out." He shook his head. "That poor guy. He's probably somewhere right now thinking about you, wondering what he could've done to make it different."

I rubbed the back of my neck. "I'm sure he's over it by now."

Lionel's eyes widened. "Over you?" He laughed. "Naomi, you're a phenomenal woman. You raised a boy, in your first year of nursing school no less, after the man you had him for up and left out of the blue."

I fidgeted in my seat. That was the story I'd told him. It was also the story I'd told Scott.

"You completed your degree and then went on to become one of the best surgical nurses in Boston." He lowered his voice. "You're loving, you're kind...you'd give the coat off your back to anyone who needed it. You always put others first. You have this way of seeing what people need and giving it to them before they even have to ask."

My lip trembled. I bit down on it to make it stop.

"And on top of all that, you're smoking hot! Him *over* you?" He grunted. "I don't think so, baby."

Lionel leaned over to kiss me, but his buzzing cell phone sliced into the exchange. As he pulled his phone off his waist and looked at the screen, his eyebrows drew in.

"What is it?" I asked.

"Nothing. I mean...it's an out of State call. Could be a client." The phone rattled in his hand. "Do you mind if I..."

"Of course not," I assured him. "I'm the one that's retired, not you."

He laughed and kissed my mouth before sliding his finger across the face of his phone.

"Lionel Weldon," he answered.

I took another slurp of my milkshake but couldn't help notice Lionel's countenance. His features began to sag until his mouth formed an upside down 'u'. He looked at me and then looked away quickly. His body turned in the chair until his shoulder was facing me.

"Who is this?"

I sat the glass down on the table and picked up a French fry, trying not to appear nosey.

"I don't understand," he said.

More silence. He nodded. His hand fled across his brow. "Wow," he said through a breath. "I can't argue with that, can I? But—" He was interrupted.

He nodded and chuckled a few times, then his shoulders dropped.

After a few seconds, he hung up. He moistened his lips and fitted a smile on them.

"That was a strange call," I said.

He shrugged and picked up his burger. "Very strange," he agreed.

I waited for him to elaborate. He didn't.

"Who was it? If you don't mind..."

"It was my partner, Hector" he said. "There are a few projects he wants to switch around."

"But you didn't recognize the voice at first," I pressed.

"He was drunk," he replied after a brief silence, pushing his unfinished burger to the side. "It's getting late. Maybe we should..."

I looked at my shake for a moment. "Yeah, sure," I replied.

WHEN WE ARRIVED at my townhouse, Lionel closed the car door behind me and followed as I walked up the stone steps to the front door.

The entire drive home had been awkward. We'd hardly said a word, and we continued in silence as I searched for my house keys. As my hands finally clasped around them in the bottom of my purse, I tightened my grip on them, unsure of what to say.

"So...you never asked," I said, trying to spark conversation.

"Asked what?"

"I told you, if you want us to be exclusive, you need to ask me. I'm an old fashioned girl. It's the way I was raised." I chuckled, feigning naiveté.

"Oh, right."

"Li, is everything okay? I mean..." I paused, searching for words again. "Did I miss something?"

He tugged at his ear.

"Because all of a sudden it feels like this is our first date when it's not and, to be honest, I'm a little confused."

His shoulders rounded. "I know," he said, "I –"

"What's going on?"

"I don't know." He paused. "Tonight was nice. It always is. I love being with you. When I'm not with you, all I do is count the minutes until I am."

I waited.

"But...I was thinking. Maybe things are moving too fast."

My head jutted forward. "What did you just say?"

"I don't know, I mean..."

"Wait a minute," I paused, running my hand over my ponytail.

"This entire relationship was your idea. Remember? I was sitting alone at the gala. I had on the blue dress. You'd been watching me all night...*Remember?*"

"I know, and all of that is true, it's just—"

"You asked me for my number. You asked me out on a date. When I said no, you begged me to change it into a yes!" I gulped. "I made myself vulnerable in front of you. After all the years I'd focused on work and dodged relationships, I opened myself up to you."

"I'm sorry," he said and nothing more.

I squared my shoulders. "Indeed," I spat, pulling my keys out of my purse.

"Sweetheart—"

"No, it's okay," I said. "I'll admit, I don't understand all this, but I will get over it. I'm a sixty-year-old woman, Lionel. I'm not some teeny-bopper who's going to cry into her pillow or wonder how I could have been whatever you wanted me to be."

"Naomi, I don't want you to walk away thinking it was something you did wrong." He groaned, running his hand over his face. "I wish I could explain," he mumbled.

"Don't feel pressured," I said, forcing a smile on my face. "Goodbye, Lionel. Thank you for the movie and dinner."

I pushed the key in the lock.

"Maybe..." he watched me turning the key and extended his hand. "Nay, maybe I can call you tonight. We can talk and—"

I spun around to look at him. "Don't bother."

Pushing open the front door to my townhouse, I stepped inside and closed it firmly behind me. I stared at it for a moment and listened to the soft crunching of footsteps as Lionel returned to his car. Releasing one last sigh of confusion and disappointment, I trudged up the stairs and crawled into bed.

15

WILLIAM

BOSTON, M.A., 1996

I marched up and down the suite while throwing clothes into an open suitcase, trying to stay focused on the task at hand.

The blaring of my phone sliced through the tense atmosphere. I looked at the number.

"Not now, Evelyn," I groaned. She'd been calling me all week, and all week I'd been ignoring her.

I had needed a clear mind, and she would offer me anything but.

So many things were competing for my attention and at the top of the list, even though it shouldn't have been, was Naomi. I sat on the edge of the bed and clamped my hands over my ears to silence the incessant ringing, which was starting to feel like a drill slowly cracking its way through my skull.

As soon as it stopped ringing, it started again.

Realizing I had no other option, I answered.

"Hello!" I barked.

"Well, it's about time I got ahold of you," Evelyn said.

"That must mean you miss me."

"Of course I miss you," she responded. "I'm counting the minutes until you get back home."

Sarcasm.

We could both play that game, if she really wanted to.

"Well, I'll be home tomorrow afternoon." I switched the phone from one ear to the other. "How are you feeling? You sound tired. Have you been resting?"

"Rest? How can I rest, William? I'm as bald as a damn billiard ball."

I closed my eyes. "It's part of the process, sweetheart. Your therapist is helping you deal with it." I paused. "You are letting the therapist help you to deal with it, aren't you?"

"And my boy is in another state with another woman..."

I groaned. "You mean his fiancée, don't you?"

"If that's what you want to call her," she said, starting to sob. "And on top of that, he's mad at me because he refuses to consider the counsel I am offering him. How the hell can I rest?"

I rubbed my brow and forced myself to remember the vows I had made to Naomi about how I was going to be a better husband to my wife. "I'll talk to Ethan," I said. "You were both emotional on that day, but now you've had some time apart, you might be able to reconnect."

"You think he'll listen to me?" she asked. "He never listens to me. I'm only trying to help, William. It's bad enough he's gone into the medical field when he should have been taking over the family shipping business, but no, he opposed that too, didn't he? And against my better judgment, I let it slide."

"The medical field is a noble profession," I said through a sigh.

"And now he's with this woman, this *Dakota*. She's no good for him for him, Will."

"He's not going to leave Dakota," I said, trying to harness patience. "Evvie, let that go and be happy for the boy. He's in love. Let him chart his own course."

Evelyn grunted. The sobbing had vanished. "I'll let it go the day I die, which is soon coming, by the way. And you're right. I am tired. I've not had a minute's rest since I landed."

"I'm not surprised. Gerald told me about all the committee meetings you've attended over the last couple of days. You're gonna have to put that stuff on the back-burner. If there's any way for you to beat this thing, you have to—"

"Beat it? Let's be real, William. I'm not going to beat it. Stop talking like I will. It's over. I have six months left. I feel weaker every day." As if trying to provide evidence, she hacked into the phone. "But I'm going to do everything I want until my time is up. Slowing down won't help me none. Sharon goes with me everywhere I want to go."

I shoved my tongue inside my cheek. "Fine. That's understandable, but I'd really like it if you'd slow down a little." I sensed a dent in her armor. "I was thinking..."

"About what?"

I paused. "Maybe we could travel. Go somewhere nice together."

"We've been everywhere already," she said.

"Sure we've been to different places on business," I said, "but it's never been the both of us...together with nothing to do. How'd you like to go to France? Or Italy or Hawaii?"

Evelyn thought about it for a second and my heart softened for her.

"I'll think about it," she said.

"Okay, good," I replied, trying to smile.

"But only if you're absolutely sure you'll be going with *me*, your wife, and not some historical figment of your imagination."

"What?"

"Every time we travel together, I see you. You get a glazed, forlorn look in your eyes. God only knows what's going through your mind, but I'm sure it has something to do with *her*."

"You cannot be serious?" I grumbled.

"I know the truth, William. It's been this way forever. I just wish you would be honest about it." Her tone had softened, and for a second, I couldn't help but wonder what that honest conversation would sound like and how she would respond.

I sighed. "Evelyn, I haven't seen or thought about the maid's daughter since I was a boy," I said.

Two lies in one breath.

"I'm *your* husband, Evelyn. I wish you would just leave the past alone."

Naomi's words burst into my mind. If only she knew how hard it had been to love this woman, maybe she'd have had some pity on me. Maybe she'd have been able to understand why I couldn't forget about her. My mind lapsed into thoughts of her.

The week had flown by and I hadn't seen her. Not even the cell phone had brought her back. It had been an instant replay of 1954. She hadn't even stopped to give my request any honest consideration. I'd gone from depressed, to angry, to desperate. I considered calling Ethan and asking for her home phone number, but that would have sparked questions. I could've found out where she lived and shown up on her doorstep, but I didn't want to chase her.

Evelyn's voice was squeaking on the phone. "So how was she, Will?"

I jolted. "Who?"

"What do you mean *who*? That girl, whatever her bloody name is."

"Dakota is a beautiful woman," I said with another sigh. "She's going to make our son very happy."

Evelyn grunted. "I can't believe you're not siding with me on this. It's not going to work. They're from different worlds."

"And you know this because you've actually taken the time to get to know her," I said, shaking my head as if she could see me.

"What was she wearing?" she continued, oblivious to my escalating irritation.

"Jesus Christ, Evelyn. You can't be serious about this. Are you really still that girl?"

I heard her breath catch on the other end of the phone. I imagined her sitting rigid, like a pole had been shoved down the back of her shirt. "I'm the same girl you married thirty years ago, William Cooper," she muttered. "The same girl you fell in love with, or at least that's what you told me."

"Evvie, I'm sorry, I'm just a little flustered right now. You're sick, Ethan's getting married..." *After forty-two goddamn years, the long-lost love of my life shows up to dinner...* "There's a lot going through my mind. I didn't mean what I said."

"Yeah, well...just make sure you choose your words more carefully next time."

I picked up the television remote and started flipping through channels, trying to take my mind off the current conversation.

A hard knock on my door made me look up. "Hold on, Evelyn," I said. "I think that's the butler with the dry cleaning."

I peeked through the peephole and saw a smartly dressed man standing with my Armani suits hanging from his hand. I pulled the door open.

"Good evening, sir. Your dry cleaning." He extended his arm.

I waved him into the room. "Just throw them over there," I instructed, pointing to the place where I'd shoved the rest of my clothes into a suitcase.

The butler frowned. "I trust your stay at the Ritz Carlton has been suitable?"

"It's been fine, but I'm ready to leave." We stared at each other. "Business calls. You know how it is."

The butler nodded as if he did. "Will that be all, sir?"

I contemplated whether he could make arrangements to kidnap a particular woman and have her delivered to my room. If I'd asked Gerald to do it, he would have made it happen. Too bad this guy wasn't Gerald.

"Apart from a slice of cheesecake and a bottle of Dom Perignon, that'll be all," I said.

The butler nodded again. "I'll have that delivered promptly, sir."

I watched him leave and then looked at my cell phone on the bed, remembering Evelyn. Groaning, I picked it up. "I was right. It was the dry cleaning."

"The Ritz is really lacking in customer service," she said.

"You're done attacking Dakota and me, and now it's The Ritz Carlton?"

"It's ten-thirty at night, William. Who delivers dry cleaning at this hour? You should file a complaint."

I shook my head and picked up the remote again. "I'll do no such thing. Listen, as soon as I get back, we're going to hire a live-in nurse."

"Well, now you sound like my husband," she said. I sensed the smile on her face. "I mean, Sharon is there but she's no nurse. I wouldn't trust her with a thermometer."

"Don't talk about Sharon that way," I said. "She's been faithful to you."

"Like a dog," she agreed. "But you're right. A nurse will be just the thing I need. Who knows, maybe she'll nurse me back to health."

"That's the kind of talk I like to hear," I said with a smile.

"You just make sure you get me somebody good. I want the best of the best."

"I know," I said, thinking about Naomi again. "I'll try. Who knows? When you tell Ethan, maybe he'll have some suggestions."

"You're right," she said after some thought. "Maybe I should call him tonight and—"

Another knock on the door diverted my attention. The cheesecake and wine had arrived.

"Evvie, I'm sorry to cut you off, but room service is at the door," I said. "How about I call you back? I need to finish packing and get ready to leave. Will you be up?"

"It's already late and like you said, I need my rest," she said. "I'll see you tomorrow when you arrive."

I offered her a few well-rehearsed words of comfort and hung up, breathing a sigh of relief.

The knock came again.

Rubbing my eyes as emotional and physical exhaustion started to crush me, I walked to the door and pulled it open. "Just rest it on the b—"

It wasn't room service.

Naomi stood in the threshold, staring at me with her hands hanging at her sides and her lips parted. She was wearing jeans and a light, loose-fitting sweater. Simple pearl earrings accented her delicate earlobes.

My mouth fell slack and my posture went rigid.

Nothing but silence filled the narrow space of the doorway as we gaped at each other from either side of it. Eventually, Naomi rolled her gaze off me and walked into the suite without an invitation. She didn't need one and she knew it.

I spun around on my heels to follow her as she sauntered into the room.

"I forgot my things," she said, walking over to the night table and picking them up. Without so much as another word, she let the watch roll over her hand and snapped it shut on her wrist.

I looked behind me at the open door and then back at her. "Is that all you forgot?" I asked.

She cocked her head to the side. "Did I miss something?"

"I was thinking a sorry might've been appropriate."

She walked over to the bed and sat on its edge. Her head and shoulders slumped.

I closed the door and turned to face her.

Silence.

"You're leaving tomorrow," she said.

I didn't say anything. It was common knowledge. Nothing sensational.

"And...your wife is sick," she added.

Again, something we all knew.

"I wanted to let you know that I'll be praying for you and your family. I came to get my things, but I also wanted to say goodbye."

My jaw clenched. Stepping over to the bar to pour myself a drink, I decided the champagne would be too weak for this occasion. "Goodbye, then."

"Will—"

"If you came back here to torture me...to remind me of the years that have gone by or of the one night we spent together, or the fact that my wife is dying and you're unwilling to help me, then you're welcome to leave. Other than that—"

"I don't deserve that, Will, and you know it," she said.

I glared at her. "What do you deserve, then? And when did this ever become about you? This is about my wife."

"No, it's not. It's about you," she said, "and that's something that has never changed, even after all these years."

My jaw muscle flexed and my voice lowered. "You're the one who walked out on me six days ago. You left me here and—"

A knock on the door interrupted me.

"Who is it?" I shouted.

"Room service. Your cheesecake and champagne, sir."

Pinching the bridge of my nose, I marched to the door and pulled it open. "You can put it on the bar," I said.

The butler walked in and set the tray on the bar counter before promptly turning around and leaving.

I inhaled. "You left me here alone in my room and told me you couldn't help me. You said it was best we act like we had never seen each other." My tone inched higher. "Then you show up at my hotel room, unannounced, casting judgment on me like I'm the one who's done something wrong."

Her lip trembled as her hand smoothed over the crumpled bedspread.

I walked over to the bar and made the wine rain into a crystal tumbler. Slamming the bottle down on the counter, I then lifted the glass to my mouth.

"Do you want the truth?" she said, looking up with wet eyes.

Without taking a drink, I set the glass back on the counter and looked at her expectantly.

"I wouldn't be a good choice of a nurse to take care of your wife."

"Why not?" I demanded.

"Because I'm angry with her," she said.

"What are you talking about?" I replied, shaking my head and almost laughing.

"Don't you get it, Will? She's the one I should have been, but there was no way I could be her. I should have looked like her, I should have talked like her. I should have *been* her, Will, but I'm not...and now you're asking me to take care of her? How the hell am I supposed to do that?" She paused, rolling her eyes and forcing tears back.

I rushed over to Naomi and placed a trembling hand on her

shoulder. "You're wrong," I said, crouching in front of her. "You never should have been her. If you had been her, you would never have been you. And I need you, Naomi. Jesus Christ, there's no one I need more."

She looked away from me.

I guided her face back toward mine with a finger under her chin. "Give me a chance to be the man I wanted to be."

"For your wife?"

I nodded. "Yes. And for you."

"What are you talking about?"

"Forty-two years ago, I was a shadow of a man," I explained. "I made promises I intended to keep but didn't have the means to. I'm a man now. I want to show you I can do the right thing. If I can be a good husband, maybe it'll prove I could've made you happy too."

Naomi raised herself from the bed and walked out onto the balcony. The cooling fall breeze toyed with her tresses as she pulled her sweater closer and looked out at the buildings below.

I tipped the remainder of my drink against the back of my throat and joined her.

We were silent for what felt like an eternity. There was nothing left for me to say. I'd used every line I had. I'd taken every available avenue.

"I'm sorry," she said.

"For what?"

She shrugged. "Earlier, you said an apology seemed appropriate. You were right. I shouldn't have walked out on you like that the other night."

I chuckled. "You used to do that when we were kids. Things would get heated, and you'd throw a tantrum and walk away from me."

She rolled her eyes as a smile tugged at her lips. After a second, her bright features dropped and she became serious again. "I'll come," she whispered.

I almost didn't hear her. My eyes widened as I turned to face her. "What?"

"I said...I'll come. I'll take care of your wife. I'll do whatever you need me to do to make this time easier for the both of you." Her mouth clenched. "I'm not saying that it's gonna be easy for me, but it's the least I can do. I don't want to abandon you again."

"What about Leonard?" I asked.

"Who's Leonard?"

"Leonard, your boyfriend. That was his name, wasn't it?"

She pressed her lips together and looked away, her eyelashes fluttering. "*Lionel* broke up with me," she muttered.

"He did what?" I took a step towards her. "What happened?"

"I don't know what happened. Everything was fine, and then out of the blue..." she cut herself off. "It doesn't matter. Everything happens for a reason, right?"

I stared at her, unsure of what to say. "I'm sorry, sweetheart. I know you cared for him."

She snorted.

"Well, he's a goddamn idiot," I whispered. "He has no idea what he's losing." Taking her hand, I rested my lips on hers and placed a delicate kiss on her mouth. Soon, primal desire took over and I pulled her into me, her breasts crushing against my chest. As I kissed her, taking her in deeper and deeper, years of pent-up passion and desire cascaded from every nerve in my body.

After a second, she pulled away, shaking her head and wiping the corner of her mouth. "I'll come, Will...but all of this," she said, gesturing in a circular motion with her index finger, "is not happening. So put that out of your mind right now. I come to South Carolina, I take care of your wife, and when my job is finished—"

"When she dies, you mean?"

She backed away and pulled at her sweater. "I leave. I come back to Boston. We move on with our lives."

Does she really think that would be possible?

"Fine," I said.

"What do you mean *fine*?"

"I mean it's a deal." I narrowed my eyes. "But how about one more kiss? Before we get down to business and all?"

"I'm a professional and business starts now," she said, but her eyes briefly dropped to my lips and her chest heaved in and out before she pulled her eyes up. "I'll see you in Beaufort."

Watching her collect her belongings and walk out of the suite, I leaned against the railing and closed my eyes.

You sure will.

WILLIAM

BEAUFORT, S.C., 1968

The new assistant was following me and my business partner, Rob, through the corridor of Cooper Shipping, trying her best to keep up.

"Your meeting at two o'clock called to cancel," she was saying, flipping through a notepad. The sound of her heels scraping the tiles was grating my eardrums.

"The meeting with Chip Rogers?"

"Yes, sir. Apparently his daughter's school called to say she had to go home sick. His wife is out of town."

I snorted. "Doesn't he have a goddamn nanny?"

Rob leaned over and whispered in my ear. "He had a *fight* with the nanny," he said and raised his eyebrows.

"But he's rescheduled for next Tuesday at the same time, Mr. Cooper," the assistant said.

"Fine. At least now I have some downtime." I stopped walking and turned to face her. She bumped into my chest. "And for future reference, Genevive, I don't like back-to-back meetings. Four meetings a day is pushing it. Three, I can handle. I need time to decompress."

She flipped another page on the legal pad and scribbled something down. I wondered what the hell she was writing as I looked at Rob and started walking down the hall again. Everyone fell in step.

"Well, I wouldn't get too excited about downtime, Mr. Cooper. Your father is here for his biweekly meeting. He's been here since eleven," she said.

I looked at my watch. *An hour early.* Why was I not surprised? When I reached my office, I could see him through the glass panels set on the sides of the door. My father was sitting at my kidney-shaped rosewood desk, despite the numerous armchairs and the suede circular couch that were available to him. He'd been complaining about the décor recently; he said it was too modern. As soon as he'd made me CEO, I'd gotten an interior decorator to come in and give the place a sprucing up to make it more compatible with the times. The color scheme was mint-green and grey. Elaborate drapery hung from the vast panoramic window and the plush carpeting was top of the line. I had become the envy of my corporate buddies.

"I'd better get it over with then," I said, pushing the wood door open.

"Oh, one more thing, Mr. Cooper," the assistant said as she handed me a piece of paper.

"What's this?"

"A telegram. It came through early this morning."

I took the paper from her and opened the office door without looking at it. "Meet me here at two o'clock," I called out to my partner as he headed towards his own office, but he waved me off and disappeared around the corner.

I entered my office to find my father's face planted in the company's financial documents. He looked up with a grimace plastered over his features.

"These numbers don't look right," he said.

"No hello, then?" I chuckled. "Mom must be rubbing off on you now you're retired."

"You could be right," he mumbled. He cleared his throat. "But about these numbers...Have you triple-checked this ledger?"

"Quadruple-checked," I said, falling onto the Luna sofa. "The accountant has been over them a thousand times. I actually made her stay late last week just to give them a final gloss over because I knew you'd be in here today saying this very thing. What's the big deal? We're in the black." I gasped, pressing my hand against my chest. "Wait a minute, are you shocked at the profit margin, Dad? Is that what this about? You can't believe the gross profit we accumulated last quarter?"

My father frowned and slapped the folder closed. "Fine, I'll say what you want to hear. You're doing a good job, Will."

"I know I'm doing a good job," I said, putting my feet up on a coffee table and crossing them at the ankles. "Dare I say better than you expected?"

"And I admit, things have been looking good ever since I gave you the business." He smiled. "I'm very proud of you, son."

"Well, fifteen years is certainly a long enough time for me to demonstrate productivity and the quality of my leadership. Harvard wasn't for naught after all," I said, smiling. "I know you didn't doubt me, though."

He shrugged. "No, I never doubted you. Your mother, however..." he chuckled and rubbed the back of his neck. "She's always had this idea that you weren't settled enough to take over the company. She didn't think you were ready."

"Because of Naomi," I mumbled.

My father didn't say anything, but he didn't need to. The thick silence that enveloped the room revealed everything he was thinking.

"How is Evelyn?" he asked.

My hands crushed the telegram I had yet to look at. "Good," I said, staring through the window. "We have an appointment tomorrow to pick out flowers for our anniversary dinner. Sounds exciting, doesn't it?" I couldn't keep the frown off my face.

My dad laughed.

"I'm a thirty-two year old man who's been hitched for ten years. That's not funny, Dad. It's pretty depressing."

"Getting married right out of college wasn't a bad idea, William.

Your grandfather did it. I did it." He grunted. "I know marriage can be tough, but it's the stability that's important. If it were up to you, I swear you'd never have gotten married. You'd have been a bachelor for the rest of your goddamn life. If your mother was right about anything, it was that."

"What's wrong with bachelorhood?" I asked, looking at him for the first time. "As a bachelor, I can do whatever the hell I please. I have no one to answer to."

"There's always someone to answer to, son. There's me, for example."

I stood up and stretched my legs. "Let's get down to business," I suggested, choosing to ignore him. My tone was stiff. I should have stretched that instead of my legs.

My father slapped his palms against his thighs and rose, heading for the meeting table at the center of the room. He looked down at the paper in my hand. "What's that about?"

I looked at him confused before I realized what he was referring to. "Oh, this." I shrugged. "I haven't had a chance to look at it yet. Genevive gave it to me when I was walking in. I'll put it with the mail and check it before the end of the day." I looked down at the memo title and scanned the note, but when I saw who it was from, my knees almost buckled. And when I saw what it was about, my vision clouded. I grabbed onto the back of a chair for support, the paper rattling under my grip.

"Are you all right? What is it?" my dad asked.

My fingers tightened around the paper. I couldn't answer.

He strode over and reached out to take it from me.

I jerked my hand away. "It's nothing, Dad," I said, but the sweat on my forehead was ratting me out.

He reached out again. "Well, it must be something. Look at you. You look like an immigrant in a sweat shop."

"I'm fine," I said, trying to assure him. "It's...from the Brooklyn office. They want me to fly up for a meeting...and you know how I hate flying."

The muscles in my father's face relaxed as he shook his head and laughed. "Oh, is that all? I didn't realize you hated airplanes so much. Anyway, you can deal with that later. Like you said, let's get down to business."

I looked at the telegram again, trying to keep the shock and maybe even horror off my face. I tugged at my goatee before setting the slip of paper face down on top of the other mail and sitting at the table with my father.

———

LATE AT NIGHT, I was still in my office, still sitting at the desk, and still staring at the words glaring up at me from the telegram. I'd read it a million times and still hadn't been able to make sense of it.

It was from Miss Carole. She said that her grandson—*so Bruce was right?*—had come to see her. She wanted to let me know, she'd written, because she knew how special Naomi was to me and thought she'd keep me abreast, especially since I hadn't seen her in so many years.

I propped my elbows on the desk and clasped my hands in front of my face. Why did she think I'd want to know about any of this? Maybe she didn't know how much it pained me to think about her daughter. I'd done a hell of a job pushing Naomi into the backdrop of my mind. All the wedding planning had helped me to do that. Making love to Evelyn, well, that hadn't helped quite so much. In fact, the first time had been really bad. She didn't have the same passion as Naomi, I remember thinking. There was no spark, no chemistry; there was no *love*.

But maybe that was my fault.

I looked at the telegram again. By now, it was totally wrinkled from where my trembling hands had assaulted it over and over again. I pulled a cigarette out of its pack, lit it, and leaned back in my office chair, staring past the wispy designs of the hazy, blue smoke. Finally, I picked up the phone and called the homestead.

My mother answered.

"Mom, is Miss Carole awake?" I asked, cutting right to the chase.

"Of course she is," my mother said. "It's eight-thirty. I'm having a luncheon tomorrow, so she's in the kitchen prepping with the rest of the staff."

I ran my hand over my face. "I need to speak to her."

"William, she's hard at work right now. I'm sure she wouldn't want to be disturbed."

"It'll just be a second," I said.

My mother was quiet. "What's this all about, anyway?"

I was ready for that question and had prepared a suitable lie. "I'm gonna need to borrow her, if that's all right with you. I have my own dinner party coming up, and we all know that Miss Carole makes the best pecan pies in all of South Carolina."

"Oh, well, in that case, that should be fine. Let's see, tomorrow she's doing the ironing and the windows, but maybe in the evening you can—"

"I'd like to talk to her myself," I said. "We're both adults. We can make our own plans."

Silence.

"Of course. Well, don't be too long. Like I said, she's got to prep and there's a lot left to do."

I heard the phone clank on something hard before my mother started to holler through the house. I took a deep, unsatisfying draw from my cigarette.

A few seconds later, Miss Carole was on the line. I busied myself with uncoiling the mint-green colored telephone cord in an effort to make my hands stop shaking.

"My sweet Will," she said. Affection immediately seeped through the telephone wire. "Lord, I'm so happy to hear from you."

We hadn't spoken in almost a month. I tried to stay in touch with her as often as I could, but being so busy, it had become difficult.

"Yes, I miss you terribly as well. It's been so long since we spoke."

Insignificant pleasantries.

"Well, if that ain't the truth," she agreed. "It's been too long in my opinion, but I figured I'd be hearing from you soon enough. You got my message, didn't you?"

I moistened my lips and let my eyes fall on the paper again before pushing it to the side. "Yes, I did. I didn't know you knew how to send a telegram, Miss Carole."

"Me either. I spent the last couple of hours wondering if you got it. But, you hang around Miss Anna long enough, and you sure 'nough gonna learn somethin' new." She lowered her voice to a whisper. "I sent it from her office. You don't think she'll find out, do you?"

"No, Miss Carole, she won't...and if she does, you just call me and I'll come deal with her." I shifted in my seat, which suddenly felt as hard as a stone. "That message...You said something about your grandson?"

"Yes, I did. His name is Scott. He came to see me a few weeks ago." There was a smile in her voice.

My lips pursed. "Wow, Miss Carole. That's great," I lied, forcing the words out of my mouth. "You must've been through the roof with excitement."

"Don't you know it? My first time seeing the boy. He's only thirteen, but he knows everything. So smart, got a good head on his shoulders, he does. The two of you would connect in a second."

"He sounds like a good kid. I didn't realize you had a grandchild, Miss Carole. I mean...I didn't know Naomi had gotten pregnant. He's thirteen?" I swallowed. *That means she got knocked up as soon as she'd landed in Seattle...* My fists clenched.

"So...your parents never said anything, huh?" It was a rhetorical question. We both knew the answer.

"No, they didn't," I said. "They want me to forget about Naomi. They want it to be like she never existed...like she was a figment of my imagination." I paused, bitterness making my mouth wrinkle. "Now I wish to God she was."

"Don't talk like that, Will," Miss Carole tried to encourage me. "Naomi made a mistake. You both did."

"What mistake did I make? She's the one who went out there and..." I couldn't finish the sentence. "The only mistake I ever made was loving her. I should have known better, and you should have warned me."

"Stop it, William," she scolded me.

My mouth clamped shut.

"You can't help who you fall in love with. Naomi *loved* you. You saw the look on her face when she left that airport."

Sure I did. It was the last memory I had of her. Miss Carole was trying to make me feel better, but her assurances meant nothing to me anymore.

"Why did you send me that message, Miss Carole?" I asked. "I'm moving on with my life, and no offense, but I don't need to be reminded of your daughter. I'm trying to live without her."

Miss Carole whispered. "I understand, Will, I do," she said. "The only reason I sent you the message was because the boy said he wants to meet you."

My head jerked back. "Meet *me*? Have you lost your mind? Has *he* lost his?"

"He's only a child," she said. "His mind is still developin'. Don't you be wishin' that on him."

I grunted. "The lack of development would explain his request then." I stood up from the chair so fast it flew back on its wheels. "No. It's not a good idea. And why does he want to meet me? He doesn't know me from a hole in the goddamn wall. I'm as good as the next stranger."

"Naomi may be in another state, but South Carolina is her home. You are her family and she's told him all about you."

The thought caused a pain to slice through my body.

"My precious grandson," Miss Carole continued, "he wants to see the place where his mother grew up. He's thirteen years old, Will, and he's very inquisitive. He wants to see the world, you know. Once you meet him, you'll understand." She lowered her voice. "Naomi doesn't know he's been to see me."

"Then how did he get to Beaufort? Plane tickets are mighty expensive, and she had to have questioned his whereabouts."

"Your father bought the ticket, and Scott told her he'd gone on an out-of-city trip with his classmates. Scott wanted to come so badly, but Naomi kept telling him no, so we had to think of something." She sighed. "I hate the thought of doing things behind my daughter's back, but she can be so stubborn sometimes."

Sometimes?

I shook my head as if Miss Carole could see me. The entire scenario sickened me, and I didn't want any part of it. Naomi had ruined our future with her hard-headedness, so I was content with letting her ruin this boy's too. I didn't know him, and the way I saw it, he was better off not knowing much about his mother's past.

"I'm really sorry, Miss Carole. I know the boy means a lot to you, and I know he wants to meet me, but there is no way I can—"

"Please, Will. If not for him, then do it for me."

My shoulders folded. Miss Carole had always been good at getting me to do the things I didn't want to do. There was a certain way she'd do her eyes and a certain tone in her voice. I leaned on the sill of the window, my head hanging. My body felt like bricks. I still didn't see what any of this had to do with me. I couldn't stop myself from asking the next question.

"Have you spoken to her recently?"

"Yes."

Silence.

"How is she?"

"She's doin' good," she replied. "She's working real hard and making her way through life, making a name for herself. She's a real good nurse, Will."

I wanted to smile but didn't have the energy. "Did she...ask anything about me?"

"I'm sorry, Will," Miss Carole whispered.

My heart sank.

"But, Scott said she talks about you all the time, and that's why he can't wait to meet you."

I pinched the bridge of my nose and cursed.

"Now you watch your mouth, you hear? There ain't no need for cussin' like that, like you ain't got no home-trainin'," she said.

"I'm sorry, Miss Carole. I just..." Throwing my arm on top of my head, I raked at my hair then rubbed my eyebrow before exhaling a deep lungful of air. If I was going to do this—for her—I would need all the courage I had, and I couldn't let a soul know that I was doing it, especially not my parents or Evelyn.

"Maybe you could...give him my number when you next talk to him. Have him call me at the office?"

"Oh, William!"

"But this is only for you, Miss Carole," I said, pointing at nothing. "I wouldn't do it for anyone else. Not for this boy, and definitely not for Naomi."

The distant shrill of my mother's voice piercing the atmosphere was a surprising and welcome distraction. I'd had enough of this conversation.

"So you don't want to see him in person? That's what he was hoping," she said. "I don't know when he'll be coming back, but maybe your father might think about sending him a ticket for year after next."

"I'm not goddamn Superman, Miss Carole," I said. "I'm not strong enough to do that."

"Okay," she said. "I won't press you right now. I don't know when little Scott will be coming back, but maybe your father will send him a ticket sometime soon." Her tone was hopeful. "I have to go, so we'll talk soon. I love you, puddin'."

"And I love you too," I mumbled through a hefty sigh.

"And, Will?"

"Yes, Miss Carole?"

"You're strong enough for anything. In fact, you're one of the strongest people I know. Hang in there. Everything is going to happen just the way it is supposed to."

"I'm sure. And if my mother asks, you're doing me a pecan pie for a dinner party."

She laughed and then hung up.

The phone trembled against my ear until I slammed it down in its cradle, sending a shrill ring through the office. I leaned my head back against the glass and silently prayed to God to let me fall through it.

17

NAOMI

BOSTON, M.A., 1996

*S*creaming in frustration, I flipped the top of my suitcase over the bulging mess of clothes I'd tossed in and sat on it, desperately trying to make it stay closed. A sudden vibration caused me to look down at the sheet-less bed beneath me, just as my cell phone began to ring. Balancing on top of the luggage, I tried to reach over and grab it but cursed when I rolled off the suitcase and landed on the bed in a heap. Once I'd crawled back over the luggage and realized who it was, I rolled my neck and sighed.

Scott.

I inhaled and listened to it ring for a second before answering.

"Happy retirement, Mama," he shouted into the phone. A warm smile spread across my face.

"Thank you, Scott. This call means a lot to me, though it's a little late," I said lightly. "The celebrations happened over a week ago, but I guess I should be grateful you even called."

"What do you mean?"

"I know how you behave when you get in your moods," I said. "I thought you might have still been upset about my relationship status."

Scott grunted. "For the record, I *am* still upset about your relationship status. Something about it just doesn't seem right. I mean, a sixty-year-old woman going out on dates and painting the town?"

I couldn't contain the laugh.

"I actually thought about calling the other night but figured that what's-his-name would want you all to himself, so I didn't bother."

I sighed. "Well, for your information, what's-his-name and I have broken up. I'm sure you're devastated by the news."

"Wait, what?" Scott's tone had changed. "What do you mean he broke up with you?"

"Just as I said," I explained. "We were out on a date, there was a phone call, and everything between us changed. I would explain it more if I could, but I'm just as confused as you are."

"Mama...I'm sorry to hear this," Scott said.

"No you're not," I said, trying to muster up another laugh. "You hated the fact I was seeing someone."

"That's not entirely true," he said. "I hated the fact you were moving on with your life without affording me the same courtesy."

The air around me got thick.

Scott waited for me to say something.

"I'm not sure what else I can say about that topic," I said, nervously rubbing my elbow. "I told you your father's name. I've looked everywhere for him, but I just can't pin him down."

Scott sighed. "I'm sorry, Mama."

"What are you sorry for now?"

"I'm sorry for bringing it up again. You've told me the truth over and over and that's all I've ever asked for."

I fought the urge to clear my throat.

"At the end of the day, it's not you I should be angry at. It's that loser of a man who left a beautiful woman and his son." He paused. "And I'm sorry it didn't work out between you and this guy. I know you were starting to really care about him."

"How can you be so sure about that?"

"You talked about him all the time!"

"And what does that have to do with anything?"

"Mama, you'd never talked about a man that much since Mr. William, and that was years ago."

"What?"

"Mr. William. Your childhood friend? The guy you grew up with?"

I shifted on the bed. "Yeah, well, none of it matters. I'm starting a new chapter. I've retired. The world is my oyster now." I looked at the luggage on my bed and my stomach started to churn. "And there's no need for you to be sorry. They say everything happens for a reason."

"How about we change the subject?" he suggested. "How is retirement so far?"

I looked at the suitcase full of clothes on the bed again and realized it wasn't much of a change of topic at all. I had been manipulated into spending the first few months of my retirement as a caretaker for my ex-boyfriend's wife.

"Ask me that in a couple of weeks, and I'll be able to give you an accurate answer," I said. "I'm only a few days in."

"Are you planning on doing any traveling?"

"Why would you ask that?" My back straightened; I needed to adjust my tone.

"It was a simple question," Scott said. "People normally plan to travel when they've retired."

I jumped off the bed. "I actually do have plans. In fact, I've decided to take a spur-of-the-moment trip."

"That's great, Mama. To where?"

My chest hitched. "To China. I leave tomorrow."

"Wow. Talk about out of the box. When I was a kid, I could barely get you to cross state lines."

"Well, I'm getting older," I said. "I figure I need to do some things before I die."

"For how long?"

"For how long what?"

Scott sighed. "For how long will you be in China, Mama?"

I looked around the room in a vain effort to come up with the right responses, but the questions were coming too quickly. I was ill-prepared for this conversation with my son. "I'm not sure," I said. "I have nothing to do, so perhaps I'll stay for a whole month. Maybe more. Who knows?"

Silence.

"Say something," I said.

"I'm happy for you," Scott said. "You deserve this. After working so hard for so many years, raising me all by yourself...Take as much time as you want. Maybe I'll join you. I have vacation days I need to use anyway."

"Don't feel pressured," I said, perhaps a little too quickly. "I mean, I don't know how long I'll be there for." I waited for him to say something again but he didn't. "But I'll be sure to keep you posted."

"Yeah, keep me posted," Scott said. "Maybe after China you might be inclined to take a local trip."

"A local trip to where?"

"Oh, I don't know, South Carolina maybe?"

My heart jumped clean up into my throat. "What on earth would I go there for? I told you I'd never go back. There's nothing there for me."

"But you haven't been there since you were a kid. Surely you would want to go and reconnect with old friends."

"You know I don't have any friends down there, Scott. You said it yourself. The only person I ever talked about was William Cooper, and I haven't seen or heard from him in years." I cursed under my breath. The lies were piling up, and I felt like I was backing myself into a corner.

"For two people who were so close, it's awfully strange that the two of you haven't reconnected," Scott said. "I mean, if he were my childhood friend—"

"The circumstances of our friendship were atypical, Scott. I was the maid's daughter. Sure, we lived in the same house, but we led totally separate lives." I paused and tried to rein my emotions in. "When I left for school, William married a rich white woman and I haven't seen or heard from him since. Life goes on. It's silly to hold on to the past." I thought about what I'd just said and cringed.

"If you say so," he replied.

"And why are we talking about him anyway?"

"We're not talking about him, Mama. We're talking about you going back to Beaufort one day."

"That's not going to happen, Scott."

Silence.

"Well, it might have been nice. You know, you've never taken me down there. Not even as a child."

My chest tightened again.

He continued. "Sometimes, I try to imagine you growing up. I try to imagine my grandma too." I sensed a smile on his face and sighed.

"Now, that's one thing I do regret," I said softly. "I wish you could have met her, Scott. You would have loved her. She was real kind and gentle. She would have spoiled you to death if she could have. She was always hard at work so I figured it never made sense to go back there, but I know the two of you would have adored each other."

"I can only imagine," he said firmly.

My eyebrows creased as I went in search of my cigarettes. "I've made huge mistakes, Scott. There was so much I should have done for you."

"You mean other than making sure I had clothes on my back, food to eat, and a solid education? You did the best you could, Mama. I'm sure of it. I'll figure the rest out on my own."

His words pierced me, causing the hair on my arms to stand on end.

"Well, I have so much to do before I leave tomorrow," I said.

"Yeah, I should let you go," he said, catching the hint. "I actually have a ton to do myself, but call me when you land in China. And if you need anything, Mama, anything at all—"

"Yes, I know, I'll call," I said and smiled. Tears suddenly collected in my throat. "I love you, Scott."

"I know, Mama." He made a kissing sound into the phone and hung up.

LATER THAT NIGHT, I was sitting on my porch smoking another cigarette. The solar yard lamps were illuminated, creating a soft glow around the perimeter of my yard. The sound of ocean waves slapping against the shoreline echoed in my ears, but I could only see the tops of the frothy, white crests as they rolled in. I took another draw of the cigarette and walked over to the big willow tree. The white mesh hammock was swaying easily as I climbed in, feeling secure as it closed around me.

My body rocked back and forth. So did my mind.

Lionel.

Scott.

William.

I was creating a web of tangled connections in my mind.

Who was I trying to fool? I was acting like I was in control of this situation with William. In reality, I was anything but. I should've stuck to my guns. I should never have agreed to go back to Beaufort to take care of his wife. I didn't owe him anything...did I? There were good reasons why I cut him off. Weren't there? But if that were true, why hadn't I yet told Scott the truth about his father's identity? The boy had no clue, and the only ones who did were dead and gone.

Feeling a sob rising in my chest, I choked it down, coughing until water filled my eyes. I lifted the cigarette to my mouth and sucked at it. The soft crackling sound instantly soothed my body in a blanket of familiar comfort.

As I swatted a mosquito that was trying to land on my arm, my cell phone rang next to me in the hammock. I looked at the screen and saw it was an out-of-state call. Bracing myself, I inhaled and answered. William had already called earlier, but I'd let it go unanswered. I couldn't avoid him, especially since I'd agreed to help him. Now it was quiet, it was a good time to have a chat.

I clicked the answer button and exhaled. "You're calling to check up on me, I guess? I'm fine. You don't have to worry. I'm a little apprehensive, but—"

"I beg your pardon?" a catty female voice with a thick southern accent shot back at me. Shocked, I jolted up straight in the hammock.

The swiftness of the motion caused me to flip out of it and land hard on the ground. Stretching to retrieve the phone that had bounced away as I'd crashed against the grass, a shooting pain bolted through my shoulder.

"Is this the nurse?"

I rubbed my shoulder and tried to pull myself together. "Yes it is. To whom am I speaking?"

"Oh good," the lady said. "When I didn't get you earlier, I began to doubt your suitability for the position." The woman exhaled loudly into the receiver. "This is Evelyn Cooper, William Cooper's wife. I've been made to understand that you will be the in home nurse who will be caring for me in the upcoming months, and I wanted to make immediate contact with you."

Still massaging my aching shoulder, I cleared my throat, trying to find the right words.

Evelyn Cooper waited for me to respond, but only for a second. "Anyhow, I've looked over your credentials and my doctor has approved you. Your in-home care experience is a tad dated, but I understand you worked closely with my son. Because of that, and *only* because of that, I might add, my confidence was boosted."

"I beg your pardon?"

She huffed. "Ideally, I wanted someone younger, someone fresh out of school with access to the latest interventions and technologies. I wasn't sure how adept you'd be, but my husband insisted you were the best of the best and I trust him."

I opened my mouth to say something, but she cut me off.

"Anyway, Nancy, I wanted to call you personally and let you know we are looking forward to having you as part of the staff."

"Nancy?"

Evelyn Cooper released another audible sigh. "Well, this is very odd indeed. Perhaps I caught you at a bad time. Or maybe this is the wrong number. You are Nancy Cameron, the nurse from Bostonwho spoke to my husband earlier this week, aren't you?"

My jaw clenched when I realized what was happening. William had given her a false name to disguise my identity. This was a calamity waiting to happen. I was being forced to act as a character in this ridiculous drama. Instead of letting my emotions get the better of me, I should have stuck to my guns and refused to go to South Carolina. Yet, here I was, and I didn't see how I could easily back out. Suddenly, a pain in my head was distracting me from the pain in my shoulder.

"I apologize, Mrs. Cooper. I admit, the phone call caught me off guard, but you have the right number. This is the nurse...Nancy."

"Oh good," she said, chuckling. "You had me concerned for a second."

"No need to be concerned," I assured her, although I wasn't sure how accurate my statement was. "I look forward to caring for you during this critical time in your life."

"Well now, that's sweet," she said. "Now, when you arrive tomorrow afternoon, I will allow you some time to settle in, of course."

Allow me some time...

"But I will require you to get right to work. I want to ensure you understand your new role. I'm very particular about my day-to-day routine, and I will have high expectations. Yes, I'll be going through chemotherapy, but I want to stick as closely to my routine as possible."

"That's understandable," I said.

"There are my dinner parties and socials...I'm the chairwoman of the Historic Beaufort Foundation...there's so much to be done."

"You're very busy, Mrs. Cooper," I said, "but your health and recovery will be my number one priority."

"Yes," she agreed, "but my expectation is that you will enable me to participate in all of the activities to which I'm accustomed."

Silence.

"Anyhow," she continued, "I've started putting your file together."

My file?

"But I'll require copies of your credentials and certifications. Also, if you could have your resume available for the meeting, that would be splendid."

I cringed. My certifications wouldn't have the name Nancy Cameron on them, that I knew for sure.

She stopped to take a breath. "So, is everything clear?"

I opened my mouth, willing the words to come out, but a searing heat in my chest was burning them up. I stared out at the open water, focusing on the light from a boat in the distance. I looked away. "Everything is very clear, Mrs. Cooper," I said. The words were like acid on my tongue. "I look forward to meeting you and your family and being a part of the team." *There I go, lying again...*

"Wonderful. Well, enjoy the rest of your evening, Nancy. I will see you tomorrow."

Click.

I stared at the illuminated clock on my cell phone, trying to wrap my mind around the conversation I'd just had. Mentally preparing myself for the role I had agreed to play, the gravity of it hit me and an icy chill passed through my body like an avalanche. I wondered if I would be able to pull this off? How could I take care of the woman who was the wife of the man I had once loved? Was I ready to stare my past in the face and put it behind me once and for all? I exhaled, pulled my knees up to my chest, and rocked back and forth as if I was still sitting in the hammock.

18

WILLIAM

BEAUFORT, S.C., 1970

The bell on the restaurant door jingled a million times, and I looked up a million times, my heart pounding against my ribcage. This time, it was a white couple coming in for a cheap dinner. I turned away, dipping my straw in and out of my glass before I picked it up and took a hefty swig of scotch. Glancing down at my watch, the door jingled again. This time, it was a group of teenagers. Double date.

I told Miss Carole I would talk to Naomi's son on the telephone, but she'd done that thing with her voice and eyes and bullied me into a physical meet and greet. He was coming into town, she'd told me, and it would be the perfect opportunity. She had told him all about me, and he couldn't wait to meet me. How could I have turned her down?

I groaned, putting my drink to my lips. "I can't help but feel like this is a huge mistake," I said to Miss Carole.

She rubbed the back of her hand and then patted mine with jerky movements. "No, baby. You doing the right thing. It's for the boy, remember? Naomi's boy."

"Even more evidence for why I shouldn't be here," I mumbled.

"Naomi doesn't want anything to do with me. Why should I be giving her son the time of day?"

"Because you're the bigger man," she said, "and you know that no matter what has happened between you and Naomi, an innocent boy doesn't deserve to suffer." She nodded, as if I'd agreed with her. I wondered which innocent, suffering boy she was referring to.

"I think it's wonderful that you've agreed to meet him. It took five weeks of convincing, but I believe you're doing the right thing and in your heart, you know it too." She lowered her voice. "He talks about you nonstop, you know?"

"Yeah well, I still don't get it." I chewed the inside of my cheek. "But maybe it's not for me to get. Maybe it's just something I have to do and get it over with."

Miss Carole frowned, and so did I as I looked at my watch again. "He's late," I noted. "Where did you say he was staying?"

"At a hostel near the airport. It will take him an hour to get here. I'm sure he's nearby."

I grimaced. "A hostel? He's your grandson. My parents wouldn't let him stay at the house?"

The spark in Miss Carole's eyes faded. "Well, your father suggested it, but Mrs. Cooper didn't think it was a good idea. She's busy this weekend, and the house will be hectic. He would get in the way."

I rubbed my brow, not fully understanding my parents' change of heart towards Naomi. Ever since she'd left for school, the relationship between her and my mother had changed. My mother didn't dote on her the way she used to, and I couldn't help but wonder why. Maybe they were as hurt as I was by the poor decision she'd made. She'd been raised better than that, I thought. Sure we'd been making love—every chance we could get—but her being with another man, having unprotected sex, getting pregnant...that was a different thing altogether. Now I thought about it, I didn't blame my parents for shutting her out. I was on the verge of doing the same.

Before I could ponder any further, the door chimed again and a tall, thin black boy marched into the restaurant. He was sporting a neatly trimmed Afro and wearing large, wire-rimmed glasses. Dressed smartly in plaid pants and a matching vest, he appeared to be clutching a thick book in his hands and had a backpack hanging off his shoulders.

I couldn't stop looking at him. There was no doubt in my mind this was Naomi's son. He had her striking eyes and her small ears. His nose was different from hers though. He'd probably gotten that from his father. And he was lighter in complexion. Again, one of his father's genes. Resentment welled up inside of me.

I ripped my eyes off him and grabbed the rest of my scotch, thinking how I probably should have had lemonade. If it was true that Naomi had told him all about me, I'm sure she hadn't told him I was a drunk. I looked at the glass and swished the brown liquid around one last time before gulping it back and pushing the empty glass to the side.

"Scott," Miss Carole said, rising to her feet.

I remained seated, running my hands over my goatee.

Scott approached the table as if he were unsure what the reception would be. I didn't blame him. He was down south, for one, and secondly, he and Miss Carole were the only colored people in the entire restaurant. Thirdly, I thought as they embraced, he was meeting me, a stranger whom he'd only heard stories about. Supposedly, I was a man who had been a good friend to his mother. I had no clue what else Naomi had told him, but I could bet my bottom dollar she hadn't told him I was in love with her.

"Mr. Cooper, sir?"

Until he spoke, I'd been engulfed in my own world of pointless thoughts, perhaps trying to delay the inevitable introduction.

I looked up and smiled. "Scott...It's a pleasure to meet you. And please, no sir for me. I'm a good friend of your mother's. Mr. William will be fine."

The boy stood staring at me, his face as blank as the linen napkins on the table.

I cleared my throat. "Why don't you have a seat, son?"

Miss Carole nodded, encouraging him to do as he was told.

Scott put the book under his arm and pulled out the chair, sliding the backpack to the floor.

My knee bounced under the table as he stared at me in awe, like I was one of the characters in the book he was reading and had just come to life before his eyes. I looked at the spine of the book. "Watership Down? I hear that's a really good book."

He glanced down at it as if he didn't know what I was talking about. "Oh yeah, this." His lips stretched, but didn't part.

The silence was deafening.

"So you like to read?"

"I'm starting to like it," he said. His vocal chords had already cracked, and the deepness of his tone surprised me. "My mother, she makes me read all the time. I've read thirty-four books in the last eighteen months. Great Expectations, The Count of Monte Cristo, To Kill a Mockingbird..."

"Big titles," I said. "Looks like your mother has the right idea. A man won't get very far in life if he doesn't read."

Miss Carole touched my shoulder. "You know how his mother is, don't you, Will? Real academic. She was always into her books. She used to live in the library, along with your father." She turned to look at her grandson. "Your mother was real smart, Scott. She did well in all of her classes."

"I know," he said. His eyes brightened a bit. "When she was in nursing school, she was always studying. I was a baby then, but she kept all of her papers to show me the A-grades she'd gotten. She thinks it'll keep me on track or somethin'."

"Yes, your mama was a nerd," I said, surprised when the boy laughed. I joined in and so did Miss Carole. A nostalgic smile settled on my mouth.

God, I missed that woman. To have her child sitting here was the closest I'd been to her in over a decade and a half. It was a bittersweet experience. I found myself wanting to connect with him, yet, he was not only a reminder of her betrayal but also a reminder of the fact that she had found someone else and given up on me.

I started to wonder about the boy's father as I assessed him again.

What did the man look like? He had to have been a fair black man, because Naomi's skin was dark compared to the boy's, like chocolate mixed with milk.

I looked into the boy's eyes. They weren't the same hue as his mother's. In fact, they were light brown. I could almost see myself in them.

A waiter came and took our orders. Miss Carole ordered a salad, and Scott ordered a cheeseburger with fries. I figured I'd order the same; let him know I was down to earth.

We were eating in relative silence, aside from the random comments Miss Carole was throwing out here and there. I could tell she was trying to fill the dead spaces, trying to make us all a little more comfortable, but I wasn't sure if she was making things better or worse.

Soon, she was looking at her watch and rising from the table. "I gotta go," she said, smoothing her hands over her skirt. "Miss Anna was so kind to let me out on this little excursion, but I got some chores to finish up."

I chewed on the tip of a cold French fry before dropping it back on the plate.

"You don't have to rush off if you'd rather stay," I said, looking over at her. "My mother..." I sighed. "You're with me. She'll understand."

She hesitated for a second but then her eyes dimmed. "No, Will, I got to do my chores. A woman won't eat if she don't work, now. You know that." She chuckled. "Besides," she nodded toward Scott. "I've had my time with Scott, and I'll be seeing him again before he leaves day after tomorrow. You two have a nice chat. It was you he wanted to see anyhow."

I looked at Scott, who was making a hopeless mess of ketchup and French fries on his plate. He didn't contribute to the conversation.

"Fine, then," I said. "You call me when you get to the house. It's dark out there and sometimes it isn't safe."

Miss Carole bent over, kissed my cheek and squeezed my shoulder. Then, she walked over to her grandson and did the same. The bell on the door jingled again as she walked through it and left.

I looked down at my plate.

Now there was no Miss Carole to temper the quiet, I tried to figure out what to say to the boy. He wanted to meet me, but he was awfully quiet for someone so apparently curious.

Scott leaned down and unzipped his fabric backpack, pulling out a spiral notebook.

I wiped my mouth on my napkin. "What are those? Notes from school?"

He didn't answer. Instead, he flipped it open to reveal pictures that had been secured onto the pages with clear Scotch tape.

My eyes widened and my breathing slowed. I put the napkin on the table, pushing it to the side with one hand as I pulled the book in front of me with the other.

Pictures of Naomi, lots of them, blasted me. In one, she was on a college campus. There was another of her in a restaurant, biting into a burger that was bigger than her face. She was radiant. Whomever had taken the picture was making her laugh, I suspected. I wondered if it was Scott's father on the other side of the camera. My body vibrated.

I flipped through the pages. Now, I was looking at pictures of her and a small boy, who I guessed was Scott. Naomi was holding his hand, smiling at the camera and he was staring up at her, his lip twisted upward.

I chuckled and pointed at it. "Is that you?"

"Yup."

"You don't seem too impressed by the photo shoot."

Scott shook his head, smiling. "She's always taking pictures," he said. "Gets on my nerves sometimes."

I smiled. She had never wanted to take pictures when we were kids. She said it was 'evidence'. I thought about the one picture I'd had in my room and flipped the page again. My fingers stiffened when I saw the next one.

"She says that's my father," Scott said, almost in a whisper.

I was staring at it. At the man. His skin was a deep brown hue, and he was big and burly, almost overweight. He was the complete opposite of me, not counting the fact he was black. If this was Scott's father, he didn't fit the mold I'd created for him. I winced at the surfacing jealousy.

Scott seemed to be reading my mind again. "I don't think that's him, though," he said with a resolute shake of the head.

My head shot up. "Why would your mother lie to you?" I asked. My tone was curt, maybe a little too emotional. I didn't want to hear any more about Naomi being someone other than who I believed she was. The fact that Scott was here, sitting in front of me, was proof enough that I'd been misguided about her, but I wanted to keep the rest of my pleasant memories intact.

"I dunno," he said, shrugging. "The guy never treated me like I was his son. You know how dads are supposed to be?"

"You mean like taking you to the ice cream shop? Tossing a ball around in the yard?"

"Yeah, alla that." Scott craned his neck to look at the picture like he'd never seen it before. "Look at him, Mr. William. I don't even *look* like him. His nose is way big. Mine is nowhere near that fat. And look at his cheekbones. He's so fat, you can hardly see them."

I looked until I could look no more. I pulled at the hair on my chin before closing the book and pushing it back toward Scott. I smiled, but it was paper-thin. "Thanks for sharing that with me. It's always a pleasure to be reminded of your mother. She was very special to me."

Scott packed the book away. "How did you guys meet anyway?" he asked, picking up his Coke and taking a slurp.

"I thought she'd told you all about me?"

"Yeah, but she never told me about that, even though I've asked like a million times. It's like some big mystery, you know?" He laughed again and I joined in, even though I didn't want to.

I scraped at the back of my neck, thinking of what to say. "Well... We kind of grew up together. You see, your grandmother has worked for my parents for many years. When she first moved into my house, your mother was with her. We were both kids."

Scott's mouth was twitching. He reached back into the bag and pulled the notebook out again, this time along with a pencil, and I watched him start scribbling words onto the page.

"What are you writing?"

He finished and then looked up at me. "I'm trying to figure something out," he said.

My mouth dried out, and I picked up the glass of lemonade I'd ordered. "You're a detective then?"

"No, but I think I wanna be a police officer when I get older Protect the community from bad guys."

"Well now, that's a fine career aspiration for a young man like yourself."

"Thanks," he said, lowering his head. "Either that or a lawyer. My mother says I'll have to work really hard, especially if I want to be a lawyer. Gotta keep my grades high and what not."

I leaned in, glad that the subject had shifted. "How are you doing in school, anyway?"

Scott's shoulders straightened. "I'm doing good," he said. "Better than good, actually. Math is a pain in the you-know-what, but other than that..."

"Math?" I sucked my teeth and put my glass on the table. "Listen, if you ever need an extra hand—"

"My mother said you were good at math. She said you used to help her when she had trouble with it."

"I was *very* good," I confirmed. "Still am. So if you ever need someone to quiz you or go over something you can't figure out—"

"You'd do that for me?" His eyes looked hopeful.

"Of course!" We stared at each other. "Any friend of your mother's is a friend of mine. And you're more than a friend, you're her bloody son!" We laughed together.

After a few minutes of saying nothing, Scott said, "Mr. William, I got something to ask you. I ain't never said this to anyone before, but I came all this way so I have to know what you think." He blew out a long breath. "Do you think…" His voice and bravado faded, and his gaze dropped back to the notebook as he fiddled nervously with the pencil.

"Well? What is it?"

He started over. "Do you think that you could be…my father, Mr. William?"

My head jerked back and I almost choked on saliva. "I'm sorry…*What*?"

"I know it's a crazy question, but I just can't help thinking it may be true." He was saying it as if we were discussing Aristotle's Ladder of Life theory. "My mother, she talks about you all the time and when she says your name, there's this crazy look she gets in her eyes."

I swallowed. "Crazy look?"

"Not crazy, like *crazy*…I mean, her eyes soften and get all gooey, and it looks like she's about to cry. And then that man, the one who she says is my father, I already told you why I ruled him out."

"I think your logic is a little farfetched, son."

"Maybe," he agreed, his eyes shifting thoughtfully. "But it's more than that, Mr. William." He pointed to the most recent note he'd written, even though I had no idea what it was. "I'm thirteen years old."

"Yeah. And what?"

"I only met the man my mother said is my father when I was five."

"Maybe you were too young to remember him before that."

He flipped the page of the notebook and jammed his index finger on a photo. "This was the first time I met him. I remember. We all went out to eat." He flipped the page to another picture, the one of Naomi smiling into the camera. "See? He was talking to my mother like he was trying to win her over. It was a first date for sure. And she never told me he was my father then. If he was, surely she would have said something at that time, right?"

I was sitting in my seat the way a street lamp sat on a sidewalk. My skin felt prickly, like a thousand needles were piercing it. What the hell was this kid talking about?

"That's real unfortunate," I said, trying not to sound cold, but I couldn't hide the chill in my tone. "It sounds like your mother has some explaining to do, but I can assure you, none of it will include me."

Scott lowered his head. "You're right." His mouth wrinkled. "I just thought that...She talked so much about you, I was sure she had feelings for you. I thought it might have gone both ways."

A muscle in my jaw twitched.

"Did you ever love her?"

I rearranged my unused cutlery on the table. "Your mother and I were like brother and sister, if you can imagine that."

"But you *weren't* brother and sister," he said. "Did you ever—"

"There was a time when feelings developed, yes," I admitted, "but that was also a time when those feelings couldn't be honored. We lived in those times. Some say they still exist. So, the short answer is yes, I loved your mother. Very much." I leaned closer to him. "But there is no way I could be your father, son. I haven't seen your mother in..." *Thirteen years?* I cleared my throat. "Such a long time, any love we made has long become insignificant. Pardon the reference to your mother and I having made love, of course."

Scott shrugged. "I'm thirteen years old, Mr. William. I know all about making love."

"You'd better not," I scolded him, grimacing. "You want to be a lawyer, don't you? Well, that won't happen if you go and make yourself a baby."

He held up his hands. "Okay, okay," he said, laughing. "Geesh. You may not have seen my mother in a long time, but you sure sound a lot like her."

Scott smiled. "Hey, I'm sorry for coming down here and throwing something like that at you. Must've taken you by surprise, huh? Some random black kid asking a white dude if he's his father."

"Maybe a little," I said, slapping his back so hard his body lurched forward.

"I just wanted to be sure, you know? Rule everything out." He pointed to the notebook again. "I keep all my records in here, observations and photographs. Just trying to piece some things together for myself. I haven't seen that man since I was seven years old when my mother broke up with him. You may not be my daddy, but that man sure ain't."

The dinner ended pretty soon after that. I couldn't help but feel relieved when Scott's bus pulled up and the doors hissed open. He extended a spindly arm and shook my hand with a firm grip.

"You still gonna help me with my math homework?" he asked.

"Of course I am," I assured him, even though I wasn't sure at all. "Like I said, any friend of your mother's is a friend of mine."

"And I'm her son, so..." Our smiles faded at the same time. "Thanks for listening, Mr. William. I can sure see why my mother thinks so highly of you. You're a cool white dude."

"Thanks," I said, realizing how stupid it sounded after it had come out.

Scott hoisted himself onto the bus and the doors hissed to a close before it chugged away. I watched its taillights until they blurred and blended with the rest of the traffic on the street, then I went back inside and ordered another couple of scotches.

19

NAOMI

BEAUFORT, S.C., 1996

*E*velyn Cooper was the first thing I saw as the limousine rumbled up the long, narrow drive that was characteristic of the old plantations down south.

During the drive, I'd been able to shove aside annoying memories of my younger years, relegating them to a deep recess in my mind. It was a beautiful day, with stratus clouds sweeping across the extra blue sky in long, curly wisps. I could only imagine what the night sky would look like. We were far away from the offensive city lights. The stars would be out en masse, the way they used to be when I was a girl. I focused on the oak trees dripping with Spanish moss like Christmas garland, lining the newly paved streets. The crisp, sweet smell of country air took over my senses. I closed my eyes and inhaled deeply.

"You're enjoying the scenery, I see," Gerald had said.

I opened my eyes and smiled. "I can't deny the nostalgic rush," I replied. "This reminds me so much of my childhood. I grew up around here, you know." I was surprised at the pride in my tone.

"Oh really?" Gerald said, catching my eye in the rearview mirror. "Which part?"

"A different town..." I said. "Close to Sheldon."

"Well that's not too far from here," Gerald said. "Yup! The good old south. It has its challenges, but at the end of the day, there's no place like home, is there?"

We continued the drive in relative silence until I could see the majestic manor I'd once called home surfacing in the distance. The drive had been pleasant, but now there was nothing to distract me from the fact that William's wife was standing on the porch awaiting my arrival. I could see her, even from this distance; round and pale, wearing a powder-blue skirt suit that had been tailored to hang perfectly on her body. Her hands were clasped in front of her like a school headmistress, and her jet-black hair curled and came to a severe rest under her earlobes. A thick string of milky-white pearls hung around her neck and shimmered against the unrelenting rays of the sun.

She was the complete opposite of me. I wondered how William could have made such a drastic adjustment. Maybe this was the kind of woman he had really wanted, I thought. I had been no match for the lifestyle he was accustomed to, and I had been a fool to ever think I might have been. My mouth pinched as we drew closer.

"Who is that woman?" I asked Gerald for confirmation.

He grunted, shifting slightly in the seat to give me a quick glance. The smell of vanilla, orange, and musk lifted into the air every time he moved. "Oh, that's the Queen of the South. A southern belle if there ever was one." He looked at me through the rear-view. "Now that's a woman you want to meet." He cleared his throat as if to get the sarcasm out.

"Looks like I'll be meeting her pretty soon," I muttered, straining my neck to see more. "She looks pretty good. One would never be able to tell how ill she was."

"And believe me when I tell you, she would have it no other way," Gerald said. "She has another surgery tomorrow. We'll see how good she looks after that." Gerald wasn't doing a good job of hiding his disdain for the woman. From the brief conversation I'd had with her, I could see why it might be justified.

"Who is the woman standing next to her?"

"That's Sharon, her right-hand woman."

The maid, I thought. Just like I was about to be. Just like my mother was. *I'm about to become my mother...*

"She doesn't go a step without Sharon nearby, but I guess that'll change too."

"What do you mean?"

"You're here," he said. "She'll push Sharon to the side the minute you step out the car. That's how Mrs. C. is, you see. Before Sharon got here, there was a woman named Luisa."

"Where is she now?"

Gerald shrugged. "Who knows," he said. "Sharon was young and strong and Luisa couldn't keep up. She was outta here before she could blink two times. Mrs. C. don't like incompetence. She'll get ridda you real quick."

I grimaced, thinking about the conversation I'd had with her.

The car inched closer at the speed of a rollercoaster going up the first steep incline. I sat back against the leather seat, trying to ease the churning in my belly.

"What do you think of the house?" Gerald asked.

"The house?"

"It was Mr. C.'s parents' house. Been in the family for generations. It's a three-story frame house, built in the classic Beaufort T-shape." His eyes glistened as if he were talking about his own property.

Views of the majestic manor were visible high above the oak trees. The white roof and five chimneys towered into the cloudless sky. My breath hitched in the back of my throat.

This was my home.

The stark white mansion became more imposing the closer we drew. Twelve pristine windows with decorative blinds reflected the bright sunlight, and tall, thick pillars accentuated the splendor of the entrance.

"It's beautiful," I whispered. "I'm surprised he still lives here. I mean, I assumed he would have upgraded to something a little more modern."

"No, no," Gerald said, shaking his head, "this place means too much to Mr. C. It has unspeakable sentimental value to it. He did some renovating—you know, to spruce it up a bit—but he didn't want to change much."

"I can only imagine how much this place means to him," I said. "His parents lived here so it's understandable."

"Yup. That and a few other people who meant a lot to him. He's told me so many stories about his childhood, some of them not so pleasant...true, but nevertheless, he has been adamant that nothing be moved out of its spot. Now, Mrs. C. had a problem with it at the start. She kept sayin' something about leaving the past in the past, but Mr. C. wasn't hearing her. But now she's the president of that historical society, it would be pretty hypocritical of her to modify a home that has so much history." Gerald rambled on. "Yup! They argued many a night over this old house, but I reckon it would have been over Mr. C's dead body that she had her way. He bought her a nice little waterfront property a few miles out, just to appease her I suppose, but this is the homestead. That William is a chip off the old block if there ever was one."

"So you met his father?"

Gerald nodded. "Sure did. I started working for his father just before the old man died. What year was that now?"

1976...

"1976," he said, snapping his fingers. "It was in the spring."

My mother died in late 1977, a year after William's father.

"He was a real good man," Gerald said. "One of the nicest white men I've ever known."

I twisted in the seat as the sprawling mansion drew closer. The spacious, double-front porches with white pillars overlooked an ample lawn dotted with new foliage and wild flowers in a rainbow of colors. The lush landscaping was surrounded by a fortress-like brick wall, meant to keep out prying eyes, no doubt. There had been no wall when I was a child. I used to watch Will and his friends pass through the lawn on their way to the garage. They'd hop into his Chrysler and peel out of the yard to meet girls. I also remembered the view from the back porch on the third story; I used to enjoy looking at the wooden dock leading out to the ocean like a bridge to nowhere.

The car jammed to a halt, making my heart rise up to my throat. Dust from the gravel formed clouds that rose to the edge of the car window.

Sharon stood next to Evelyn Cooper like a pawn guarding the queen.

Evelyn twirled her hand, and Sharon leaped into action and approached the car as Gerald hopped out and opened my door. The gravel crunched as I pressed my foot against the ground. I reached into the car to grab one of my bags

"You're late, Gerald," Evelyn shouted from the top step.

Gerald's pace didn't change as he shut the door and sauntered to the trunk of the car.

"I'll take that," Sharon said as she gestured toward my bag. Her tone was blunt, and I was surprised by her Jamaican accent. I stalled, but handed her my bag nevertheless.

Sharon nodded and hurried into the house with it.

I looked up just in time to see Evelyn's hand twirling again. "Nurse Nancy, it is a real pleasure to meet you," she said with a voice that sounded like it had been dipped in syrup.

Use of the faux name was making me uncomfortable, but I needed to put my game-face on and get with the program if I was going to be successful at keeping up this appearance.

Evelyn continued. "We spoke on the phone yesterday, but I'm horrible at picturing faces. I was up all night trying to imagine what you could possibly look like."

I extended my hand to shake hers in spite of my internal frown. "I guess the file you compiled didn't include a picture then?" I chuckled, but she didn't join in. "It's a pleasure to finally be here, Mrs. Cooper. I am honored that you've chosen me for this task."

She pulled her hand out of mine and brushed the palm of it against her hip. "Oh right, well, I'm not really the one responsible for choosing you. That was all my husband's idea."

I moved to the side as Gerald walked past us holding multiple pieces of luggage.

"But," she continued, "William assures me you're the best of the best, and that's all I require. We'll get into those details later." She spun around and stretched out her arms. "Welcome to my humble abode. Well, not so humble, is it? Seven rooms, eight and a half bathrooms..."

A powder room, a library...

"But you get the point." She giggled as a manicured hand pressed against her chest.

"It's lovely," I said, forcibly pasting an enthusiastic smile on my face.

Sharon returned and resumed her position on the right of the self-appointed Queen of the South.

Evelyn snapped around as if she'd forgotten the woman all together. "Oh yes, so this is Sharon. She's my personal assistant." She leaned closer and whispered in my ear. "I swear, she goes everywhere I go, even to the bathroom on occasion. I'm mighty grateful for her dedication, but sometimes I wish she'd give me a little space." Her hand flew to her chest as she laughed, causing her waist to rattle under the powder-blue suit. "Anyway, she's served me well, but now that you're here I'll be grateful for the specialized care you can provide. Sharon's been doing her best, but unfortunately, her best is mediocre. She's worked hard, poor dear. Maybe now I can give her a little time off."

Sharon's mouth twitched slightly, but nothing else moved.

Gerald walked past us again, heading for the limo. He caught my eye with a knowing look before continuing with his tasks.

"As you can imagine, Nancy, this is a very frightening time for me," Evelyn continued. "They said I have six months. What's a girl to do with six months?" As if on cue, she pulled out a hankie and started to weep. I looked at Sharon, who continued with her stoic stance next to the apparently heartbroken woman.

I turned around to look for Gerald. Maybe he was rushing to her rescue, but the only thing he was rescuing was my luggage from the back of the car.

"Now, now, Mrs. Cooper we shouldn't focus on that. What we need to do is make sure your upcoming days are the best they can be." I reached out to rub her shoulder, but she backed away and held up her hand.

"Yes, you're right," she said. "I just get so emotional at times. I'm a strong woman, Nancy, I swear I am. I've weathered many storms and I've stood the tests of time, but sometimes a gal just needs to give in to her emotions, you know?"

"Of course. As a woman, I can definitely identify with that."

She sniffed. "But enough of that." She cleared the tears from her face as if by magic and shoved the hankie in the top of her suit. "How about we get you settled? You have a long day ahead of you."

Gerald walked past us again, carrying the final pieces of luggage. I turned to look at him.

"Gerald, don't worry yourself with the suitcases," I said. "I can handle them. Unlike Mrs. Cooper here, I'm not used to having someone do everything for me." I reached out to take them from him, but in an instant, Evelyn whipped her arm out and pushed me back with such force I almost lost my balance.

"Gerald will do no such thing," she said, pointing at me. "You may not be used to people doing things for you, but you'd do well to adjust. Quickly. You're going to be at my beck and call. You'll hardly have time to shower. Besides, Gerald gets paid very well to do what he does, don't you, Gerald? Put his son through school with this paycheck."

The taste of lemons filled my mouth. An oppressive cloud hovered over the front porch, threatening to burst.

She twirled her hand toward the house again. I was waiting for it to detach from her wrist. "Gerald, take her things to the guest room on the second floor. It's all ready for her." She looked at me. "And once you've refreshed yourself, we can have tea and get right down to business. Sharon?" She twisted her wrist again, causing thick gold bangles to crash one into the other down her forearm.

Sharon stepped forward. Her hair was in bantu knots. "Show the nurse to her room, will you? We will have an important meeting at five o'clock. You need a rest, Nancy, I'm sure, but I'm eager to get to the details of what I will require of you while you're here."

I glanced at my watch. It was three-thirty. Not much time for the kind of rest I'd been looking forward to, but Evelyn was right. We needed to get down to business. I needed to know if I was emotionally prepared to handle the task of taking care of this woman. So far, the scale was tipping toward highly unlikely.

Sharon started toward the house, and I looked around before falling into step. It was like a witch's spell; the wrist twisted and everyone did what the woman said.

I forced myself to slow down.

As we forged ahead in silence, I could almost hear the rattle and clank of the ball and chain attached at our ankles.

"She's a formidable woman," I said. "Very strong in personality."

Sharon grunted.

I paused, trying to think of what else to say.

"Have you been working for the Coopers long?"

"Two years," she said.

"You must be very close to Mrs. Cooper," I said. "I can tell she depends on you quite a bit. I guess I'll need to talk to you if I want to know the ropes. Maybe you can give me some advice, you know, tell me the ins-and-outs."

Sharon stopped walking and looked at me.

"I beg your pardon?" she said.

My pace slowed to a halt, and I quickly found myself staring into Sharon's stone-faced expression.

"I was hoping you'd be able to give me the inside track," I clarified. "Her likes, dislikes. I want to make sure I do a good job. She's very ill, but if I can make this time any easier for her, for all of us, I'd certainly like to do that. I was hoping we could work together." I smiled at the woman, even though I didn't want to.

Sharon's eyes narrowed and her lip curled up. "If you want to know anything about Mrs. Cooper, then you're gonna have to learn for yourself...the way I did."

I stood back.

"I know why you're here," Sharon said, pointing at me.

"And why's that?"

"You think you can outshine me... take my job...the job I've worked so hard to secure. You think you can just show up here and snatch it away."

"Take your job?" I shook my head. "Sharon, I can assure you, I have no intention of encroaching on your territory. I'm a retired nurse. I've been asked to take care of Mrs. Cooper and that's all." I lowered my voice. "And if you want to know the truth, I'd rather not be here."

"Mm. And that's what they all say. I heard what the woman said. I can't afford time off, and if you being here is going to make that happen, then there's no way I will be giving you any kind of advice. You just make sure you do your job, you hear? No need to be askin' me any questions about Mrs. Cooper or any of them that live here. Anything you need to know, you gon' have to find out for yourself."

A thick silence dropped between us like a brick wall.

"Now, if we're all clear, let me show you to your room, *Nurse Nancy*."

I straightened my clothes and followed Sharon without further conversation. We passed through the grand Victorian-style foyer. My feet glided across marble floors so shiny, my reflection glared back up at me. An exceptional solid oak table, holding the biggest flower arrangement I had ever seen, sat in the center of the room. A light, delicate floral aroma consumed me. Above me, a dazzling chandelier hung suspended from the ceiling. The staircase that seemed never ending when I was a little girl was still there, and it still seemed endless. Behind it, a wall of glass doors let the marvelous sunlight stream in, unrestricted.

As if watching a movie, I saw myself standing at the windows, peering out onto the lush lawn, watching William play croquet with his friends from private school. Miss Anna came and gently put her hand on my shoulder before leading me away from the window and over to the piano to practice my arpeggios.

"This way," Sharon said, breaking the silence.

When we reached upstairs, more memories played in my mind. I was seventeen again. I saw Will walking through the hall late at night.

I felt a smile pull at my lips.

When we reached my room, I almost choked when I realized it was the same room that had once been my mother's. Like Gerald said, everything was the same. It was simple and quaint. Radiant yellow with drapes hung from the windows, and a new double bed now replaced the single bed my mother had slept on. An en suite bathroom, positioned off to the left, was the only renovation to the room. An eerie but pleasant aura was suspended in the air.

"There's your luggage," Sharon said, looking into the room. "Meeting at five, on the dot."

I turned to look at her. "Thank you," I said. She nodded and headed out of the room. I watched her for a second. "Sharon?"

She stopped but didn't turn around. "I didn't mean to offend you earlier," I said. "I hope we can be friends."

She simply grunted again and disappeared.

As the thud of her shoes became weaker and weaker, so did my confidence. Already, I could tell; I knew. This was a mistake.

20

NAOMI

BEAUFORT, S.C., 1996

Five o'clock arrived in a flash. By then, I had showered and gotten a nap before peeling myself from the plush bed and readying myself for Evelyn's meeting. I searched through my purse for my cosmetics kit and freshened my face, then I raked a paddle brush through my hair, pulling it up into a sleek ponytail. I slipped into a pair of hot-pink scrubs and headed for the door.

The house was quiet. I hadn't heard any more from Sharon or Gerald since I'd come into the room and closed the door. Neither had I heard or seen anything of William.

I blotted my nude lipstick on a tissue before slipping into a pair of flats and stepping outside of the room. I jumped, startled to find Sharon on the other side of the door.

"You're late," she said.

I looked at my watch.

"Mrs. Cooper ain't gonna like that. Not one bit."

"I thought we agreed that you wouldn't tell me anything about her likes and dislikes," I said, adjusting my scrubs.

"I would've thought you'd figure that out by yourself," she replied, exhaling an exasperated sigh. "This way."

We made our way through a maze of secretly familiar hallways before ending up in the library. Nostalgia consumed me. William's father and I had spent countless hours in this room when I was a child. My eyes darted over to the far corner where his worn leather armchair used to be. It wasn't there anymore, but I could almost see him lounging there with his long legs crossed over one another and his salt and pepper hair combed neatly over his head. In the evenings, I'd sit next to him reading the book he'd assigned while he read his daily newspaper. Then, when he'd finished his paper, he'd quiz me on a chapter of my book and if I impressed him enough, we'd go out for ice cream. Something tugged at my heart.

The walls were lined with bookshelves, stacked with hardback books that looked as if they hadn't been read since he'd been alive. A ladder on wheels propped against one of them, giving the illusion that someone was actually interested in the books on the higher shelves.

Evelyn sat at a long oak meeting table in the center of the room, with rimless glasses supported by the tip of her nose

Sharon extended her hand and I approached the table, then she scurried around preparing tea and biscuits.

I had no doubt that *The Wrist* would be twisted several times during the meeting.

"Come," Evelyn said, not bothering to raise her head from the documents she was looking at. Her tone was clipped, and she made a point of looking at her watch.

I didn't move. There was no way she could be talking to me. Maybe she was calling Sharon, but when no one reacted to her instructions, her eyes peered over the top of her glasses and she glared at me. "Sweet Jesus. The nurse is deaf."

"I beg your pardon?"

"Oh, so you *can* hear me." She wiped imaginary sweat off her brow and slid her glasses closer to her eyes. "For a second, I thought you were hard of hearing. I summoned you, and you just stood there like you didn't know what was going on."

My jaw tightened as I swallowed choice responses.

"I apologize," I said. "I didn't realize you were speaking to me." I headed toward the table, uncurling my fingers.

"You'll learn soon enough," was her tepid response. "Sharon knows very well when I'm addressing her. When I want tea, I go like this," she said, demonstrating the *wrist flick*. "And when I require anything else, I do this..." She did the same wrist flick, then she laughed. "Sharon basically moves when I move, so there's never really a need to call her, isn't that right, Shay?" She sighed like she was bored, then beckoned me with a hooked finger. "Sit there, Nurse Nancy. Let's get this thing started. You're already late."

I looked at a grandfather clock standing majestically behind her, the pendulum swinging like my patience.

She licked the tip of the pen and began scribbling. "I've been hiring and firing for as long as I've been married, and I can always pick up bad traits. For example, I already know you can't keep time." She *tsked* three times. "That may be a problem. I will have various appointments in the upcoming weeks and if you're longwinded or... lazy, then I don't see how it's going to work."

I adjusted my clothes for no reason. "I'm not lazy, Mrs. Cooper. It's been a long day of traveling and I overslept."

"Of course," she said with another flick of the wrist.

Sharon brought the tea.

"Let's begin, shall we?" Evelyn wriggled her shoulders and then flipped open a file, which I assumed contained the details of my life. She pulled out a few pieces of paper and pushed them across the table.

"Thank you for sending your certification documents," she said. "My husband gave them to me early this morning. He said you'd given them to him prior to his departure from Boston. I was surprised. You didn't mention having sent them when we spoke on the phone last night."

I peered down at the documents. They were fabricated certificates bearing the name *Nancy Cameron*.

"You're welcome," I said, looking up quickly. "It must've slipped my mind. There's been so much to do over the last few weeks."

Evelyn's eyes narrowed. "Right. Well, aside from the fact that these documents are dated, all is satisfactory." She rummaged through the file and pulled out another document, sliding it with ease across the highly polished table in my direction.

"What's this?" I asked.

"It's your daily schedule," she said. She pulled out a copy for herself and adjusted her glasses with a thumb and forefinger. "As you can see, your day begins at five-thirty."

"Five-thirty...in the morning?"

She took the glasses off her face and leaned closer to me. "Well, yes," she said and paused. "Is that going to be a problem, Nancy? I would have imagined in your profession you would be accustomed to waking up with the first rays of sunlight."

Her poetry made me want to vomit. I kept my eyes focused on the schedule.

"You're right," I agreed. "I worked the early shift for many years. Five-thirty will not be a problem." I smiled.

"Well, thank heavens for that," she said and laughed, pressing her hand against her chest. "Let's continue, shall we? I like to have my breakfast at six-thirty. At the back of this folder, you will find a comprehensive menu."

"So I'll be cooking too?"

"Oh heavens no, dear," she said, cackling again. "Of course we have chefs who run our very busy kitchens. They've studied under the finest, you know...the likes of Wolfgang Puck and Eric Ripert. The newest one worked with Gordon Ramsay. He's positively fabulous!"

"Then what's the purpose of the menus?" I asked, cutting through the accolades.

"I'll require you to provide the chefs with a specialized meal plan," she explained. "I'm known for my spectacular dinner parties and socials, so of course, they are very busy. You'll need to advise them of what I should be eating during my recovery."

Silence.

Evelyn raised an eyebrow. "You understand of course..."

I shifted in the seat. "Yes."

"Good. Let's continue." She looked at her watch and grimaced. "By seven-fifteen, I want to be in the gym."

"You want me to be your personal trainer?" I asked. "You'd have been better off asking me to cook." Evelyn glared at me as my moment of humor vanished into thin air.

"As an accomplished nurse, I would have assumed you to be familiar with the fundamentals of fitness," she said.

"You'd assume correctly," I replied.

"In which case, the expectation is that you'll create a suitable workout regimen for me."

My jaw clenched. I cleared my throat. "Perhaps we could hire someone who could assist you with that. You mentioned my credentials being outdated, and that is definitely one area of expertise that I have not kept current."

"Hire someone?" Evelyn laughed. "Nancy, do you think that money grows on trees? If I wanted to hire someone, don't you think I would've done so by now?"

I dry-washed my hands. "I was under the impression you wanted the best of the best," I said. "I can research workout regimens and exercise programs, but I figured—"

"I know what you figured," she cut me off, swiping the glasses from her face. "You saw this lavish home, the kind of which you've probably never had the opportunity to experience before, and figured we had access to it all. Well, we *do* have access to it all, Nancy, but we're very selective in how we use what we have access to. That's why we're wealthy. We understand the principles of budgeting and frugality. Some people don't understand those things." Her eyes fell to the Rolex on my wrist.

I clasped my hands together to stop them from shaking.

She put the glasses back on and looked down at the schedule again. "At eight o'clock—"

"I'm sorry I'm late."

We both looked up as William walked into the library, shrugging out of his blazer to reveal a crisp, white shirt and a lime green and navy blue woven tie. The fresh smell of his aftershave reminded me of a couple of days ago, when my body was wrapped around his. The deepness of his voice caused a flutter in my belly, and the smile on his lips produced the taste of sweet and spicy gin in my mouth. His piercing eyes captured me in an instant.

I moistened my lips and looked away from him for fear that the images in my mind would somehow show up on my face.

Evelyn rubbed her forehead as he came over and pecked her on the lips. "William. Well, I'm so glad you could grace us with your presence. I thought you'd clean forgotten about our scheduled rendezvous," she muttered.

"I'm sorry. I had a board meeting that ran overtime," he said, caressing her back.

A surge of jealousy arose in me, and I swallowed it like a slice of lemon.

"Darling, I'd like for you to meet the nurse you hired. Nancy Cameron."

"Nancy..." William called my faux name and gave me a cautious eye.

I sucked in air. "It's a pleasure to meet you, Mr. Cooper," I said, glaring at him. He approached me in my seat, and I reluctantly extended my hand to greet him.

"I guess she's never heard about southern charm," he said to Evelyn, but he wasn't looking at her. "We hug around here," he said. "You'll need to get used to that."

William pulled me from the seat and wrapped his arms around my shoulders. I stood stiff as a board, trying not to melt under the pleasant yet excruciating heat of his touch.

"What the hell are you doing?" I mumbled like a ventriloquist.

He gave me another squeeze and whispered, "I'm here."

In less than a second, the physical exchange had been broken, but the emotional one persisted long after I had taken my seat.

Evelyn's face looked sour. "Don't mind my husband," Evelyn said. "He tends to go overboard with the southern charm thing. You'll find we're complete opposites, Nancy. Sometimes I wonder how on earth I ended up with someone like him."

William sat down and leaned back in the chair. "I've wondered the same thing myself on occasion," he said, chuckling. "What did I miss?"

"Mrs. Cooper was advising me of my schedule," I said, crossing my legs under the table.

"We were clarifying her duties," Evelyn said. "She had quite a bit to say about the things I've laid out so far."

"What do you mean?" William asked, adjusting his position in his seat.

"Well, first she queried the start time."

"I didn't *query* the start time," I said. "I merely mentioned that I hadn't worked the early shift in a while and that I would have to get used to it again."

William's eyes shifted from me to Evelyn.

"Then," Evelyn continued, "she had questions regarding the menu."

"Mm-hmm," William hummed.

An awkward silence followed as he took the schedule Evelyn had provided and peered at it with drawn eyebrows. We both watched him, waiting to see what his response would be. He pushed the paper back in my direction but didn't say anything.

"We just finished talking about my workout regimen, and I was about to introduce her to Kibbles and Bits."

My eyes shot down to the schedule. "I'm sorry, who are Kibbles and Bits?"

"Kibbles and Bits are her poodles," William said, running his hand across his forehead.

In the corner of the room, a teacup rattled, and everyone turned back to see an apologetic looking Sharon.

The skin under my eyes grew tight and I shifted in my seat. "If I may," I began.

Evelyn groaned. "Here we go again..."

"What is it, Nancy?" William asked, clasping his hands on the table.

"It's not a problem really..."

"Then what is it?" Evelyn repeated, crossing her arms. The severe black wig rattled against her jawline.

I paused. "I would prefer to limit my duties to those directly associated with taking care of your health needs, Mrs. Cooper," I said.

"Excuse me?" she said through tight teeth.

"What do you mean, nurse?" William chimed in.

His reaction surprised me.

I blinked and paused again. "What I mean is, I wouldn't want to encroach on anyone else's duties. I'm sure Kibbles and Bits have enjoyed their walks with whoever was taking them before I arrived." I glanced at Sharon. "I was under the impression that my role would be to care for Mrs. Cooper. Not take care of the pets. What's more, as your wife's nurse, especially at this stage of her illness, I really think my time would be better spent making sure she has everything she needs, medically." I grabbed at Evelyn's medical records, which I had brought to the meeting. "According to the doctor's orders—"

Evelyn leaned forward. Her pale skin had taken on a reddish hue. "What business is it of yours to whom I assign tasks?" she asked. "You have been hired to do my bidding."

I held my temple, watching as she reached into the file and pulled out a lengthy document. She almost threw it across the table.

William arrested it before it reached me. "Listen," he said, "I think it might be best if we put this Kibbles and Bits discussion on ice for a moment. I agree with the nurse," he said, tilting his head towards me. "She's been hired for a specific purpose, so perhaps we need to focus on that."

Evelyn glared at him. "Are you siding with this woman? We're paying her good money, William. These are my final days and I'm in constant pain." We watched as she pressed the hankie against her nose and manufactured intense sobs. "You brought her here, William. You said she was the best, but it seems like everything I'm asking is too much."

Her wails reverberated off the library walls.

"All I want is for someone to understand what I need right now. I'm not asking too much," she said. "Am I asking too much?"

William's throat constricted as he reached over to console his lamenting wife. "No, sweetheart, you're not asking too much," he said, pulling her into an awkward embrace. "We're going to make sure that everything works out. I promised I'd take care of you, didn't I?"

Over Evelyn's shoulder, William's pleading eyes connected with my cold gaze. I scowled at him, shaking my head in disbelief. He released her.

Evelyn patted her eyes dry and straightened her posture in the chair. As if by magic, all evidence of her suffering was erased in an instant.

William ran his hands through his hair and forced breath from his mouth. He gaped at the table, his reflection staring back up at him from the over-buffed oak. "Listen, Nurse Na...Nancy," he cleared his throat, "I understand your concerns, but we have hired you to take care of my wife as she transitions through the stages of this illness. Now, Mrs. Cooper seems to really need your assistance with the duties she has chosen. If overseeing the menu, creating a workout regimen, and walking the dogs are things she would like you to take on, maybe you could just...do them. So we can all get along here." He paused. "I'm sorry."

I glared at William, trying not to let my eyes reveal the extent of my disdain for what he'd just said. "Mr. Cooper—"

"I'd be happy to review the schedule and the contract," he interrupted, shuffling through the paperwork. "I certainly wouldn't want you doing anything you're not comfortable with."

The edges of my eyes quivered.

"You don't have to apologize to her," Evelyn spat. "It's very simple. Either she signs the contract and agrees to the terms, or she doesn't, and she leaves."

I looked from Evelyn to William. A tight lip was locked between his teeth and deep creases had spread across his damp forehead.

"Nurse Nancy, you've been touted as being the very best," he said softly. "We want you to stay. Please take some time and consider this."

Evelyn smirked and leaned over to William, throwing her arms around his neck. "Well, maybe we're not so opposite after all," she purred.

I placed a hard smile on my lips. "Maybe you're not," I agreed.

Taking the contract in my hands, I let my eyes gloss over it but the words seemed blurred and fuzzy. I'd been double-teamed. William had deceived me into thinking he would be supportive of my emotional needs while I was in Beaufort, but it was obvious his allegiance was to his wife.

"I'll look at this in the privacy of my room," I said, pushing my chair back from the table. "If I may be excused."

But I didn't wait for permission.

21

NAOMI

BEAUFORT, S.C., 1996

I made it back to my room, despite the hallways spinning like they would in a funhouse at the circus. That's where I was, I decided; the Ringling Brothers had landed in Beaufort and set up shop in William's house. I used to like circuses as a little girl. Mr. Cooper had taken me to one when I was seven years old. I'd asked for popcorn. He'd gotten peanuts. We sat in a row near the front and watched clowns trip about in their oversized shoes. Then the elephants had come out, standing on their back legs and turning around in circles. I'd clapped until the palms of my hands were beet-red.

Well, many years may had passed since that day at the circus, but there was most certainly still an elephant in the room. It lived in the Cooper's house now, but there was no way I'd be clapping for this one.

I pressed my hand against my stomach and threw the bedroom door open, rushing to the toilet where I regurgitated nothing. My back arched as bile scraped the back of my throat. I heard the bedroom door close and footsteps come in behind me. A satisfying, yet unwelcome aroma followed. My stomach muscles tightened as I grabbed the edge of the commode, shoving my face deep into it again.

William approached and put his hand on my back, drawing small, rhythmic circles, applying just the right amount of pressure.

Water filled my eyes as my muscles began to relax. "What the hell is the matter with you?" I muttered through clenched teeth.

His hand froze. "What?"

"You fed me to the goddamn wolves, William," I said, pulling myself up from the rim of the toilet. "You tag-teamed me with your *wife* and took me down in the first round."

"Jesus, Naomi..."

"Naomi...Nancy...I'm glad it's so easy for you to remember which name to use and when." I pulled myself to my feet.

"Naomi, you're overreacting," he whispered. "Please—"

I put my palm up to his face. "I get here, a house I didn't want to be at in the first place, and I'm about to have an emotional meltdown after being bombarded with all these memories and being placed in my late mother's room...all the while, you were nowhere to be found! And then *that*?"

He stood and followed me out of the room. "Sweetheart, I told you, I had a business meeting that ran overtime. I was trying to get here, I swear to God, but I couldn't leave those men at the table."

I spun around and pointed at him. "Don't call me that," I said.

"What?"

"I told you, this is a business relationship. Besides, that's what you call your wife." I walked over to my suitcase and flipped it open. "And another thing. You told your *wife* that you'd been in a business meeting. That exchange had nothing to do with me."

William groaned, raking his hands over his head. "Naomi, do you have any idea how much of a nightmare this is for me? I'm stuck between a rock and a hard place."

I ignored him.

I sensed the heat emanating from him as he approached me from behind, towering over me. "Arguing with my wife is not something I want to do," he said.

I grunted.

"Neither is arguing with you," he added in a whisper. "How about you put yourself in my shoes for a minute?" he said. "You're on the right, she's on the left, and I'm literally in the middle trying my best to make each of you happy. It's an impossible task if there ever there was one."

"And there it is again," I murmured, pitching a t-shirt into the suitcase.

"There's what again?"

"There you go putting everyone else's feelings above mine. You could have done more to defend me, William. But of course, that's always been your weakness."

"I'm trying to defend you," he said, "but the woman is dying, Naomi. The least you can do is buy into her program. If she wants you to walk the damn dogs, walk the damn dogs, and we can figure out the rest later. What's the big deal?"

The article of clothing I was holding dropped from my hands. "Do you want to know what the *big deal* is, Will? The big deal is that I didn't come here to walk dogs. I came here to provide medical care to a dying woman. And if I walk the dogs, what will Sharon do? She already thinks I'm here to steal her job. I'm not trying to make enemies."

"This has nothing to do with Sharon. It's about you doing what you've been hired—" He pinched the bridge of his nose and closed his eyes. "I mean, it's about you doing what I'm *asking* you to do."

His words pierced me in the heart. My fingers stiffened at the feeling of my blood running hot through my veins.

"Hired..." I let the word roll around on my tongue, thinking about the contract I had yet to read. "Fair enough, William. But you hired me to be the nurse. Not the goddamn maid. That was my mother's role. I don't know what's in that contract the two of you drafted—"

"I had nothing to do with that," he interjected.

"Well, whatever it is, doesn't sound like it's something I'll be comfortable with. It's bad enough that I agreed to come here in the first place, especially under these circumstances. I can't believe you!

We grew up together," I said, pointing at him. "We've...been intimate. You told me you loved me. Now, you're nothing more to me than your father was to my mother."

"My father loved your mother," he whispered through tight teeth.

"Right. Like Pharaoh loved the Jews," I said.

"You're blowing this thing out of proportion," he said, rubbing his brow.

"Of course you would say that," I replied. "You're all the same. You have no clue what I'm experiencing, and you just don't care. Just like when we were kids." I started throwing clothes into the suitcase.

"What are you doing?"

"There's a simple solution to this problem. You need to hire somebody else. This whole idea was a bad one. I never should have come here."

William's body stood rigid, his mouth drawn into a tight line. After a second, his eyes shifted. "You know what I notice?" he said, walking over to the suitcase and running his hand over its worn edges. His long fingers caressed the fabric.

My mind wandered to the other night when he'd run them through my hair.

I shook my head and continued to pack my things.

"You keep saying that this is a business relationship, but it's obvious that your feelings have nothing to do with business. Be honest, Naomi. All of this drama has nothing to do with tasks or responsibilities. This is about how you feel about me and how I feel about you." He paused. "This is about *us*."

My throat tightened. "There is no *us*," I said.

Slamming the suitcase lid closed, he looked me square in the face. "I'm not going to allow you to cop out with that. Need I remind you that the whole business thing was your idea? I had other ideas." He lowered his head. "Do you really want to know what I'd rather be doing right now?"

Silence.

My body trembled.

He looked at the bed and then back at me. "I would rather be making up for forty-two goddamn years of not seeing the woman I love more than anything in this world. I would rather take you out to dinner and dancing. I want to hop on that private jet and fly away with you and not care about coming back."

My chest rose and fell with intensity, fighting against the rigid atmosphere. He was suffocating me and I wanted to die.

His voice lowered. "I want to sit on the dock in those two chairs and look for shooting stars while I hold you in my arms and never, *ever* let you go." His head rose and he backed away from me. "*You* wanted to make this about business, and as difficult as it is for me to do that, I'm willing to do it. For you and for my wife. The least you can do is put your ego to the side and act like a goddamn professional. I'm not going to beg you to stay. I've been on my knees for the last four decades praying and waiting. If you're too weak to do this, then leave. I'm not going to stop you."

Without so much as a glance in my direction, William turned and walked out of the room. When the door closed, I spun around to look at it, but I couldn't see anything through the curtain of tears.

22

WILLIAM

BERMUDA, 1977

he rain from a passing sun shower slickened the golf green, but I'd already told Rob there was no way he should expect it to ruin my game. We were surrounded by lush flora; vibrant hibiscus flowers in shades of red, pink, and yellow. Bluebells climbed on vines, choking the thin branches of shrubs that surrounded the course, and ahead of me, the pink sand in a bunker glistened under the radiant, scorching sun. I inhaled the deep, earthy aroma of a nearby crowd of Bermuda cedar. The gnarled, bleached branches reached into the sky.

Rob pulled out his nine-iron. "After I beat you on this last hole, how about we make our way to the beach. One last swim before we hit the boardroom this afternoon."

I reached into the golf cart and pulled out my hand towel. "First of all, you're not going to beat me. You never have, and you never will."

Rob leaned on his club and gave me a sarcastic face.

"Second of all, I'm not sure that'd be a good idea. This sun is killer, and it's only ten o'clock." I looked up to the sky, shielding my eyes. "It'll drain us, and we won't be able to close the deal because we'll be snoring on the meeting table."

Rob laughed. "I doubt that," he said, perfecting his stance. "Snoring or not, you blow this deal and your father will roll over in his grave for sure. He's not even been dead a year."

"God rest his soul," I murmured. A dull pain made my heart throb for a second.

Rob's club smacked the ball and we watched it sail through the air. It landed close to a billowing flag in the distance, but not close enough.

Choosing my next club with careful consideration, I didn't hesitate to then smack my ball from the tee in the same direction as Rob's. I shaded my eyes and tracked its path across the backdrop of blue sky. It landed and bounced a few times, coming to rest mere inches from the hole. I grinned.

Rob sucked his teeth and started putting his clubs away.

"What's the matter?" I asked. "The game's not done. I need to put that thing in the hole."

"It's as good as done," he said, flinging the bag in the back of the cart. "Let's get out of here. We need to get ready for that meeting anyway."

"Suit yourself," I said, shrugging and slipping my club back in the bag.

We jumped into the golf cart and bumbled along the narrow roadway back to the Princess Hotel. The huge, coral-pink building was perched atop a hill, affording a splendid, unrestricted view of the shimmering Atlantic Ocean. It was the same Atlantic Ocean I saw everyday in Beaufort, but the turquoise shade, with the baby and deep blue patches, was far different from anything I'd ever see back home.

I nodded to a group of women dressed in saris and sunhats, smelling like five bottles of suntan lotion each. I rubbed my nose.

"Mr. Cooper?"

I turned around to see a smartly dressed black man standing at the concierge desk. We made eye contact and he smiled. I glanced at his nametag.

Allan. He'd introduced himself yesterday, but remembering

names was not my strong point, so I never tried. Over the years, I had learned to work my strengths and forget about the weaknesses.

"How was golf?" he asked.

"Ask Rob," I suggested, pointing at him. "For me, it was spectacular, for him..." I shrugged.

Allan laughed. "Your taxi will be here in another few hours," he said. "I trust you gentlemen will want to get some rest before you head out, but your dinner reservations at Four Ways are set."

"Wonderful," I said and slapped the desk.

"Before you go, Mr. Cooper..." Allan handed me a *While You Were Out* paper. "You received a call. The person didn't leave a message, other than to ask that you return the call."

I looked at the paper and saw the name. *Naomi Jackson?* A number with a New York area code had been scribbled next to her name.

My mouth slackened to the point where saliva threatened to spill out of it. I closed it with a snap and folded my hand over the paper. I turned to look at Rob. "Why don't we meet up in the lobby at two-thirty?" I suggested.

"Sounds like a plan."

"I'll have a look at that report."

"For the hundredth time? Will, we've got this. *You've* got this. How many deals have you closed in the last twelve months?"

I shrugged and scratched my jaw. "Fine. I'll see you later."

I caught the elevator to my suite and rushed into the room. A comforting breeze greeted me through the swaying curtains as they glided in and out of the sliding glass door I'd left open.

I sat on the bed and picked up the phone.

"This is the operator."

"212-738-4993."

"Collect, sir?"

"Of course not," I said.

"One minute please."

Ringing.

A male voice answered.

"Scott?" I couldn't disguise the irritation in my voice.

"Mr. William, thank God you called back," he said. His breathing was out of sync and his tone was rushed, indicating he only had a few minutes to talk.

I ran my hand over my face before clenching it into a fist in the air. "Scott! What the hell—"

"I'm sorry, but I had to do it that way. I knew if I said it was my mother you'd call back. I didn't think you would if you knew it was me. You're a busy man."

I sighed. He was right, but it was pretty underhanded of him to do such a thing. I was now bothered by the fact that I'd called back so quickly. Naomi still controlled me, even after all those years of not seeing or hearing her voice. "What is it?"

All of a sudden, Scott burst out crying. The sound of his tears coming through the phone made my heart leap into my throat. What was going on? What had happened to Naomi? I clutched the phone with two hands, pressing it against my face until began to slide against the glow of my hot skin. "Scott, talk to me. What's happened?"

More crying. The sniveling sort. He started coughing and moaning simultaneously.

I stood up and paced the floor as far as the telephone cord would allow. "Jesus Christ, Scott, say something. Is it Naomi?"

"No," he finally answered.

I slumped down onto the bed as relief washed over me. "For heaven's sake, you can't be calling and crying like that. You trying to give me a heart attack?"

Still unable to speak, he released a woeful moan before a loud clatter suggested he had dropped the phone drop.

"Scott?"

Nothing.

"Scott! Are you there?"

Silence. I sat on the bed, running my hand over my hot face. I wanted to hang up, but that wouldn't be right; the kid was sobbing like a two-year-old on the other end of the phone. What kind of heel would I be to leave him hanging? This was Naomi's son. Even if I wanted to hang up, I couldn't. In some ways, having him was like having her.

Groaning, I picked up the television remote and started flipping through the various channels, trying to be patient. As I flipped to the fifth channel, a rumbling on the other end of the phone caused me to sit bolt upright again and shut the television off.

After a few more sniffles and deep breaths to compose himself, he finally spoke again, although the tears were still evident in his shaky voice. "Thank you for calling me back," he said again.

He was wasting my time. I needed him to get to the point. "No problem. I've always been here for you, haven't I? But like you said, I'm very busy. I'm actually about to go into a business meeting and I need to get some rest before I do." I waited for him to say something, but the crying was starting again. I cut him off before he could dissolve too much further. "Whatever is bothering you, it sounds pretty serious, but if you need some time to think about it, maybe pull yourself together before you—"

"It's my grandmother," he said.

My mouth clamped shut. It took me a second to unstick it. "What about her?"

"She's in the hospital," he said, "and they say she's not gonna make it through the night."

I tried to swallow my Adam's apple. "Tell me you're joking, Scott."

"I wish I could." He coughed. "My mama said she was getting better, but—"

"Where is your mother?" I asked.

"She's gone. To Beaufort, I think. She left last night."

That meant hours had passed, at least twelve of them, and no one had reached out to tell me anything. No one had called to tell me that the woman, my surrogate mother, was on the brink of her demise?

My thoughts fled back to Naomi. Not that I would have spoken to her if she were there. She had no idea Scott and I were in communication. It was an unspoken thing between us. I hadn't asked him not to tell her, and he hadn't requested it of me. It just seemed obvious.

But what was not obvious was why I was the last one to find out that Miss Carole had been hospitalized.

"Why has no one called me?" I demanded of Scott. "Where's my mother?"

He didn't respond. He was crying again. I wanted to reach through the phone and shake him. My extremities began to tremble. I listened to Scott's lamentations and an urge to join in crept over me, but blasts of anger suffocated the sadness. I could only imagine him, sitting there in New York, confused and alone. My eyes blurred over as the phone began to shudder in my hand.

"Scott, I have to go," I mumbled between tight lips. "I need to make some calls, find out what's going on."

"Mr. William? I need to get to South Carolina and see my grandmother." He sucked in snot. "I *need* to go to the funeral, and I don't have a dime to my name. You know I don't ask you for anything, but you gotta help me with this one."

He was right about that. From the first time we'd met, he hadn't asked a thing of me, other than if I was his father and some occasional help with calculus equations. The boy was in law school now, so of course he didn't have any money.

I inhaled, pulling back emotion. "You'll be on the next flight out of New York, Scott. Don't you worry about a thing."

He sniffled into the phone. "Thanks. I don't have to tell you I appreciate it. You know how much I do."

"Yes, I do," I said.

Silence.

"So, when are you flying up?" he asked.

My muscles rattled. I had been waiting for him to ask me that.

"You are coming, aren't you?" he persisted when I didn't respond.

"I would like to," I said, tears stinging the back of my throat, "but I'm not sure if I'll make it down there by tomorrow. I have this meeting tonight and I'm scheduled to land in Tokyo on Friday. It's a huge business deal, Scott. I can't back out of it." I winced as soon as the words hit the atmosphere.

"But it's my grandmother," he said. "She means just as much to you as she does to me, if not more." Scott waited for me to say something, but it was in vain. "Okay, well..." He sniffled again. "I know how business is."

"It's brutal."

"I know."

I swallowed. Was I really making the decision not to fly down to Beaufort to be with Miss Carole? Was I really that selfish? I scratched through the smooth stubble growing on my cheek.

"Well, thanks for the ticket. I'll pay you back as soon as I get the money."

"Scott, you don't have to pay me back."

"No, I do have to," he insisted. "I'm a man, Mr. William. I can make my own way. Just need a leg up sometimes."

"Fine," I relented. "So where are you gonna stay while you're down there?"

"With my mama," he said. "She's at a bed and breakfast close to the hospital."

"A bed and breakfast?"

"Said she'd be more comfortable."

I laughed, shaking my head in disbelief, but decided against saying anything. Scott was clueless about anything that was going on beneath the surface, but the information he was giving me burned me up on the inside.

I hung up from Scott and raked my shaking hand through my hair, almost pulling it out. I picked up the phone and called my mother. She came on the line instantly. The paradox of her feeble, yet strong tone never ceased to amaze me, but not in a good way.

"So you heard about Carole?" she asked after a robotic greeting, which seemed inappropriate and insensitive given the circumstances.

"Yeah, I heard," I confirmed. "Why didn't you call me, Mom? Didn't you think Miss Carole being sick was something I should've known about?"

My mother sighed. "I was going to call you, but—"

"You were *going* to call me," I mocked her, shaking my head. I tried to rein in the emotion. "Okay." I paused. "Have you seen Naomi yet?"

My mother laughed. "And you're still worrying about that girl. You still haven't let it go, have you? This isn't about Naomi, William. It's about Carole, and you should be ashamed of yourself."

Fire consumed me. I rose to my feet, pulling the phone base off the nightstand in the process. "If anyone should be ashamed, it should be you, Mom," I shouted. "How dare you say something like that to me? Naomi is staying at a goddamn bed and breakfast! Her son comes into town and you act like he doesn't exist."

"How do you know about her son?"

"If you didn't want Naomi and me together that badly, there were other ways you could've handled the situation. You could've talked to me about it. You could've shared your concerns about our relationship."

"Don't be a damn fool," she spat. The feebleness in her tone had dissipated, and in an instant, I was eighteen all over again. "You didn't know what was good for you then, and you sure as hell don't know any better now." She lowered her voice. "I kept the two of you apart for good reasons. You were so stubborn. You never would have listened to reason and logic. You're just like your father! There are things you don't know about that girl and her family. Things I've protected you from, for your own good!"

My mouth trembled and my eyes flickered.

"Carole is on her deathbed," my mother said. "Prayerfully, she's going to be with the good Lord, and you have the audacity, the imprudence to call this house on such an occasion talking about yourself! You don't care about Carole any more than your father did."

I tried to make sense of her disjointed speech. For years, she had tried to control me. For years, she had succeeded in doing so. I was a man now, and she still couldn't give me the pleasure of living my own life the way I wanted to live it.

She continued. "The woman is dying, and I know she would want to see you. So the questions have nothing to do with Naomi or her bastard son. There is only one question...are you coming or not?"

Silence.

"If you are, I'll see you when you get here, but if not..."

This was where I was supposed to jump in and say something. I was supposed to acquiesce. I was supposed to apologize for disrespecting her. I was supposed to thank her for protecting me from the dreadful unknown. I was supposed to curl up and play her game the way I had for my entire life.

I thought of Naomi, who was probably somewhere nearby getting ready to face the biggest loss she had ever encountered. Not even she had called to say anything. She didn't even know that Scott and I had met. She was so disconnected, so deep in the fake world she had created for herself that she didn't want to know the truth. Just like she'd been when we were teenagers.

My hands rolled into fists and my face burned as a barrage of emotion threatened to overflow and turn me crazy. "No, I'm not coming," I said.

"William Frederick Cooper—"

"You don't want me there. You said it yourself. No one wants me there."

"This isn't about you," she shot back.

"And neither is it about you," I said, jabbing my finger into the air. "Give Carole Jackson my regards. And just so you know, I will *never* forgive you for ruining my life. Ever!"

"You're making a mistake," she said, "just like you did before, and this time, I'm not going to be the one to bail you out."

"Then let me make it," I said. My heavy breathing suspended in the air between the phone and my mouth. "I have to go."

"William, you listen to me," my mother demanded.

"I'm done listening, Mom." I shrugged, looking up at the ceiling. "It's over," I spat and hung up.

23

NAOMI

BEAUFORT, S.C., 1996

The following morning, I rolled over and looked at the digital clock on the nightstand. It was 5:15 a.m. I sighed and squeezed my eyes together. My suitcase was still open and spilling with clothes strewn over the bed. I'd tossed and turned on top of them all night, unable to get William's disturbing monologue out of my head. I was angered by the things he had said, but I was angrier at the fact that he was right. I'd lost focus and allowed outdated emotions to cloud my judgment. Evelyn was being a witch, but that was no reason to abandon my assignment. I had committed to this. If I walked away from it, especially after the way she had treated me and the things William had said, it would mean I was weak. I didn't want to be my mother, but if I couldn't stay and handle this situation, it would mean I was worse than she was.

I pulled myself out of the bed and walked to the window. Pulling the curtain to the side, I was just in time to see Gerald buffing the last spot off the sleek, black limousine he'd just washed. He pulled at the tip of his cap and got down on one knee to inspect the rims before pulling the cloth back out scrubbing them to a high shine.

I pushed the sill up and listened to him whistle "Singing in the Rain".

As the southern sun rose above the oaks, bands of red and pink ribbons smeared across the sky. Not a rain cloud in sight, I thought, at least not ones visible to the naked eye. Somehow, I could identify with the song.

I huffed.

"Good morning, Gerald," I sang out, fitting a smile onto my face.

He stopped what he was doing and peered up at the window. In an instant, a warm, bright smile appeared on his face. "Well, good morning, Nurse Nancy. And it certainly is a fine one. How was your night?" He raised an all-knowing eyebrow.

I shrugged.

He mouthed a silent whistle.

"Today will be better," he said before resuming his task.

I stared at him for a second longer.

Turning away and pulling the window down, a knock sounded at the door.

"Come in," I said.

Sharon entered. She was wearing the same thing she had on yesterday. I assumed it to be her uniform.

"Good morning, Nurse Nancy," she said, stepping just inside the threshold. "Mrs. Cooper sent me to fetch you. She's ready to go to the car."

"Of course," I said, forcing myself to smile. "I'll be right down."

Sharon stalled but then nodded slightly and walked out of the room.

I skipped into the bathroom and freshened up. Then I put on pink scrubs and stepped into my sneakers before heading toward the sitting room where I knew Evelyn Cooper would be. Per the special schedule for today, she should be having tea. I was right.

"Good morning, nurse," she said, putting a dainty teacup to her lips. She rested it back on the saucer and looked at her watch. "You're on time today." She smiled and so did I. "I assume your presence is indication that you have agreed to the terms of the contract."

I inhaled. It was obvious that the woman wouldn't let the matter rest until she had evidence of my submission.

"I'm a professional, Mrs. Cooper. I'm aware of your standards, and it is my job to meet them." I walked over to her and touched her hand. "Big day today. Your third round of chemo."

"And a mastectomy," she added.

"How are you feeling about it?"

She sighed and pushed the tea away from her. "I'm a strong woman, Nancy."

"Yes, I know," I said, "but even strong women have times of vulnerability. I have learned to find strength in being vulnerable."

Her lip trembled and she grabbed her handkerchief to wipe it. "Yes, well, I appreciate your concern for my mental health, but with all due respect, you're a nurse. Not a counselor." She shoved the suddenly redundant hankie into her Louis Vuitton purse.

The smile on my face faltered.

"Fair enough," I said with a nod. "Would you like for me to meet you at the hospital? I can help get you settled."

She flicked the wrist. "That's not necessary. My husband will be there," she said. "You just make sure everything is in order for when I come home in a few days. You have the list, don't you?"

"Yes, ma'am."

"Good. And what about the groceries? I'll be famished when I arrive. It's not like I'm staying at The Ritz. The food will be horrible. Please make sure to liaise with the chefs."

"I'll make sure your meals are prepared and ready for your arrival," I assured her.

"I'll do you one better than that," she said. "I would like a home-cooked meal for breakfast, lunch, and dinner while I'm at that godforsaken place. Have Gerald deliver those, will you?"

I nodded once.

Evelyn eyed me for a second. Her tone softened. "I'm sorry if yesterday we got off to a bad start," she said. "I was very emotional and perhaps I came off too strongly."

I straightened my shoulders. "We all have bad days, Mrs. Cooper. In reflection, I don't think I was on my best behavior yesterday either."

She nodded, still eyeing me, and then pushed her chair back. She released a light groan and I rushed over to help her from her seat. I held her by the arm, but she jerked away from my grasp.

"I'm fine, nurse," she said. "I told you, I'm strong."

I backed away from her, holding my hands up in defense. She composed herself and raised her frail body out of the seat.

After a few more arduous minutes of wrist flicking and declarations of self-pity, I was finally accompanying her down to the foyer and into the courtyard where Gerald had finished cleaning the car. Upon seeing us, he hurried to the back door and opened it for Mrs. Cooper. Sharon appeared on the steps holding two pieces of expensive luggage and I went to assist.

Before long, William strode out onto the doorstep dressed in a heather-gray, three-piece suit and a powder-pink tie. I couldn't help but notice the way the suit was melded against his body, like he had been born in it. His thick hair was perfectly arranged, and his clear brown eyes captured me in an instant. I looked away, unwilling to maintain his gaze.

William shoved his hands into his pockets and walked past me towards the car. He leaned through the open window and kissed Evelyn. I stretched my neck.

"Everything will be alright, sweetheart," I heard him say. "I'm spending the entire day with you. I've got people handling business at the office and my secretary has cleared my schedule. I won't leave your side."

I smoothed the front of my clothes as my heart crumbled in my chest.

"Oh, William," Evelyn purred, just as the waterworks began.

William caressed her black wig and they snuggled for a second. I watched him whisper in her ear.

Sharon was standing next to me, rigid like a wrought iron pole. I glimpsed her in my periphery, trying to get a sense of what might be going through her mind. Her flat affect revealed little.

It felt like hours had passed by the time the limousine was finally rumbling down the path and the Queen of the South was leaving the premises. My shoulders folded as I released the breath I'd been hold-ing. Sharon turned and headed back up to the house. I looked at William, who was watching the car as it disappeared from view, then I turned and followed Sharon in silence.

I headed to the library, where Evelyn's notes still laid strewn on the table from the meeting yesterday evening. I picked up my schedule and grimaced. My chest tightened for a moment, but I closed my eyes and exhaled, reminding myself of the decision I'd made this morning and the things I'd said to Evelyn earlier.

"I can do this," I said softly.

I started to clear the table but paused with a déjà vu when I caught sight of the place where Mr. Cooper's old leather chair used to be. I stood erect and again stared at the spot, another warm smile appearing on my face. In an instant, I could see him sitting there, flipping through the newspaper and sucking at a cigar. I put the schedule down and walked over to the bookshelf, running my fingertips over the spines of the aged books. The ridges, set deep in the old leather, tickled my fingertips and sent a rush of something through me. After searching for a few seconds, my eyes landed on The Count of Monte Cristo, the book he'd made me read when I was fifteen.

Pulling it out and flipping it open, I inhaled and read aloud. "On the 24th of February, 1815, the look-out at Notre-Dame de la Garde signaled the three-master, the Pharaoh from Smyrna, Trieste, and Naples."

A nostalgic smile settled on my mouth. I turned towards where his chair would have been. "Mr. Cooper, I'm very tired," I whined, trying to mimic the voice I had when I was a girl. "May I stop and have tea with Miss Anna?"

I cleared my throat and dug deep to lower my tone. "Darling, you should never tire of reading. Reading is the key to the universe. If the water goes cold, we'll boil some more."

I laughed when I realized I sounded nothing like him.

Flipping to another random page deep within the book, I started reading again, pacing the floor. "When you compare the sorrows of real life to the pleasures of the imaginary one, you will never want to live again, only to dream forever."

My lips parted as I considered the words. My shoulders shrunk back, and unshed tears made my eyes burn as I swiped at them and prepared to close the book. This was just wasting time, I thought. I needed to begin working on the list Evelyn had left.

I snapped the book shut but froze when I noticed something strange. A curious piece of loose-leaf paper had been tucked between the yellowed, frayed edges of the novel. I opened the book to the section that housed the document, which was folded in half. I opened it and gasped when I realized that I was face to face with Mr. Cooper's peculiar penmanship. I read the first words and crumbled to the ground.

My dearest Carole...

My eyes squinted. I read the line again.

My dearest Carole...

My breath hitched and stung my chest.

I miss you as soon as you're gone...

My neck snapped back and my vision blurred. My fingers tightened around the edges of the antique paper and my eyes searched the page, trying to read more, but I couldn't see anything.

Suddenly, the door opening averted my attention.

"Nurse Nancy." It was Sharon.

I re-folded the letter with trembling hands and shoved it in the pocket of my scrubs. It felt like I had shoved a brick back there.

"Jesus, Sharon, you startled me," I said, rubbing my hands together. My heart was pounding. I scurried back over to the desk and continued to tidy it. "Was there something you wanted?"

"Yes, there was." She looked behind her and pushed the door to a close before taking a step into the room. She paused. "I wanted to say thank you."

"Thank you? For what?"

"For what you did yesterday."

I moved a humongous arrangement of flowers in the center of the table, trying to get my mind off the letter so I could attend to what she was saying. "There's no need to thank me, Sharon. I told you, I'm not here for your job."

"I know," she said. "I mean, I know that now." She watched me struggle for a second before walking up to the table and helping me to reposition the arrangement. We worked together in silence then stood back to look at each other.

"I was rude to you yesterday," she admitted. "There was no need for it. My mother raised me better than that."

I smiled and leaned against the table, folding my shaking arms across my chest.

"Apology accepted," I said. "Hopefully, it'll all get better from here on." I swallowed, thinking again about the letter I'd just discovered.

Sharon smiled and walked over to the cabinet where I'd seen her preparing Evelyn's tea; however, instead of Earl Grey, she pulled out a carafe filled with a rich, dark liquid. She selected two tumblers and filled each of them halfway. Setting them down on the table, she dropped into a chair with a sigh.

"So do you want to know the scoop on the Coopers, or what?" She put her feet up on the table and took a swig from one of the tumblers.

I snickered and sat down across from her, pulling the remaining glass close. "It sounds like this is going to be good," I said. My insides quivered with nerves, so I took a sip of the beverage and tried to adjust to the burning sensation as it went down my throat.

"Where do I begin?' She tapped her chin. "Evelyn Cooper is a very proud woman, but I think you figured that much out already."

"I think so," I agreed.

"That's how it may appear, but underneath that saditty façade, the woman is very insecure."

"What do you mean?"

"The united front that she puts on with Mr. C. is just that...a *front*. He doesn't really love her, Nancy. Ray Charles can see that much. And why would he? She's pompous and rude, not to mention a complete bitch. The only reason I done put up with her crap for these last two years is because I need the paycheck. I'm working on my Associate's degree."

"Good for you, Sharon," I commended her.

Her chest puffed out. "Yes ma'am. Finished my GED and working on the next piece of paper. I can't afford to not work. But as soon as I can find something else, you can bet your boots I'll be outta here before the wicked witch of the south can bat her pretty little eyelashes."

"I'm so happy to hear about the goals you've set for yourself," I said. "But I do feel bad for Evelyn. It must be horrible to be in an unhappy relationship."

"She's happy enough," Sharon clarified.

"But I thought you said—"

"She's not the one you need to be concerned about. It's Mr. C. you should really be feeling sorry for." Sharon threw her head back and finished what was in her glass. "Now, I don't know the full story," Sharon said, leaning in, "but apparently there's another woman."

"What makes you say that?" I picked up my glass and put it to my mouth.

"No one has ever seen her, of course..."

"Then if there's no evidence..."

"But he's talked about her. To Gerald. You can't get a good word out of Gerald, though. That's why he and Mr. C. are so close, but there's some woman that Mr. C. has been pining over for quite a while."

I swallowed the rest of my drink, wondering who the other woman could be and what Gerald knew. "Does Evelyn know about it?"

"I think so," she said, "but because there's never been any *evidence*, the most she's been able to do is try and live up to some unspoken standard. Hence the insecurity and the overbearing nature." Sharon stared into the distance. "It's all pretty sad, when you really think about it, huh?"

I looked down at my empty cup and thought about Evelyn's faux bravado. Here was a woman facing the battle of a lifetime while trying to prove to her husband that she was good enough. It was very sad, indeed.

Sharon pushed her chair back and collected our glasses. "I need to get back to work," she said, "and you should too. I don't want another night like last night to happen. That meeting was so intense."

I stood on wobbly legs. "It certainly was. Like I said, hopefully things will get better, especially now that you've given me some more insight into the complicated woman."

Sharon found a tray and put the empty glasses on it before heading for the library door.

"We've got a few days without her," she said, turning back to look at me. "That's plenty of time to chat and learn more. In the meantime, If you need help with anything . . ."

"Sharon, you've got your own work to do," I said with a smile. "I can handle my to-do list, and I can handle Mrs. Cooper. But if I need anything, I'll be sure to call you. And you don't hesitate to do the same, okay?"

Sharon nodded, her mouth pressed together, and then she walked out.

When the coast was clear, I fell back into the empty seat and reflected on the information I'd received, both from Sharon and from deep within the pages of The Count of Monte Cristo. I rested my hand on the pocket in which I had shoved the old paper, and my shoulders crumbled. I had mounted my pedestal and preached to Evelyn about strength and vulnerability, but now I felt like a hypocrite. I was in over my head.

24

WILLIAM

FLORIDA, 1978

This would make my eighth time seeing Scott in person. I had started counting. A few years ago, when Miss Carole had twisted my arm and forced me to meet him for the first time, I never imagined I would stay in contact. He'd taken me up on my initial offer to help him with algebra, and before I knew it, it had become something else.

This.

It was our standing appointment.

I'd buy him a plane ticket and we'd meet somewhere new every time. It was my way of exposing him to the world outside of New York where he and his mother were stationed. He was Naomi's son so it was the least I could do, I told myself.

I was used to him by now, even if his appearance changed every time I saw him. That first night, in the restaurant, he'd been tall, lanky, and awkward, almost like his arms were too long and his head too big. Now, at twenty-three years old, he was a man and he looked different. He had filled out and finally grown into his head and limbs. His arms were thick and strong looking. He might be described as strapping, like a football player. Or maybe a basketball player, neither of which he was interested in becoming. It was cliché and stereotypical, he told me. That was all white people ever expected black boys to become. It was a good thing I hadn't suggested either of them as a possible career option.

This year, we were in Florida sitting on a porch under a huge umbrella at a beach-front restaurant. It was our first time meeting since Miss Carole had died and the atmosphere was jaded, like there were a million elephants in the room and we were snaking our way through them. We'd been doing the small-talk thing for the past twenty minutes. There hadn't even been this much small talk when we first met.

I sipped my vodka through a too-small straw. "There's something on your mind," I said.

Scott grunted. "You think you know me now, huh?"

"We've been meeting long enough," I said. "I think it's safe to say I know a good bit about you." I tilted my head to the side. "So, let's have it. What's on your mind?"

He sipped his Long Island Iced Tea and licked his lips. "Truth is, I shouldn't have anything to say to you," he said, looking past me.

I glanced over my shoulder and got a glimpse of what had caught his eye. Three women walked past. One offered him a sweet smile as she tucked a strand of hair behind her ear.

Scott smirked and turned his eyes back on me. He rolled them as if he was bored.

"So you're into girls now?"

"*Now*?" He snickered. "I'm a grown man, Mr. William. I've been into girls since the day we met in Beaufort. I was into girls last year. And the one before that," he said, pulling the thickening tuft of brown hair on his chin and twirling it around his finger.

"You got a girlfriend, then?"

"Maybe."

I shifted in the seat. I didn't like his quick responses and the trivial talk was starting to get on my nerves. "So, I'll ask again, I don't mind. What you got to say to me?"

"I already told you, I shouldn't even be talking to you right now," he said again. "That's what my mama says anyway."

I put the straw to my lips. "Your mother?" I snorted. "You told your mother about our meetings?"

"No, she doesn't know about them," he said, sighing. "I tell her I'm going over a friend's house for the weekend, and she never asks any questions when I get home. She'd kill me if she ever found out, though." He stared at me. "But that's what she says about you. She says she's not speaking to you ever again."

That was funny, I thought. She was acting as if we had spoken since she'd absconded from my life.

"She's angry that you didn't come to the funeral," he continued.

"How do you know that?"

"Are you kidding? She dogged you out for two weeks straight. Wouldn't stop."

"That must have been comical," I said, unable to restrain myself. "I would have loved to have been a fly on the wall for that!"

Scott chuckled and so did I.

"Well, she didn't come to my father's funeral the year before, so it's one for one, as far as I'm concerned."

"You wanna' know what I think? Both of you are acting like kids," Scott mumbled, shaking his head.

I sighed. "Maybe you're right. Listen, Scott. The truth is, I regret not going to the funeral. Your grandmother, Miss Carole...she was a very special woman to me. Sometimes I wonder if I made a mistake not bidding her farewell."

"So why didn't you show up?" Scott placed his glass down on the table and the cutlery shifted. "I know you said you had a business meeting and everything, but I figured you would have at least..." He shook his head and scratched the side of his face. His hands balled into fists. "Whatever, Mr. William. Listen, you know me. I'm cool about it. I mean, I'm not *cool* about it, but I can get over it. My mom though..." He laughed. It sounded like he'd pushed it out from the bowels of his stomach.

I pressed my finger on the tip of the straw and looked at the indentation it had made on my skin. "Business shouldn't have kept me away, Scott," I said. I looked up at him. "And about your mother, with all due respect, your mother and I...we're not on the best of terms."

"You ain't telling me anything I didn't already know."

"I haven't spoken to her in so long. *Years*. She doesn't want anything to do with me. My not coming to the funeral wouldn't have made a difference in the things she says about me or even how she feels."

"I still don't get that," he muttered.

"Get what?"

"She hates your guts," he said. "She says she can't stand the thought of you. She wants you under a moving train." He had been looking at his hands, but now he looked up at me. "She walks around the house like a zombie, feet dragging, wearing the same dirty house-coat. I don't even think she washes it."

Silence.

"In fact, I know she doesn't. I've started washing my own clothes now because I don't know when she's going to do them."

The thought of Naomi bedraggled and depressed shredded my insides, and in an instant, a primal desire to find and protect her rose up on the inside of me.

She was so close yet so far away, I thought. All I had to do was ask Scott to tell me where he lived and I'd have access to her, but the conversation never came up.

It was best this way anyway. We had both moved on. Her problems were not my problems anymore. And if you asked her, they never had been.

"You shouldn't be having her wash your clothes anymore anyway," I said, content to shift the angle of discussion. "You're twenty-three. You got hair on your balls, don't you?"

Scott burst into laughter and after a second, I laughed too.

We spent the next few hours eating and laughing, the way we had come to do, before we jumped into a taxi and headed for the airport.

"So where we meeting next time, Mr. William?" he asked, adjusting his backpack on his shoulders.

"Where have we been so far? I'm not keeping track."

Scott started counting off on his fingers. "L.A., Connecticut, Puerto Rico—"

"How about we do Vegas next time," I suggested, cutting him off. "Who knows? Maybe you'll hit the jackpot and strike it rich! That'll pay for law school next year."

Scott smiled. "Oh! Speaking of striking it rich..." He dug into his pocket and pulled out a wad of cash.

"What's this for?"

"The ticket you bought me for the funeral," he said, flipping through it. "Remember, I said I'd pay you back."

I ran my fingers through my hair. "I don't need your money, Scott."

"I know you don't need it, but I owe it to you. A man has to pay his debts. Plus, I got a job and the pay is pretty good so..." He extended his hand.

"Fine," I said, snatching it from him and shoving it into my jeans pocket.

We engaged in a firm handshake and he started to walk away.

I watched him shuffle through the crowd, his cumbersome backpack threatening to knock people over. He was still a kid, I thought. A kid without a father; a kid with a mother who was down in the dumps.

Suddenly, my throat grew dry and the skin around my eyes tightened. I opened my mouth to say something, but then I closed it again, staring after him until he threatened to blend completely into the masses.

"Scott!" I shouted.

His backpack slammed into someone as he swung around.

I started shoving my way through the wall of people to meet him.

His eyebrows were bunched. "Yeah?" he shouted back. "What is it?"

I pushed through a few more people before I caught up with him. Now that I was standing in front of him, I didn't know what I wanted to say. I mean, I knew what I wanted to say, but I didn't know how I should say it.

"I've been thinking about it. For a long time," I said. "I know you wonder who your father is. It's probably been bothering you since that time we met in the restaurant with your grandmother."

Scott's head dropped and he rubbed the back of his neck. "Mr. William—"

"I'm going to help you."

"Help me with what?"

I rested my hand on his shoulder. "Help you *find* him."

Scott's mouth went tight and his shoulders slumped. "I already did," he said. "I found him."

I pulled my hand back. "What? I mean, when?"

"Seven months ago. My mother and I had a heart to heart...well, that's what she called it." He shook his head like he was trying to get the memory out. "Anyway...She finally told me his name. Some guy named Danny Hightower. They hooked up the week before she left for college, and she hasn't seen him since."

I shoved my hands into my pockets so hard they almost came through the fabric.

Scott shrugged, oblivious to my agony. "Apparently, she's tried to track him down but hasn't been able to."

"Have you tried looking him up in the telephone directory?"

Scott pushed his lips out. "Really, Mr. William? The telephone directory?"

"Well, why not?"

"So how would that work? I look up and call every Danny Hightower in the book and ask if they had a child with a woman named Naomi Jackson?"

"Maybe not..." I said.

Scott shrugged. "Besides, I already looked. There are only six Hightowers in the local directory, but when I picked up the telephone to call the first one, I couldn't do it." A lopsided smile spread over his face.

I rubbed my temple and my eyelids fluttered, but I fixed a smile on my face the best I could. "Well, I'm glad you found your father, son."

Scott shrugged. "I didn't *find* him..."

"You know what I mean," I said and sighed. "You're a great kid, Scott. You deserve the best that life has to offer. I'm really glad things are looking up for you." I put a jab on his arm. "Everything is gonna be just fine."

"Thanks," he said, rubbing the spot and offering me a tight-lipped smile as he adjusted his backpack. "I gotta run," he said. "Next year. Same time, different place?"

"No doubt." I smiled and watched him disappear into the billowing crowd before yanking myself from the fog in my head and heading toward my terminal.

25

NAOMI

BEAUFORT, S.C., 1996

I dug my pink scrubs out of the hamper and pulled the folded note from the pocket. I'd been in possession of the document for two days, but only now did I have the courage to look at it and see what it was really all about. I hadn't been able to stop thinking about it since its discovery. The questions and memories it evoked were almost debilitating. There were so many things I needed to be doing, yet knowing there was a letter that William's father had written to my mother hindered my performance.

It was late at night, and the lamp from the desk cast an eerie glow about the room. As I walked over to the window and slid the lemon curtains open, I drew in a breath of courage, then returned to the table and attempted to finish reading the letter Mr. Cooper had written:

My dearest Carole,

I miss you as soon as you're gone. Mere words cannot express the way I feel about you. I know it hasn't been easy for us. The secrets we've kept and the lies we've told have eroded your confidence in me as a man; as your lover.

Looking up from the letter, tears obstructing my vision, I walked over to the nightstand and pulled a tissue out of the box. Sitting back at the desk, I dabbed at my eyes and continued to read.

I cannot promise you that things will change, but I can promise you that one thing will remain the same: I will never stop loving you. I vow to protect you from anyone who will seek to hurt you. I know why you did what you did. There was no way you could have given birth to the gift that God had given us, but I want you to know that I hurt just as much as you hurt. Maybe even more.

I lurched backward, staring at the yellowing paper and fading words.

"Mama was pregnant?"

I searched my mind, trying to conjure up any long-lost images of my mother with morning sickness. She worked hard and was rarely ill. I couldn't recall a scenario. What about with a big belly? Of course not! If she'd had an abortion, I'd never have seen that either.

Frustration began to set in. I didn't want to read anymore. I didn't think I could stomach it, but the compulsion to continue was too strong.

If we lived in a perfect world, our love would have been perfect, but regrettably, we must make do with what we have be given. It's not much in comparison to what I want to give you, but I will give you all of it; unashamedly, without reservation...

The end of the page.

I was sucking at the air trying to catch my breath, but a mounting pressure started making my head tight. I grabbed my temples. Pushing the chair back with force, I slid away from the desk until I crashed against the corner of the room and smashed the tissue against my face to catch the sobs lifting from my throat. Questions rolled through my brain like waves on top of a disturbed ocean.

Who had written that letter? Wait, I knew the answer to that. Mr. Cooper's handwriting was unmistakable. *Who had he written the letter to?* I knew the answer to that too. My mother's name was as clear as day in it. So what was left to ask? Everything had been made plain. The facts were evident. So why did I feel more in the dark now than ever before?

I pulled my robe across my back and made my way to the library. There had to be more, I thought. If Mr. Cooper and my mother had an affair going on, there was no way he would have only written one letter.

Returning to the shelf where I'd found the book in which the letter had been hidden, I started ripping books off one by one, flipping through their pages, looking for evidence, clues, anything. The distinct sound of fanning pages filled the room as I scoured the books. Tears blinded my progress. I threw useless literature to the ground. But, book after book, page after page, there was nothing more.

I looked at the corner where Mr. Cooper used to sit, tall and stately. His brown hair combed back, not one strand out of place. I could see him sitting there with me at his feet.

I closed my eyes as pain shredded me. Opening them, I walked to the corner and ran my hand over the undulating rows of book spines. His energy blasted me: Pleasant, anxious, kind, frustrated.

Slowly, I pulled one book off the shelf and dropped it to the ground. My eyes widened. An old, wooden box was tucked at the very back, shoved against the bookshelf like a forgotten ornament. My heart clamored against my ribcage as I reached in and grabbed it. A silver latch with a lock had meant to secure it, but the lock hadn't been closed. My fingers toyed with the lock. I wanted to flip the lid open, but something was holding me back. Was I emotionally prepared to know more about the truth of my past? Could I handle the uncovering of even more secrets?

Suddenly, a light from somewhere in the house clicked on, followed by the muffled sound of distant footsteps. My fingers tightened around the box as a blast of cold breeze whipped through my body. I'd had enough for one night, I thought. Panicked, I looked at the floor, messy with books, and hastily started sliding them back into their spots. Then, I hurried back to my quarters and sealed the door behind me.

NAOMI

BEAUFORT, S.C., 1996

The days flew by faster than I'd expected them to, and in no time at all, the car was pulling up outside the house with Evelyn perched in the back seat. Her shoulders were not as erect as they'd been in the library during our meeting. They slumped a little, almost as if waterlogged from her ordeal. Without makeup, I could see pomegranate-red swells under her eyes. Even the jet-black wig looked limp, as if tired of its performance. Her lipstick-less lips were pushed out and her eyebrows slanted downward toward the tip of her pointy nose.

Sharon and I stood on the top step as I squinted ahead, like the sun was in my eyes even though it wasn't. My mouth was pinched together as I braced myself for round two. I'd almost lost round one, but I'd be damned if I let William or his witch of a wife make me a quitter.

Sharon's eyes were fixed on the car, but she addressed me. "Has everything been taken care of inside?"

I nodded, my eyes still focused ahead. "Yup," I said. "Lunch ready, bath drawn, bedcovers pulled back."

Sharon's eyes shot to my face. "Did you pull the left corner down in a right angle?"

I patted the air. "Of course I did," I said, smiling. "Your lessons were not in vain. You said we were in this together. That means I need to be a good student."

"Cheesums," she said, looking ahead again. "The way you're performing, my job might really be in jeopardy." She nudged me playfully. We giggled but settled down as the sleek, black car came to a halt. William and Gerald exited first.

I fixed my shoulders straight.

William's nose was stuck in his cell phone, but he looked up and his gaze seized mine.

Today, he was wearing a navy suit, fitted to expensive perfection.

I swallowed and bit the inside of my lip. I could smell him from the steps. *Jasmine and vanilla...Bergamot...Musk...*

"Shall I get her from the car?" Sharon asked, breaking the connection.

I ripped my eyes off him. "We should both go," I said. "I don't want it to be said that I didn't do my job."

Sharon nodded.

We stepped off the porch and reached the car just as Gerald was helping Evelyn out of the back seat. I hooked my arm under her left one as Sharon took the right.

"Welcome home, Mrs. Cooper," I said with a frozen smile. "How are you feeling?"

"How am I feeling? I feel like I have stage four breast cancer, Nancy. I feel like I had radiation therapy. I feel like they cut my breast off. What kind of a ridiculous question is that?" She huffed. "I would expect a little more tact from a highly recommended nurse," she spat.

"Of course," I said, opting for anything other than my preferred response. "It's been a long few days for you. How about we get you upstairs and settled."

"That would be nice," she mumbled. "It was horrible at the hospital. The meals you had delivered were good, but I expected a little more variety."

I inhaled. "I selected items from the menu you provided," I said.

"Yes, well, perhaps we should review that. We will need another meeting to review how things have progressed."

"Let's worry about getting some rest right now, Mrs. Cooper. I imagine you're exhausted."

Sharon and I tried to hoist Evelyn up from the car as she groaned and grunted with each and every movement.

"Where is my husband?" she demanded, dissatisfied with our efforts. Suddenly, she burst into tears and William raced over to the commotion. My body brushed against his as he reached out for his wife. A charged current zipped through me at the brief contact. I backed away from them.

"Everything is alright, sweetheart," he said, gathering her into his arms. He turned to Sharon. "She's very emotional. She's a strong girl, but this one really took her to the limit. I'll handle it from here."

I moved to the side of the car.

William turned and nodded to Gerald. "Take her things up to the house," he instructed. "Sharon, if you wouldn't mind preparing her an afternoon snack." I waited for him to issue me an instruction, but he turned silent.

I squared my shoulders in an attempt to be unaffected by his coolness. I flexed my fingers and looked at Gerald, who was the only one who seemed to be paying me any attention. "I'll go and prepare her bed," I said.

Evelyn's head whipped around so fast that the black hair fell loose over one of her mascara-stained eyes. "Prepare my bed? It's not already done?" She groaned like a terrible two-year-old. "I specifically instructed you to be prepared for my arrival and this is what I get? The least you could've done was have my bed made."

William glared at me. The muscle in his jaw flexed. "Is her bed made, Na...Nancy?" he whispered.

"Of course her goddamn bed is made," I whispered back through tight teeth. "Who the hell do you think I am?" I spun around and marched up the steps into the house, through to Evelyn's bedroom. I closed the door just as tears began to pour down my face.

"I'm not gonna cry," I said over and over until they stopped. I rushed to the bathroom and splashed water on my face, then I ripped through the medicine cabinet, looking for anything I could put into my eyes that would take the red out. When I found something suitable, I tilted my head back and squeezed the contents of the tiny bottle into each eye until it had been drained. Then, I stared into the mirror until the red disappeared and walked back into the spacious bedroom.

The bed in question stood before me, and I forced my muscles to relax. It had been perfectly prepared with fresh linen, turned down at a ninety-degree angle on the left-hand side. I walked over and ran my hand over the bedspread, just in case there was a wrinkle I'd missed.

My mother would have been proud...

I grimaced at the thought.

My eyes drifted to the vase of fresh roses that had arrived that morning. I'd placed it carefully in the center of the bureau so Evelyn would be able to see it even when she was lying down. The small card sticking out from the middle of it caught my eye, and I walked over and picked it up.

'I love you, forever.'

It was in William's penmanship. He still wrote his 'y's the same way, with an extra curl on the tail. Fresh tears blurred my vision. I shoved the note back into its envelope and replaced it in the vase just as the door flew open and Evelyn entered, supported by her two bodyguards, William and Gerald.

When William saw the room, his face relaxed and then fell. He tried to look at me, but I avoided eye contact. There was no point for us to connect on.

I walked over to the window and pushed it up a little further, allowing a warm, fresh breeze to flow inside the bedroom.

"The room looks lovely, Evvie. I told you there would be nothing to worry about," I heard him say to his wife.

She grunted.

I walked over to the bed as they escorted her closer and pulled the covers back. As William lowered her to the bed, I helped her into it, making sure she was comfortable. Lifting the linen to her chin and offering a polite smile, I walked over to the bureau where a steaming pot of lemongrass tea waited for her.

"I like it sweet, Nancy," she said.

"I know. Three and a half sugars."

Evelyn looked at me sideways and slid the wig off her head with a trembling hand. The wig fell to the floor, and I stared at it for a second before picking it up and placing it on a mannequin head next to the pot of tea.

Huffing, Evelyn laid her head back against the pillow and snuggled against it.

After setting the cup of tea down next to Mrs. Cooper's side of the bed, I strode over to the corner of the room where I had prepared my medical supplies and dragged a tray over to the bed. The squeaking sound of the wheels navigating through the carpet pile filled the room.

From an untraditional hot-pink bag, I pulled out my stethoscope and slung it around my neck. In my periphery, I saw William staring at me, and I was more aware than ever of how his presence grated against my nerves.

"If you could sit up, Mrs. Cooper..." I instructed. "Just a little."

"Do I really have to? You watched me struggle to get comfortable and didn't offer to help. Now, you want me to sit up?"

"Evelyn..." William warned as he stood back.

I inhaled and pulled out a thermometer. I placed it under her tongue, then pushed up her sleeve and strapped a blood pressure monitor around her arm. I started pumping the end of the device. "Where's the file?" I asked behind me to William.

"You mean you haven't spoken to the doctor yet?" Evelyn asked. "There's an updated file. I've been in the hospital for almost a week. Surely some communication between you and the hospital staff should have occurred during that time."

My jaw clenched, but I fixed a smile on my face nonetheless. "I've spoken to your doctor many times," I said. "The most recent time being this morning. We had a verbal discussion, but I would like to review the notes in your chart. That's what professionals do." I threw the comment out there.

William shifted his weight from one foot to the other. "It's in her bag," he said.

I nodded to Sharon who went and retrieved it.

I pulled the thermometer from her mouth and then reviewed the reading on the blood pressure monitor. Grimacing, I pulled it off her arm.

"Your blood pressure is low," I said.

"I know."

"We'll work on raising that. I'll bring your meds with your lunch."

Sharon handed me the file, and I added a written note under the last. I stuck the pen through my ponytail and pulled the covers back from her chest. "I need to do a brief exam," I informed her. "I'll be applying pressure to your abdomen. You need to tell me if you feel any pain."

I slid the top of her shirt up and started pressing against her soft flesh. She winced a few times, but didn't say anything. "Does this hurt?" I asked.

"What do you think?" she snapped.

William took a step toward the bed. "Evvie, just answer the questions," he said.

I bit the inside of my lip, pulled the pen out of my hair and wrote another note. As I attempted to lift the shirt up further to inspect her surgical wound, with a strength that surprised me, she gripped my wrist.

"What do you think you're doing?"

"I need to see the wound," I informed her. "I need to monitor its progress as it heals."

"You think you would've told me that before you tried to invade my privacy," she said. "Some professional you are."

I ripped my hand from her grasp and stood back. The skin on my face felt like I'd had plastic surgery. "Mrs. Cooper, I am here to take care of you. You've not been the easiest patient so far and I've tolerated it. However, I'm not willing to take jabs about my bedside manner or professional composure."

"Nancy," William said, reaching out to me.

I sidestepped him.

"No, Mr. Cooper. I don't need you to intervene. I'm a big girl now. I can advocate for myself, just fine."

Evelyn narrowed her eyes.

I huffed. "I'm going to take a walk," I said. "I need a moment."

Evelyn sat upright in the bed and audibly winced. "Now you wait one minute," she demanded, flicking her wrist. "Your schedule doesn't indicate a break. There are things that need to be done around here. The dogs are dying to be walked. I hope to God they haven't messed the house!"

"Evelyn, your tone is not warranted," William said.

I held my hand up. "The dogs have had their morning walk, Mrs. Cooper," I said. "We were all up bright and early at five-thirty, and both of them shit on the sidewalk just outside the fence. I know because I picked it up with the pooper scooper."

She gasped. "Well I never!"

"Now, I am going for my walk, and no one is going to stop me. I'll be back when I have calmed down."

My shoes left imprints in the perfectly vacuumed carpet as I marched through the hall. My mind raced. There was no way I could do much more of this, I thought. How had my mother done it? Day in and out; the degradation and negativity? And William; how could he side with his wife seeing how her behavior was affecting me and everyone else on staff?

Other than the airport, there was only one place I could think of where I would find peace. The dock.

The sound of Evelyn's bedroom door closing interrupted my thoughts.

"Nancy," William called out.

I didn't answer.

"Nancy!" he called again.

My pace quickened.

"Naomi!" he whispered forcefully.

"Shh," I said. "Don't let your wife hear you call me by my real name. Your secret will be blown, just like it was when we were kids."

I kept walking but could feel his presence closing in on me. As he reached out to grab my arm, I stopped and yanked it out of his grasp.

He scrubbed his hands over his face. "Where are you going?"

"You're talking to me now? After ignoring me for almost a week and a half?"

"You're being ridiculous," he seethed.

I grunted. "Am I?"

We stared at each other.

"You don't have to talk to her like that, Naomi. She's dying."

"And that's a good enough excuse for you, isn't it? Because she's knocking on death's door, that's a reason for her to talk to people any way she pleases? You make me want to spit," I said, shaking my head. "I don't know who's worse, her or you."

His shoulders slumped. "I'm trying," he whispered in my face. "You told me to be a good man."

"So that's what this is? Is this what you thought I meant when I made the suggestion? You're throwing me under the bus to make up for the years you lost not being a good husband? You're so pathetic!"

"I would *never* throw you under the bus."

"It's like déjà vu. I'm the sacrificial lamb...*again*. You did the same thing when your mother found us together. You're always so quick to save your own ass, you never take the time to stop and think about my emotions."

He pointed at me, glaring. "Don't you dare do that," he said. I watched the rise and fall of his chest. "That night was just as traumatic for me as it was for you, and it's not fair for you to throw it in my face like this. I promised you that I would defend us and I did."

"Well, you're not doing it now," I said, taking a feeble step backwards. "But there is no us..." My eyes fell to the floor as the words reverberated in my ears. Tears filled my chest, making it tight.

"There's always an *us*," he contradicted me. "That's the problem. I can't stop loving you."

My thoughts traveled to the letter I'd discovered, and I backed away from him.

"Nay, this is just as hard for me as it is for you. What do you expect me to do?

Give me the solution to the problem and I'll do it."

"There's nothing you *can* do," I said, thinking about his father's words to my mother. This was our destiny, I thought. This was the only way it could play out. My mother and his father had been evidence of that. I needed to accept it.

"Naomi..."

"William, please," I begged. "Just...leave me alone."

"Fine." He nodded. "I won't bother you anymore."

27

NAOMI

BEAUFORT, S.C., 1996

*I*t was late afternoon when I finally raised myself from the dock and considered heading back to Evelyn's quarters. I had been out there for hours, pondering my present circumstances; trying to overcome my emotional instability and strengthen my resolve. I was a mess. I hated William for what he was doing. I was angry at him for not being able to stand up for me the way I thought he should have. But somehow, I loved him. I loved him just as much now as I had when I was a girl. And for that, I hated myself.

I wondered if my mama had ever hated herself.

I wondered how she had done it—day in and out—serving the wife of the man who loved her; the man she loved...

I pushed air out of my nostrils.

The sun was heading westward, beginning its slow descent behind the oak trees, and the family of ducks I'd spied on all afternoon had long disappeared beyond the glade. I looked at my watch. It was four-thirty. The glassy lake at the edge of the property had offered me the serenity I desperately longed for, and I'd gratefully accepted it. Ingesting the sights and sounds of nature had soothed my tortured soul. It was enough to refocus me and strengthen my resolve. The only variable I could control in this triangle was me. I had to conquer my emotions and maintain my composure.

It was time to go back inside and finish the job I had started.

I tapped my knuckles against the door and waited. No one answered, so I slid the door open and peeked inside just in time to see Evelyn struggling to hoist herself out of the bed. I rushed in to assist.

"Mrs. Cooper, you shouldn't be trying to move around on your own," I scolded her, linking my arm through hers and repositioning her on the bed. "You're in the throes of recovery. You're not strong enough to do these kinds of things."

"No one was here to help me, so I had to do it myself," she grumbled. "You've been gone for hours, and Sharon is on her break."

"That doesn't negate the facts," I challenged her.

She glared at me with wavering eyes.

I stared back.

"Now," I said, "how about we pick up where we left off? I'm going to check your vitals and do an examination of the surgical site. As I mentioned, I need to clean it and make sure it's healing properly."

Evelyn rolled her eyes. "Well, let's get on with it," she said. "We don't have all day and I'm hungry. I'm ready for a snack."

I retrieved my tools from my tray, which had been pushed to the side, and placed the thermometer under her tongue. I strapped the blood pressure monitor around her arm and pumped it, looking at the meter. "Systolic blood pressure is 110 mmHg. Diastolic blood pressure is 70 mmHg," I muttered. I looked up at her. "Like I said, your blood pressure is low." I looked at the thermometer, which indicated she had a slight fever. I put the tools back on my tray and wrote a note in her chart. "Now," I said. "Let's get that examination underway."

I paused. "I'm going to press on your abdomen and I want you to tell me if there's any pain." I proceeded with the examination and Evelyn cooperated without complaint.

"How was that?" I asked.

"It was fine," she said. "A little tender."

"Which is to be expected," I said. "Your body is in recuperation mode. You'll be tender for a while. Now for the wound." I touched the edge of her pajama top and paused. "Are you ready?"

Evelyn's mouth went tight. I sighed and sat on the edge of the bed next to her. "I know this isn't easy," I said, gently placing my hand over her arm.

"How would you know?" she questioned me. "You're not the one with one breast. You're healthy and...beautiful...How can you possibly know what I'm going through?"

"I may not have breast cancer, but I can imagine how degrading this must be for you," I snapped. "You feel vulnerable and uncertain. You've been thrust into this scary situation and it's taking a toll on you. I *get* that."

We were silent for many minutes. Finally, Evelyn inhaled and her shoulders rounded. "I am afraid," she whispered, and then she laughed. "I don't recall the last time I've been afraid of anything, and that makes everything even more scary."

I looked at her and noticed tears on her pale face. I reached for a tissue from my bag and handed it to her, but she pushed my hand away. I crumpled the unwanted tissue in my fist as she smeared tears across her cheek and looked up at the ceiling.

"Now, I'm not afraid to die," she clarified. "I reckon I'll be at peace when I do. What I'm really afraid of is what people will say about me after I'm dead and gone. I wonder what I'll be remembered for. They'll say all sorts of wonderful things at my funeral, I'm sure of that. But what will be in their hearts?"

I shifted on the bed as she continued.

"Before I go to bed every night, I say my prayers. I ask the good Lord to forgive me for my sins and to help me to forgive others for the things they've done to me. I wake up every morning and vow to do good things for people. I give to charities, and I hire people who are good and honest and need a good wage. But somehow, I always think it isn't enough. I think I've hurt a few people, Nancy." She gulped in air. "I've hurt people who are really close to me, and I don't know how to fix it. I don't even know where to begin."

My eyes fluttered as I ran my hand over my ponytail. "Sometimes, it's hard to admit when you've been wrong and say you're sorry," I said, carefully considering my words. "I've had to apologize to my son." I paused. "In fact, there are still some things I need to say sorry for, and that's gonna be real tough. I keep putting it off, but I can't forever."

I turned to look at her and was surprised to find her staring at me. The intensity behind her eyes was unsettling. My eyes moved away from hers.

"Maybe we have more in common than we think." Evelyn smiled, and an awkwardness permeated the room. Unable to conjure an appropriate response, I raised myself from the bed and went over to her teapot to prepare some more lemongrass tea.

"Let's make a deal, Nurse Nancy," she suggested, suddenly.

"Now, this sounds interesting," I said with a chuckle.

Evelyn tried to adjust herself against the pillows. I bought the steaming teacup over and assisted her.

"How about...we both apologize to the people we love...together?"

I exhaled and rubbed the back of my neck, which was now burning. "That's pretty heavy," I said. "How would we do that?"

"We'll give ourselves a deadline and hold each other accountable," she said. "We don't have much time, though. Let's say we do it by the end of the week, huh? I'll call Ethan and you call your son, whatever his name is."

"Fine," I agreed. "It's Tuesday, so that gives us some time to get our scripts together so we can rehearse."

For the first time, Evelyn released a hearty laugh and I joined in. When a coughing spell interrupted our merriment, I rubbed her back and sat on the edge of the bed again. Evelyn then leaned back against the pillows with a sigh.

"Are you ready now?" I asked.

Evelyn nodded and closed her eyes. "Yes, I'm ready."

28

WILLIAM

BEAUFORT, S.C., 1996

*T*he wind whipped through my hair as I stood on the bow of the M2-42 and unwound the mainsail. I attached it to the mast and pulled at the line, hoisting it higher and higher into the air while Rob fed the other side into the track. Soon, the mainsail was billowing against a crisp, blue sky. Not wanting to waste time, we quickly did the same for the jib, and within minutes, the sloop was pointing against the wind and zipping away from the shoreline.

I positioned myself behind the steering wheel and inhaled the scent of the salty seawater.

"It would have been a lot easier to take the yacht," Rob whined from the other end of the boat.

"Today isn't a yacht day," I responded, guiding the craft easily against the chops. "Sailing is more fun when you have to do the work. Setting this baby up and getting her into the waves is like therapy for me."

Rob *hmphed.* "If you wanted to do work, you could have gone into the office." He inhaled and leaned back against the edge of the sloop, closing his eyes. "I gotta admit though, there's nothing like an impromptu sail on the day before your wedding."

My throat tightened. There were only a few hours left before I tied the knot around my neck and committed myself to something I wasn't really sold on. It was like a business deal I had a bad feeling about, but I was signing off on it anyway; it made no sense.

Suddenly, in the distance, a band of thick, black clouds manifested on the horizon. The seagulls, which had been gliding overhead, had disappeared, and a dense curtain of rain was advancing towards us. I grabbed the wheel with both hands and twisted it, making the sloop take a tight turn to the right.

"Rob!" I shouted his name above the whistling wind as the boat dipped to the side and water poured into the hull. "We've got to turn back. The weather has shifted!"

No response.

I twisted the wheel again and looked over at Rob, but there was no sign of him. I shouted his name again, wondering how he could have disappeared so quickly and to where.

Now the storm was on top of me.

Heavy raindrops pelted against my face, and flashes of forked lightening struck the surface of the angry ocean ahead of me. I twisted the wheel, left and right, trying to regain control.

"No..." I groaned as the boat became increasingly vulnerable to the tempest. "No! No!"

"Mr. C!"

Gerald was shaking me so hard the bed frame was rocking.

"Mr. Cooper, wake up. You all right?"

I jolted to an upright position and looked around the room, trying to figure out where I was. Beams of unrestricted light poured through the windows, and I rubbed my eyes against the brightness, trying to get my bearings. After a second, the blurriness cleared from my eyes and Gerald came into full view.

"Mr. C., wake up. You were having a bad dream."

I exhaled, wiping beads of sweat off my brow.

Gerald straightened his posture and marched over to the curtains, pulling them all the way open. "Are you all right, Mr. C.? The way you were thrashing around in that bed...I thought I was gonna have to call the medics for you."

"I'm fine," I said, dismissing his concern. "Like you said, it was nothing more

than a bad dream. I'm sure you've had a few of them."

He was shaking his head. "If you say so." He fiddled with the tangled curtain material on one side of the window, and I could tell he wanted to say more.

"What's on your mind, Gerald? I know you well. When was the last time you came into my bedroom to wake me out of a dream?"

"I guess I'm just a little concerned for you, that's all," he said, spinning around to look at me. "I mean, you seem stressed out. To tell the truth, you ain't been the same since that nurse woman arrived on the property."

My shoulders dropped and I fell back against the plush pillows on my bed, closing my eyes. If I had known that this was what he wanted to talk about, I would never have asked.

"I'm fine, Gerald. There's nothing for you to worry about."

"You say you're fine, but I'm not convinced." Gerald dragged an armchair from the corner of the room to the edge of the bed and plopped himself into it. He crossed his long legs at the knee and rested his arms on the sides of the chair. "You can't fool me, Mr. C. I mean...I done seen you stressed before." He put up his index finger and started counting off. "There was that time your in-laws popped in for a visit. You was drinkin' and smokin' like a vagabond on the street, and the kitchen had to restock the wine cellar three times in three weeks."

I held my forehead. "It was not three times—"

"Then there was the time Mrs. C. meddled in your business matters—"

"Do you always have to bring that up, Gerald?"

He continued like he didn't hear me. "You was *really* stressed that time. You were even contemplating calling your lawyer and advising him to draw up papers."

I groaned and pulled the covers over my head.

"And let's not forget the most recent time..."

"And what time was that?" I asked from under the sheets.

"The time with Ethan and his fiancée. You was stressed, and so was Ethan. Like I said, I've *seen* you stressed out." He paused. "But this seems different."

I peeked at Gerald from under the sheet and we fell silent.

He uncrossed his legs and leaned forward, lowering his voice to a whisper. "Last night, I heard Naomi in her room and she was sobbing."

My head shot up, and I stared Gerald in the face. My mouth slackened.

"How..." I moistened my lips. "Gerald, how on earth did you know?" I whispered.

Gerald sat back against the chair. His eyes looked wet. "How many stories have you told me about this woman? The one woman you've been desirin' since you was sixteen years old?" he asked. "Did you really think I wouldn't see it? That I wouldn't feel the connection the minute I met her?"

Tears stung my eyes as I ripped my gaze off him, unable to look at him any longer. Embarrassment threatened to consume me. I wanted to disappear.

"Why did you do it?" he asked.

"Do what?" I mumbled.

"Why did you ask her to come here? Why did you expose her to Evelyn?"

I pulled my trembling lip between my teeth. "It was the only thing I could think of to keep her near me when I bumped into her in Boston last month," I muttered. "It was selfish and self-serving, I know. But what else was I supposed to do? Lose her again?" I scratched the side of my face, trying to come to terms with my flaws; the flaws that had been in existence since I was a kid. Naomi was right when she said I hadn't changed. I wondered if it was too late to change. I also wondered how I could prove that I had changed.

Gerald sighed. "You're always so hard on yourself," he said.

I shook my hanging head. "No, I'm not, Gerald. I've made so many mistakes. I am hurting two women. How can you even fix your mouth to say something like that?"

"You're a good man, Mr. C.," he insisted. "You've been loyal to both of these women. You've stayed by Evelyn's side, in sickness and in health."

"That was the expectation when I married her," I said. "It's not noble."

"And Naomi...even after all these years, after all you've been through with her and her son, Scott, you still love her just the same as when you were kids."

My chin dipped down.

"And now, you're in a catch-twenty-two," he continued. "You've got the woman that you love and the woman that you're in love with under the same roof. What's a man to do?" He let the question sink in. "Now, I ain't sayin' you been entirely right in this situation. You let Evelyn treat that woman like a servant and you didn't come to her defense, not once."

"And how the hell was I supposed to do that?" I asked. "How am I supposed to stand up for Naomi without catching hell from Evelyn?"

"Well, I don't quite know," he admitted, throwing his hands up. "But part of me thinks that if your daddy were here, he might have had an answer for you. He was a good man. Your father had a noble character, and he never tolerated disrespect. He would have known what to do, I know it."

We fell silent, each of us lost in a reverie of historical reflection. I chewed on the inside of my lip.

Gerald broke the silence. "Scott called."

My eyes rose. I swallowed. "When?"

"Early this morning," Gerald said. "He asked me to tell you that his flight arrives in an hour. He needs someone to pick him up from the airport."

"His flight? His flight to where?"

"To Beaufort, sir," Gerald responded slowly, widening his eyes. "He's on his way here."

I PARKED my car and walked into the arrivals section just as Scott appeared through the sliding glass doors with a simple carry-on, wearing jeans, a button up, and a baseball cap. We met in the middle of the hall and embraced. He squeezed me tight.

"I know you're upset," he said by my ear.

I released him. "Upset is the biggest understatement of the year," I said. "What the hell are you doing here, and why didn't you tell me you were coming? A heads up would have been nice."

"I didn't tell you because you would have told me not to come," he said, swinging the carry-on over his shoulder. "I figured if I didn't ask, you wouldn't be able to say no."

I rolled my eyes and we exited the airport, heading toward my car. "Well you're here now," I said. "Where are you staying?"

"I got a room at the Hilton on Queen Street."

"The Hilton?" I grunted. "For a man as learned as yourself? Surely you could have afforded something a little more upscale," I suggested. "You're a goddamn lawyer, after all. You graduated years ago."

Scott threw his luggage into the back of the car and dipped into the passenger seat as I searched for the hotel address in the GPS.

"It was a spur-of-the-moment trip, and I don't plan to be here for long," he said. "But next time I'll be sure to follow your lead when it comes to accommodation."

"So to what do I owe the pleasure?" I asked, piggy-backing on his statement. "We're not due to be in Rio for another eight weeks."

"I know," he said, "but I got something to show you and it couldn't wait."

"A phone call wouldn't have sufficed?" I asked, glancing at him. "Don't get me wrong, I'm happy to see you. I'm always happy to see you, it's just that..." I ran my free hand over my head. "You're playing it close, Scott. You know I told you your mother is here looking after my wife at the moment. If she finds out that we know each other..."

"Well, maybe it's about time the truth came out, and I don't mean about her not being in China," he interrupted.

My head jerked around. "What are you talking about?"

"I mean it," he said. "For years, she's kept these secrets. For years, she's encouraged me to live my life without the truth." He paused. "Maybe it's time we made her a little uncomfortable." He reached into the back seat and pulled a notebook out of the carry-on.

My heart lurched. "What the hell is that?"

His fingers tightened around the edges of the book. "Maybe you should pull over," he said.

I glanced at him. "Why? What is it?"

His eyes started to glaze over.

My hands gripped the steering wheel. "Don't do this, Scott," I warned him. "The last time you did this, your grandmother was dying. Now is not the time for games. What's going on?"

He drew in a deep breath. "Last year we were in Naples for our annual trip," he said.

"Yeah..."

"We were at the Blue Martini and you had the signature drink, with the glow stick. Do you remember?"

"Of course I remember," I snapped, wishing he would get to the point. "You chided me for chewing on my straw."

Scott laughed. "No, I chided you for getting drunk and trying to pick up women." His smile faded. "My mother lied to me, Mr. William," he said. "She lied to us."

"About what?"

He fell silent yet again. When I looked at him, his mouth was bunched and his chin was wrinkled. "I practice family law, and I see this kind of shit all the time. Kids looking for their fathers...mothers being evasive..."

"Scott..."

"But for it to come to my door...for it to be *my* life? It's unacceptable."

"What is it?" I demanded. "What happened?"

Scott exhaled and opened the notebook.

My chest hitched. It was the same notebook he'd pulled out in the restaurant the day we first met. By now, more pages had been filled out. In fact, I could now see that he'd purchased two more notebooks just like it and bound them together as one. He flipped past pages and pages of pictures and diagrams and letters until he finally stopped.

The edges of my eyes crinkled as I tried to focus on the traffic at the same time as glancing at the book in his lap. "That's Danny Hightower," I muttered.

"So you knew him?"

I flicked on the indicator. I was pulling over. When the car came to a stop in a lay-by, I stared at the picture until it blurred. "Your mother knew him," I said. "He tried to date her when we were kids. She was adamant she was never interested in him and that nothing ever happened between them. I guess she was just saying it to make me feel better and throw me off his scent." I sighed. "So imagine my shock years ago, when you told me that he was your father. I was glad you'd found the man, but something deep inside me hurt." I looked at him and smiled, but Scott shook his head and squared his jaw.

"Well, he's *not* my father, Mr. William."

He sounded like a panelist on a talk show.

My eyebrows drew in. "But your mother said—"

"I know what she said," he cut me off, "but she was lying. She's always... *lying*..." His chin quivered.

I shook my head, trying to put together a puzzle with missing pieces. "What are you talking about, Scott? How do you know that?"

"I *know*," he said.

I stared at him, waiting for him to offer more information. He didn't.

"Scott, why would your mother lie to you?"

"I don't know," he whispered, "but it's the same reason she would lie to you." Scott flipped the page over and handed me the book. Stapled to the page was a document. My eyes scanned it blindly. It was filled with numbers, none of which made any sense to me.

Scott's long finger pointing on the page, averting my attention to what I needed to see. A statement, in bold font, identified William Frederick Cooper as being the father of Scott Reggie Jackson.

It was a paternity test.

The book rattled in my hand until it crashed to the floor of the car.

Feeling my stomach harden into knots, I pushed the door open and fell out of the car, gasping, choking, and trying to take in as much air as I could. After a second, Scott got out and joined me on the side of the road as cars zipped by.

"Are you okay?" he asked.

My hand covered my mouth as I swallowed bile and blinked my eyes, trying to shove tears away. "Yeah, I'm good," I whispered, but now, I was the one who was lying.

Scott walked over to a railing and sat on its edge, staring ahead at the traffic.

"I'm sorry," he said. "I know I asked you years ago, and you were adamant that you weren't my father."

I wanted to chime in, but I couldn't find my voice.

"How is it possible?" he whispered.

I blinked at a sixteen-wheeler speeding past.

I knew the answer to his question.

"In the weeks before I left for school, we must've made love tens of times," I recalled. "In our juvenile ignorance, we'd never used protection. I'd always released outside of her, but, admittedly, there were times the passion was so intense, disconnecting was impossible."

My eyes shot closed and pain ripped through me as visions of my mother assaulting Naomi flashed before my eyes. "It had to have happened then." I was talking to myself. "It all makes sense to me now. Why they refused to bring her home, why they kept us separated. They knew all along."

"Your parents knew?" he asked rhetorically.

"Yes." I pulled my eyes away from the road and looked at the boy. My son.

I rubbed my palms against my pants. My racing heartbeat was contrasted by a pleasant warmth radiating through my body. Scott and I had been meeting for so long that we'd already developed a strong relationship. That was the good thing. I'd always been there for him; I had taken him on like he was my own kid, even before I knew that he was. I searched his face. In the past, all I'd been able to see was Naomi, but now I looked with fresh eyes, the more I looked, the more I could see myself: the nose, the eyes, the cheekbones.

"I'm sorry, Mr. William," he whispered. He covered his face trying to disguise his emotion, but his shuddering shoulders gave him away. "What's the point in telling you any of this, anyway? You've got a wife and kids, and I'm forty-one years old. I'm a man. I should be over it by now. I should have kept this to myself." He huffed and his shoulders dropped.

I reached out and cupped the back of his head, pulling him towards me until our foreheads touched.

I shook him. "What are you talking about?" I asked, forcing him to look at me. "There's no need for you to be sorry, Scott. It wouldn't matter if you were forty-one or one. It wouldn't matter if I was married with ten kids. *You* are my *son*." I searched his face through the veil of tears that collected in my eyes. "We're good, Scott. In fact, we're better than we've ever been. And I love you. I always have."

Scott shook his head, smearing tears across his face. "You don't have to say that, you know," he said with a chuckle. "Nothing has to change between us, right?"

I smiled. "Right. Nothing has to change. Everything is perfect... has been since the moment we met."

29

WILLIAM
BEAUFORT, S.C., 1996

*a*t three o'clock in the morning, I stood outside of Naomi's door with my hands hanging at my sides, debating whether I should knock. I paced the floor. There was a slither of light coming from the crack beneath the door. She was up. Just like she always was. Nothing had changed. On second thought, that was a lie. Everything had changed, just as she'd predicted.

I lifted my hand to knock on the door, but dropped it again.

What the hell was I going to say to her? When we were kids, I could use homework as an excuse. Now, the only excuse I had was that I loved her, and that sure as hell wouldn't be good enough. Not now. Not after the argument we'd had earlier that day. Not after how I'd been treating her since she got to the house. I was supposed to be being a better husband, but my standing outside her door like a lost puppy was proof that nothing had changed about me.

There was nothing I could do to fix this. It was messier and more complicated than I envisioned it would be. Naomi had been right. It was a modern day version of everything we had been through when we were kids, and I still didn't have it in me to do the right thing.

But what was the right thing?

This was the question that plagued me. As far as I could tell, there were two right things to do. Which one was more right, I didn't know.

I groaned and turned away from the door, deciding I would go back to my room and take a cold shower. Then, I'd slide under the covers of a too-big bed and toss and turn until the sun came up. I started down the hall, but suddenly, Naomi's bedroom door pulled open and she was standing at the threshold.

I stopped walking and turned around to face her.

"What is it, Will?" she asked.

I squinted in the dim light of the hallway and took a step closer to her. Her face was wet with red and swollen eyes. Naomi had been in her room, crying.

"Sweetheart, are you okay?"

"I'm fine," she said, sweeping her hand across her brow. She wiped at the corner of her eye, trying to clear away the evidence.

"Naomi, what's wrong?" I asked, approaching her.

"What were you doing outside of my bedroom door?" she snapped.

"I was..." I looked behind me. "On my way to get a drink of water."

Her bloodshot eyes narrowed. "The kitchen is on the first floor," she reminded me.

"I have to go past your room to get there, don't I?"

We stared at each other.

She folded her arms across her chest, obstructing my view of her full bosom. "What do you want, Will? We're not kids. I don't have time for this."

"I want to talk," I said, my throat as dry as a desert. "We need to talk."

"You're right, we do." She walked into the room and returned with a wooden box. "What the hell is this?" She demanded.

My eyebrows furrowed. "How am I supposed to know what that is?" I said as I walked past her and into the room.

"Aren't you tired of lying?" she asked, following me. "Aren't you tired of keeping secrets?"

Her words stabbed at me and heat flushed my face. I swallowed.

"What are you talking about?" I whispered.

"Why are you acting like you don't know about this? The letter says he was going to tell you everything!"

"Who was going to tell me what?"

She flipped the lid of the box open and pulled a piece of paper out of it. She waved it in my face.

"What the hell is that?" I asked.

"Read it for yourself, why don't you?"

I snatched it out of her hand and squinted in the dim light, trying to see what she was talking about. In a matter of seconds, it became apparent. The words raced through my mind, and my eyes blurred until all I saw were blobs of black ink. The paper dropped from my hands and fluttered to the ground.

"Jesus Christ..." I stared at the letter like it was about to grow legs and walk around the room. I stumbled over to a chair and fell into it, my trembling hands covering my mouth.

"What..." I swallowed. "Who wrote that?"

Naomi stared at me. "You didn't know about this either?"

I shook my head, unable to take my eyes off her. "I guess..." I paused, searching my mind for clues. "When I think about it...I mean, I knew he loved her. Like, I knew that your mother was special to my father. He always smiled when she walked in the room. His eyes would light up like candles." I thought about the past: the way my father would rush to Miss Carole's defense, the way he was adamant that I leave Naomi alone because it wouldn't work, the way he and my mother used to argue late into the night...

"I should have known," I whispered. "I guess I was too busy being in love with you to notice." I looked at Naomi, desperate to connect with her.

The silence was deafening. The sound of the wooden box falling out of Naomi's grasp and crashing to the carpet cut through the thick atmosphere like a hot knife, jolting me out of my trance. Photographs, letters, and notes, all of which bore my father's antique handwriting, spilled across the floor. It felt like he was in the room. Vivid memories gripped me, and my body began to vibrate.

I knelt on the floor next to the box and its contents, surveying the pictures in the shadows. They were of my father and Naomi's mother someplace together, alone. They were smiling. They were happy. They depicted a time of which I had been unaware.

Naomi walked over to the bay window and curled up in the corner. I listened to her soft sobbing as deep emotion extracted itself from her petite frame.

After looking at a few more of the artifacts, I hoisted myself up off the floor, squeezed myself into the window next to her and gathered her into my arms.

"Sweetheart, I had no idea," I whispered. "If I had known about your mother and my father, I would have..." My words died. I squeezed her, burying my face in her neck, pressing my eyes together, trying to make the tears disappear. My chest felt tight enough to explode at any moment. "I can't believe she was *pregnant...*"

I thought about Scott and my heart wrenched.

"Why were you standing outside of my door, William?" she whispered, easing out of my embrace. She walked to the middle of the room, stepping on a few of the letters as she did so.

My hands rolled into fists, trying to capture the shadows she had left in them.

"I wanted to talk," I said. "I wanted to apologize for everything that has happened since you got to Beaufort. I've been wrong. I've been unfair. I want to make it right between us."

"I don't need an apology," she said, "and we have nothing to talk about. Certainly not after this."

"Don't be silly, Naomi. This has nothing to do with me," I said, pointing at the box. "It has nothing to do with *us.*"

"It has everything to do with us, Will," she snapped. "Don't you see? It represents the legacy of lies and deception that have characterized our entire existence. This *is* us."

I pursed my lips and lifted myself from the window. "Lies..." I repeated. "Are you suggesting that I'm the only one who has been untruthful all these years?"

Her neck whipped back. "William, never once have I lied to you about anything concerning us. I've always been honest about how I felt."

"You've always been honest," I said, almost laughing, "yet you never told me about Scott."

Silence.

Naomi's mouth opened and closed. "How do you know about Scott?" she whispered.

"You're not answering the question," I said. "You purport to be indignant about the fact that I have kept so many secrets and told so many lies, yet you never mentioned the fact that you bore my child... my son..." I choked. "A secret you intended to keep for God only knows how long!"

"Will..." Naomi took a step towards me.

This time, I backed away from her.

She froze. "William, wait...I can explain..."

"You could have explained a long time ago," I said, shaking my head. "It's too late now."

I pushed the door open and burst into the hallway.

Evelyn, wigless, pale, and bearing a horrified expression, immediately stepped in front of me. My heart leaped into my throat as I instinctively jumped backwards. Her eyes were sunken and bright with fury, and her lips were dry and taut. The whites of her eyes pierced straight through me in the darkness as her thin voice broke the stark silence.

"It's never too late," she said. "Isn't that right...*Naomi*?"

30

NAOMI

BEAUFORT, S.C., 1996

I was waiting for the floor to open and swallow me, but it didn't happen. Evelyn stood in the hallway like a menacing illusion, pale and ghostly. A pin dropping onto the carpet would have been thunderous. Shame engulfed me.

Her eyes narrowed. "I knew it was you," she whispered, trembling. "I knew there was a reason he wanted you to come here. There were other nurses he could have hired, but no, it had to be *you*."

"Mrs. Cooper—"

"Yes, I had a feeling. Even after you left my room last night, I thought about it. Something didn't sit right with me. You were trying too hard to be nice. After the way I treated you, anyone else would have left by now, but you...you stayed. Why? To get close to my husband!"

"Evvie, listen to me," William pleaded, taking a step towards her.

"Don't you *Evvie* me!" she shrieked. The suddenness of her high-pitched response made William and me jump. "So *this* is the woman! This is the black bitch you've been on about for years, ever since you were a bloody teenager. This is the woman you couldn't stop thinking about! This is the woman I could never live up to!"

"Don't call her names," William said through gritted teeth.

"Oh, right," Evelyn responded. "I forgot, you don't like that. That makes you angry, doesn't it? So how did you find her, William? You've been seeking her out behind my back, is that it? You couldn't let it go, could you?"

"Mrs. Cooper," I whispered, "please calm down. All of this excitement is not good for your condition. You should be upstairs in bed."

Her neck whipped around and she glared at me. Her breathing was ragged and her pale face glowed with a hint of red.

"Don't you dare try to suggest what's good for me, you lying whore," she seethed. "How dare you waltz back into this house after the way you left it? I know the story. William's mother told me all of the gory details. How you got yourself pregnant so you could lay claim to William's fortune. She tried her best to keep the two of you apart, but you couldn't stay away. You and your bastard son were not welcome here back then, and you're not welcome here now!" Evelyn advanced towards me.

"Please leave my son out of this," I whispered back. "He has nothing to do with any of this."

"You're right," she chirped with a twisted smile. "This has nothing to do with your mixed-breed son. This is all your fault. It always has been!" Unexpectedly, Evelyn charged at me with her arms outstretched and her hands spread wide like the talons of an eagle swooping for its prey. Her eyes bulged with rage.

I closed my eyes and braced myself for the tremendous impact. I waited for Evelyn's feeble frame to slam into me. I waited, but it didn't happen. Upon opening my eyes, I saw William stood in between us like a wall. Evelyn's face, only inches from mine, craned around the side of his arm. Her wriggling fingers stretched out with all her might as she tried to snatch me by the throat. Spittle flew from her lips as she growled and flared her nostrils like a wild animal.

"It's all her fault," Evelyn screamed from behind William. "It's all because of her!"

William pulled her into a tight embrace, but her hands were still reaching for me.

"It's not her fault," William was saying. "It's not because of her."

As he squeezed her tenderly, I could see her flailing hands withering. Tears seeped from my eyes as we continued to stare at one another. I took a feeble step towards them and reached my hand out toward Evelyn's. If I could connect with her, maybe I could make her see that I had never meant to hurt anyone. Maybe she would realize that all I had ever wanted was to be free.

As if with a renewed energy, she lunged for me again, but her attempts proved useless as William continued to smother her with empathy.

She groaned and grunted in frustration. "You love her," she accused William with low, raspy breaths. "You're still in love with her!"

William's mouth wrinkled. "I do love her," he whispered in confirmation. "I *am* in love with her." His face was wet with tears.

"You *love* her!" Evelyn said again. Her tone was less intense, but pain and anger dribbled from her mouth like venom.

William squeezed her tighter and closed his eyes, resting his chin atop her bald head. "I do."

I reached out and grabbed Evelyn's hand in mine. I squeezed it in an effort to ignore the agony caused by the crumbling of my heart. Suddenly, Evelyn's eyes softened and her expression shifted. Her mouth trembled. "You...you love him..."

I opened my mouth to say something, but no words came out. I swallowed and tried again. "I'm sorry, Evelyn," I whispered. "I never meant to..."

Her hand fell as she leaned her head against William's chest and began to sob.

I walked up to the couple and joined the embrace. William squeezed her from behind. I embraced her from the front. Emotion poured out of me into her as we all wept together. Finally, Evelyn took my hand with her trembling one and held it tightly. Then, she crumbled, becoming motionless and heavy in William's arms as her hands dropped to her sides.

William stumbled backwards from the force of her weight and looked at me with fear splattered across his face. I rushed over and grabbed Evelyn's wrist, searching for a pulse, a sign of life, anything. I breathed a sigh of relief when I found it; strong and sturdy.

"She's okay," I assured William. "She's...overwhelmed. We need to get her to the bedroom."

Gerald and Sharon flew around the corner at speed, their eyes wide with confusion and shock at the apparent commotion.

"Mrs. Cooper!" Sharon cried, falling to her knees next to William.

I grabbed Sharon by the shoulders. "She's okay, just a little rattled." I looked at Gerald. "Help William take her upstairs," I instructed. I looked back at Sharon. "Sharon, you go and call nine-one-one. In the meantime, I'll check her vitals and get her stabilized."

Sharon stared at me, shaking like a leaf in a December breeze. I did my best to smile and reassure her.

"We've got this," I said.

She nodded before picking herself up from the ground and rushing out of sight. As Gerald and William began to carry Evelyn to her bedroom, William turned around to look at me.

"Naomi..."

"Not now, Will," I said, cutting him off.

He nodded and disappeared around the corner.

Now, I was alone.

The adrenaline spike was starting to wear off, and the room began to close in on me. I clutched my breast with both hands, gasping for air as tears poured onto my face. Everything was spinning. I pressed myself against the wall, desperate for some form of support, and slid down it until I was sitting on the floor with my knees pulled up against my chest.

I grabbed my temples, trying to stop the sudden and incessant pounding in my head. I needed to pull myself together, I thought. There was no time to process everything that had just happened.

Not right now.

Right now, I needed to put my emotions to the side and do what I had been hired to do. I could think about everything else later.

I tried to pull myself from the floor, but my legs gave out and I fell back down. As I slumped in defeat, someone rounded the corner and I sensed a shadow looming over me.

"I'm coming," I said. "I just need to..."

The person extended their hand, and I reached out to take it.

Soon, another person arrived and rushed to my aid, taking me by the arm and gently lifting me to my feet.

"Nurse Naomi, we need to get upstairs!"

My head jerked up. *Ethan?*

The other person chimed in: "Ethan is right. Pull yourself together, Mama."

Scott?

31

NAOMI

BOSTON, M.A., 1996

ix Weeks Later

S I balanced a bag of groceries on one arm and my purse on the other, all while trying to get my house keys. I finally fished them from the purse, but they fell to the ground with a jingle and I cursed before squatting carefully to retrieve them. After a minute more of fumbling, I was making my way inside. I dropped the bag of groceries onto the kitchen counter, but not before pulling out a six-pack of Heineken beer. I didn't bother getting a bottle opener. I flipped the serrated lid off the top and put the cold bottle against my mouth, chugging back a few hefty swigs, then I plopped myself on the couch and grabbed the remote.

A bowl of popcorn I had made the day before waited in all its glory on the coffee table. I picked it up and shoved my hand into it, chewing on the flat kernels before I turned the television on. I flipped through a few channels and selected one, pretending to be watching it. In reality, the only show I was watching was the one that had been playing over and over in my mind for the last six weeks, since I'd fled Beaufort and come back to Boston.

Before I left, there had been a *family meeting*. That's what Scott had insisted on calling it. A few days after Evelyn had been relocated to the hospital for monitoring, I had been summoned to the library. It had been a full house: Ethan, Dakota, Scott, and William were all seated at the long table awaiting my arrival. Gerald was there too. Questions had been asked. Why hadn't I told him? That's what Ethan wanted to know. He wasn't sure how to take everything, but a large part of him understood...at least, that's what he'd said.

Scott was more emotional as he clued me into the relationship he and his father had developed over many, many years; all thanks to my deceased mother, and no thanks to me.

Other than explaining the way in which the reunion had been made possible—Scott had just showed up, and Ethan and Dakota had flown in after Evelyn had called to apologize—William had remained silent, frequently releasing heavy sighs and running his hand through his hair or scraping the back of his neck. Gerald served as an emotional support system, though I wasn't quite sure for whom.

I sat at the table under the intense scrutiny and judgment of everyone present. My shoulders were rounded and my eyes were low. I was ashamed and sorry, I had said, and I understood if none of them ever wanted to see or speak to me again.

No one responded.

The next day, I was on the first flight back to Boston. I didn't tell anyone I was leaving, but my blaring cell phone a few hours later let me know they had figured it out.

I took another swig from the green bottle and looked at it, then I searched for my cigarettes. I didn't bother going outside on the hammock. I had no energy to move anyway. All I wanted to do was sink deep into the couch until I disappeared.

A SUDDEN KNOCKING STARTLED me out of my sleep. My eyes popped open, and I looked around at the five empty beer bottles scattered around me and the half-full ashtray in front of me. The knocks sounded again, but I couldn't tell if it was someone at the door or just the pounding in my head. I smeared my palm against my bottom lip, wiping the dribble away as I stared at the door.

Bam, bam, bam!

"I'm coming," I slurred, pulling myself from the couch. I steadied myself on the arm of the sofa and straightened my posture before stumbling to the door, tip-toeing to look through the glass at the top. When I saw who it was, I stood back.

Lionel?

Bam, bam, bam!

"Open up, Naomi," he insisted. "I know you're in there."

I leaned against the door and ran my hand over my face. I sighed. "Lionel, what do you want?" I asked through the closed door.

"I want to come in," he answered. "I want to talk."

"Talk about what?"

"About us," he said. It sounded like it should have been a question.

I rolled my eyes. "If you're here talk about us, there's nothing to discuss. *We* don't exist," I reminded him. "Please just go away."

"I'm not going away. Just open the door," he insisted. "If you want me to leave, even after you hear what I have to say, I promise that I will and I won't bother you anymore."

I considered his words, still not convinced. As far as I could remember, everything that needed to be said, had been, the night he dumped me out of the blue. I looked around my townhouse. I had been alone for six weeks. Not even my friends were aware I had returned, and that was the way I wanted it to be; however, there couldn't be much harm in hearing whatever it was Lionel had to say. At least he promised to leave me alone after I heard him out.

I looked into the decorative mirror, which was on the wall next to the door, and realized that I looked like a creature from the depths of hell. I rearranged my ponytail and tried to rub the dark spots from under my eyes. Then, I inhaled and opened the door. Lionel and I stood staring at each other for a moment before I turned around and walked back into the house.

"You don't look good," he said, following me inside.

"That's a fine thing to say after not having seen me for almost two months," I said sarcastically.

"I didn't mean it like that," he said, "I just meant..." His voice faded. He looked around the room. "This place is a mess," he said. He walked over to a discarded beer bottle and picked it up. "Nay, you've been drinking?"

"Yup! And chain smoking," I added. "Don't judge me, though. I had no clue that retirement would be so stressful." I made my way to the couch but tripped in the process, almost falling to the ground. Lionel rushed over and caught me before I could land on anything solid and hurt myself.

"You need to sit down," he said, guiding me to the couch. He helped me settle in and began cleaning up the mess. I watched him pick up the beer bottles and put them into the kitchen trash bin. He pulled out the broom and quickly swept the tiles in the hallway and the kitchen. Finally, he filled the kettle and turned the fire on under it. When the kettle began to whistle, he made me a cup of tea and brought it to me, resting it on the coffee table in front of me. He eased himself next to me on the couch and watched me take a sip.

"That should help you to feel better," he said.

I eased back against the couch and closed my eyes.

"Where have you been?" he asked. "The day after—"

"After you dumped me?" I inserted.

His head dropped and he sighed. "I tried to call you," he said. "I even came by, but the place was in darkness. In fact, days went by and you never came home. I know because I drove by every evening hoping to see you or bump into you."

I took another sip of tea. "After we broke up, someone offered me an out-of-state gig," I said. "And I decided to take it."

Lionel nodded as if he understood, but I knew he had no clue.

"About that," he said.

"About what? The out-of-state gig?"

"No. About what happened with us."

I waved my hand in the air, dismissing whatever he was going to say before he'd said it. "There's no need to talk about that," I said, resting the mug on the coffee table. "We've both moved on, and as far as I can tell, it's pointless to bring it back up."

"I disagree," he challenged me. "It's not pointless. And the fact is, I haven't moved on. If you want to know the truth, the whole breaking up thing was never my idea."

My expression slackened. "Of course it was your idea," I reminded him. "You told me that things were moving too quickly and that you needed some time to think about where the relationship might be going."

"Let me explain," he pleaded. "Everything was perfect. Everything is always perfect when I'm with you."

"Lionel—"

"And then, do you remember when my phone rang with some guy on the other end of the line and—"

"Wait, what are you talking about?" I asked, shaking my head. "When I asked you who had called, you said it was your partner. You said something about a project and him being drunk."

Lionel hunched his shoulders. "It wasn't Hector," he admitted in a whisper.

I stared at him, trying to make sense of what he was saying to me. My mouth opened then closed. "Then who was it?" I asked.

"I don't know," he said. "But the person was adamant that—"

As if on cue, his cell phone began to hum on his belt. He stared at me, trying to ignore it, but the incessant buzzing was rattling the couch.

"Go ahead and answer it," I urged him, picking up my mug again.

Lionel sighed and pulled the phone out of its holster. He peered at the number on the screen, and a look of confusion washed across his face. I was raising the mug to my mouth, but froze when I saw his expression.

"Unbelievable," he muttered.

"What is it?"

Lionel presented me with the phone. The screen displayed an

out-of-state number. We stared at each other. Lionel clicked the phone on and put it to his ear.

"Hello...Yes..." He pushed his tongue into this cheek and looked up at the ceiling.

I put the mug back on the coffee table before it could crash to the floor.

Lionel got up from the couch and began to pace the room. "Yes, I'm here," he was saying. "I came by to check on her, but—"

The person on the other line had cut him off.

"Now wait a minute," Lionel asserted himself. "If you think you can just—"

The caller interrupted again.

Finally, Lionel heaved a sigh and clicked the phone off.

"What the hell is going on?" I demanded as tears crowded in my throat.

"I can't do it," he mumbled to himself, looking at his shoes.

"What are you talking about?" I shouted. "You can't do what?"

He looked up at me. His eyes were wet. "I can't be with you," he shouted back. "I *want* to be with you, but there's someone out there who wants to be with you more."

Another knock on the door startled me, but Lionel did not appear shocked. Instead, he picked his keys up from the counter and headed to the door as if he was leaving.

My eyes bulged and my head was on a swivel. "Where are you going?"

"I'm going home," he said with a shrug.

"Lionel!" I jumped off the couch and grabbed his arm. "We're not finished talking!"

"I think we are." He leaned down and sweetly kissed my cheek, then he walked to the door and pulled it open.

Behind it, William stood staring in, holding a cell phone in his hand.

In an instant, the breath left my lungs and I gasped, covering my mouth with my hands. Lionel approached the threshold and stood in front of William. They stared at each other for a few seconds before Lionel looked back at me and smiled. He turned back to William and extended his hand. William nodded and accepted Lionel's firm handshake. Then, Lionel skipped down the steps and disappeared.

32

WILLIAM

BOSTON, M.A., 1996

*L*ionel disappeared, and I softly closed the door to Naomi's townhouse. I paused and moistened my lips before turning to face her.

She glared at me, her eyes and mouth trembling. Her chin dipped down and her head tilted to the side. "Was that you who called Lionel's phone?" she asked.

"Yes," I whispered.

She approached me slowly. With each step, her light and delicate fragrance took a stronger hold of me.

Naomi swallowed and her mouth went tight. "Were you the one who called his phone before? At the restaurant?"

I stalled. "Yes. I got his number from your phone when you left it in my suite at the hotel."

Her lips flattened and her eyes narrowed as she cocked her hand back and slapped me hard across my cheek. A penetrating, burning sensation swept across the left side of my face. My eyes fluttered, but I stood tall before her.

Naomi scowled at me. "Where is Evelyn?" she asked with a low voice.

I pulled my bottom lip between my teeth. "She's at a board

meeting for the Historic Beaufort Foundation," I answered. "We're divorced. Evelyn served me with the papers the week after you left, and Scott went through them with me. It was a fair deal, so I didn't waste any time in signing them. After everything that happened, I knew it didn't make sense to do so. I gave her the waterfront property and half of the assets. I didn't put up a fight." I shrugged and sighed. "She told me she wasn't angry anymore. She said she knew how much I loved you and didn't want to hold me in a marriage I didn't want to be in."

Naomi didn't respond.

I continued. "She's recovering nicely. The doctors say she's going to be all right, and I have no doubt that she will be." I put my hand against my hot cheek and then looked back at Naomi.

"What the hell are you doing here?" she whispered.

I shrugged. The answer was obvious. "I've come to get you," I answered.

"You cannot be serious…"

"How could you think that I wouldn't be?"

Silence.

"William," she said as she straightened her shoulders, "after everything we have been through!"

I continued her sentence, "After everything we have been through, I now know how to love you," I said. "I now know how to protect you. Thanks to your mother and my father, I have learned how to defend *us*."

Naomi gasped. "There is no way," she muttered, backing away from me.

I advanced.

"There is no way we can even think about being together now," she claimed.

"Why? Because I'm married? Because the children don't know about us?"

"Because you still don't get it," was her succinct response. Her mouth bunched and her shoulders crumbled. Naomi ran trembling hands over her face and walked deep into the house.

I stared after her trying to make sense of her words.

When she turned to face me, her features were taut with lines of concern etched around the edges of her mouth. Her eyes shimmered with unshed tears. She shook her head and an expression of sorrow and anger marred her pretty face. "You *still* don't get it," she whispered through a rough chuckle.

"What don't I get?" I pleaded, my voice strained. The distance she had created between us was unbearable, but I stood frozen in my spot, not certain what move I should make.

"Damnit, Will, you don't get *me*," she said wringing her hands in the air. "It's always the same thing with you: what William wants and what William needs. What about me?" she demanded. "What about what *I* need? When have you ever stopped to think about that?"

I exhaled and meandered into the house until I was standing in front of her. I wanted to pull her into my arms. I was dying to reach out and touch her supple skin. My heart throbbed mercilessly with a longing and intoxicating desire. I stared at her, desperately trying to understand what she was saying. I could meet her needs, I thought. Whatever they were – all she had to do was ask and I'd give them to her. That was all I'd ever wanted. I had defended her in front of my parents and my ex-wife, just as I promised her I would. I had walked away from all of it in an attempt to show her that she could depend on me. What more did she require?

I searched her face looking for answers to the questions that had plagued me since I was sixteen years old.

Her brown eyes quivered and when she blinked a splash of water fell onto her face.

Then suddenly I *saw* her.

Naomi stood before me. She was sixteen and we were in Beaufort standing in her bedroom next to the open window. She was wearing a poodle skirt and saddle shoes. Her hair was in ringlets, but humidity was forcing it to transform.

My breath caught in my throat.

Now I saw her face, and for the first time I noticed expressions that had always been there: turmoil, anguish, and fear. I recoiled and backed away from her in one swift motion.

Other faces flashed before my eyes: Miss Carole, Gerald and Sharon. Scott, my very son...

My throat constricted and I fell onto the couch. "Oh my God," I breathed. I covered my burning face with my hands trying to stifle raw emotion. "What have I done?" I stared blindly into the distance as the images continued to plague me. I shook my head, trying to get them out. "You're right. We *can't.*"

Naomi's face twisted and her hand flew to cover her mouth, stifling a gasp.

My head dropped into my hands and I tried to reconcile reality and fantasy in my tortured mind. I had loved this woman more than anything I could think of. It had been that way for as long as I could remember, yet I had systematically dismantled her, using my privileged status to my advantage, ignoring her cries for emotional support. I had strong-armed Naomi into meeting my selfish needs without taking the time to understand the depths of her own.

Did she even love me? Or had I cajoled her into doing that as well?

My shoulders hunched and I pressed my clammy palm against my mouth. The purity of her presence was like a refining fire, scorching my dishonorable character. I was a disgrace. I did not deserve her; not the way that I was...

Pulling courage from the pit of my stomach, I stood and lifted my eyes to hers. I opened my mouth to say something, but it snapped shut. I was struggling to find appropriate words.

"Sweetheart... I'm sorry," I said. I swallowed. "I was trying to prove to you how much I loved you and all I did was let you down."

Her eyes shifted away from mine.

I tugged at my collar hoping it would relieve some of the dull, aching pain in the back of my throat. "What can I do?" I stuttered. "Tell me and whatever is it, I swear I'll do it."

Naomi's mouth quivered. "I *need* space," she whispered. "I *need* to be alone." She paused. "I need to be able to think, and process, and heal... and as we stand here, face to face, after everything that has happened, I just don't know how I can do any of that with you being so close."

A heavy silence crushed me and I tried to swallow back the dread that was overtaking me. My eyes, round as saucers, fell to the ground again and my heart thumped deep inside of my chest.

"Yet..."

Her trembling voice forced my eyes to rise.

Naomi moistened her lips, shaking her head. Her voice was feather-soft. "After everything that has happened and after everything we've been through, I wonder how I could ever allow myself to let you go..." She swallowed. "I would be a fool to let you go," she concluded.

My lips parted as smidgens of hope elevated me from my low place. I took a feeble step towards her, unsure of what to say. There were a million things yearning to pour from my overzealous heart, but the moment was fragile.

Naomi straightened her shoulders and smeared tears and mascara across her face. She lifted her chin. "So how would we do it?" she asked. "How would we heal from the pain of the past and move forward?" She paused. "Together?" Her tone was businesslike, but there was no way I'd miss the sparkle that flashed in her brown eyes.

I took another step towards her; this one, more confident, though not much. I paused, considering my words thoughtfully. "From the very first time I came into your bedroom to tell you how much I loved you, all I ever wanted to do was be everything you needed," I said. I inhaled. "I did everything I thought would prove that to you, but now I understand. It wasn't about what I said. It was about what I *did*." I paused. "I let you down in Beaufort. And not just when we were kids, either. I took too long to defend you and stand up for what was right."

My mouth twisted. "There's a lot I have yet to learn, Nay," I confessed, "but I swear to God, I'm *willing* to learn and if you give me a chance, a real chance, I swear I will prove it to you. You *can* depend on me, Naomi," I reminded her.

I was standing in front of her now, staring into her eyes will an emotional intensity that threatened to consume me whole. I lifted my hand to touch her soft cheek and my heart swelled when she didn't thwart the connection. Instead, her small hand clasped over mine and her eyes closed. Tears leaked onto her face and I wiped them away with my thumb. Then I bent close to her ear, swallowing, trying to ward off my own emotions.

"I want you to be my girl," I whispered.

Naomi laughed and pulled away from me, wiping the remaining tears off her cheek. "What are you on about now?" she demanded shaking her head at me.

"You heard me," I said with a smile. "Don't act like you didn't. And don't act like I'm the only one who feels this way either, because I know I'm not."

Naomi shrugged one shoulder and crossed her arms, amused.

"I'm real gone," I continued. "In fact, I think I'm in love with you. I dream about kissing you almost every night. Sometimes I dream about more. And when I'm around you, I get this heavy feeling right here." I pointed to the left side of my chest and she tracked my finger with her eyes.

"You're such a Cooper," she mumbled, closing the gap between us. In the most elegant way, Naomi lifted her arms and circled them around my neck. Her fingers tickled my nape and my eyes fluttered. The delicate kiss she finally placed on my lips released an explosion of emotion, and I wrapped her in my strong embrace.

The past and present had collided.

We stood there for many minutes, basking in each other's unrestricted presence. There was nothing between us anymore. We were free to be in love.

"What are we going to do now?" she whispered close to my ear.

I smiled. "We can do whatever we want," I answered after a second, "because finally, it's just you and me."

Made in the USA
Coppell, TX
22 January 2021